Chihuahua

of the

Baskervilles

Chihuahua
of the
Baskervilles

—◄○►—

Esri Allbritten

Minotaur Books

A Thomas Dunne Book ⚹ New York

A THOMAS DUNNE BOOK FOR MINOTAUR BOOKS.

An imprint of St. Martin's Publishing Group.

CHIHUAHUA OF THE BASKERVILLES. Copyright © 2011 by Esri Allbritten. All rights reserved. Printed in the United States of America. For information, address St. Martin's Press, 175 Fifth Avenue, New York, N.Y. 10010.

www.thomasdunnebooks.com

www.minotaurbooks.com

Library of Congress Cataloging-in-Publication Data

Allbritten, Esri.

Chihuahua of the Baskervilles / Esri Allbritten. — 1st ed.

p.   cm.

ISBN 978-0-312-56915-0

1. Dogs—Fiction.   2. Parapsychology—Investigation—Fiction.   3. Periodicals—Publishing—Fiction.   4. Colorado—Fiction.   I. Title.

PS3601.L415C47 2011

813'.6—dc22   2011007135

First Edition: July 2011

10 9 8 7 6 5 4 3 2 1

To Angel Joe and the 'Rents,
and to the people of
Manitou Springs, Colorado

Acknowledgments

Thanks go to Jennifer Unter, my agent. She does an awful lot for me. Thanks to Marcia Markland, my editor; Kat Brzozowski, assistant editor; and all the fine folks at Thomas Dunne Books.

Thanks to everyone involved in Author Fest of the Rockies, and thanks as well to the rest of the fine folks of Manitou Springs.

Thanks to Bonnie Frank and Boni Bruntz, for medical information, and the rest of Angel Joe's kin, for being my family. Thanks to Dan and Bonnie French, for their enthusiastic support of my books.

Thanks to authors Laura Levine, Nancy Atherton, Kate Carlisle, and Rosemary Harris, for saying nice things about *Chi of B,* and authors Lynda Hilburn and Colleen Gleason, for friendship, support, and advice. Thank you, Suzan Grenier, for your Best Boy video skills, and photographer John Poplin, for making sure Suki knew her stuff.

Thanks to all my friends, especially Dominick, Uncle Dennis, Red Leather Heather, and Thanksgiving Sheila.

Though I use a different title, I allude to a famous Chihuahua movie. Let it be known that the costumes in *Beverly Hills Chihuahua* came from FunnyFur.com.

My apologies for the various inaccuracies I have included, unknowingly or for plot convenience, when describing Manitou Springs. Visit www.TrippingMagazine.com and find out why I love this town so much.

And finally, thanks to all the dog-rescue organizations out there. You put more love into the world.

You can find me at www.EsriAllbritten.com. I hope to hear from you.

Chihuahua
of the
Baskervilles

One

The heavy tick of a grandfather clock filled the parlor, as if to convince the listener that this was a serious timepiece, despite the Chihuahua toy in a fairy costume perched on its mahogany case.

Victorian-style lamps illuminated the walls, which were crowded with framed photos of costumed Chihuahuas. Looking at dogs dressed in tiny cowboy hats and sailor suits, a visitor might think he'd stumbled on a canine version of the Village People, except for the slogan at the bottom of each photo: *Petey's Closet—Where the Well-Dressed Pooch Shops.*

With a preliminary click and whir, the clock struck the first chimes of 10 P.M. The bells were soon accompanied by the sound of footsteps in the hallway outside—light, heeled taps overlaid by heavy, resounding thumps.

Charlotte Baskerville trotted into the parlor, barely staying ahead of her husband. She was just shy of five feet and seventy years, her fine hair tinted champagne blond and beautifully set. In deference to Colorado's cool evening temperature, she wore a pale pink sweater over her lilac blouse. A rhinestone Chihuahua pin rested below her collarbone.

Thomas Baskerville stalked close behind her, tall frame stooped, gray hair disarrayed, and long face angry. "For God's sake, just give me the money."

She turned to face him. "Thomas, I can't. It's going to take a lot of advertising to establish Petey's Closet in England and Australia. Maybe if the greeting cards take off. Did I tell you about those? We're going to dress Lila as Cupid for Valentine's Day, and the back of each card will have a little blurb about our company."

"*Your* company, not ours," Thomas snapped.

Charlotte's expression turned thoughtful. "I think we'll have a contest. People can send pictures of their dogs dressed in outfits from Petey's Closet. We'll use the winner's photo on a special Christmas card." Her gaze focused on Thomas again. "If the cards make a profit, I'll let you and Bob have that money."

"And how long will that take? A year? Two?"

"Maybe nine months." Her tone became tart. "If Bob hasn't moved on to some other scheme by then, I'll think your faith in him is a little more justified."

Thomas drew himself up. "You make it sound like some wild scheme, but even your little rats have to eat, and high-quality dog food is a respectable business, not like . . . this." His waving arm took in the entire room. "It's pathetic. Animals aren't meant to wear clothes."

"Babies are animals," Charlotte countered, "but at some point, someone decided to dress them. It's part of the domestication process." She walked to a chair upholstered in rose velvet and sat down.

Thomas leaned over to grip the arms of her chair, glaring down at her. "Do you hear yourself? You ought to be committed!"

Instead of withdrawing, Charlotte leaned forward until they were nose to nose. "And all those customers of mine? Are you going to have them committed, too? Face it, Thomas. Batty old women don't run successful businesses." Her smile went from angry to wistful. "You were a wonderful breadwinner for years—decades. Why can't you be happy for my success, or be part of it? You could work on promotion of the new line, manufacturing contracts—"

"For the last time, *no!*" He straightened and walked a few steps away. "It's a matter of dignity."

Charlotte stood. "Jealousy is more like it," she snapped. She went to the door and gripped the handle, then heaved a sigh and turned. "For God's sake, Thomas. It's not as though I'm asking you to *wear* the clothes." Shaking her head, she left the room.

Thomas looked at the empty doorway for a moment, breathing heavily. Then he strode to the rear of the parlor and jerked open a door, revealing a bedroom decorated in brown and black. He entered and slammed the door shut behind him.

Charlotte was halfway up the ornate staircase when she heard the door slam. She flinched, but continued to climb. At the top of the stairs, a puppy gate blocked the hallway to the second floor. Behind this, a long-haired black Chihuahua paced, the marabou trim on her tiny pink sweater vibrating with tension. She gave a sharp yip as Charlotte came into view.

"Hush, Lila," Charlotte whispered. She opened and closed the gate, then picked up the dog, who nestled her face against Charlotte's chest. Charlotte's shoulders slumped as some of the tension left them.

Doors on either side of the second-floor hallway led to bedrooms and a few bathrooms. A door on the left opened, and Ellen Froehlich emerged, wearing a blue terry cloth bathrobe. A gray headband held her brown bob away from her face, and her skin was shiny with moisturizer. She lifted a hand in greeting and headed toward her bedroom.

"Wait!" Charlotte whispered loudly.

Ellen put her hands in her pockets as Charlotte approached. "What is it?"

"Let's move our meeting from nine to eight tomorrow morning. We'll eat breakfast in the workshop and have a nice relaxing time."

Ellen nodded. "Okay."

"And you'll have new designs to show me, right?" Charlotte smiled encouragingly.

Ellen fussed with the tie of her robe. "I have some jewelry designs worked up."

Charlotte shook her head. "The jewelry market is swamped. We need new clothes."

Ellen blew out a breath. "Give me a week and I'll have something exciting for you, I promise."

"How about four days?" Charlotte squeezed Ellen's arm with her free hand. "You and me, kid. We built this together. Don't stop now."

Ellen smiled briefly. "Good night, Char."

"Good night, sweetie." Charlotte continued down the hall as Ellen's door closed quietly behind her. She had almost reached her room when she heard a girlish laugh from inside one of the rooms. She tiptoed back a few steps and listened.

The sound of Ivan Blotski's Russian-accented voice rumbled through the door, followed by the higher tones of Cheri Baskerville, Charlotte's granddaughter.

Charlotte raised a hand to knock, then stopped herself. They were probably talking about the next catalog. Ivan trained the dogs to pose, and Cheri was currently helping with photography. There was every reason for them to talk, even if it was late. Anyway, Cheri was twenty now. There were only so many limitations Charlotte could put on her, and only one real threat to back them up.

Lila wriggled impatiently, and Charlotte went to her own bedroom.

Teeth brushed, face washed, and medication taken, Charlotte switched off the bathroom light and walked to her bed, rubbing lotion along the backs of her hands.

The four-poster was high enough that she had a wooden step next to it, although that was mostly for the dogs.

Chum lay in the middle of the duvet, where she had put him earlier. The older of her two Chihuahuas, he wore a tartan sweater vest against the cold. Cataracts clouded his eyes, but his head followed Charlotte as she turned off the overhead light and came to bed.

Lila bounded up the little stairs and onto the mattress, where she poked her nose under the edge of the spread.

"Wait a minute," Charlotte said. She made Lila sit before taking off her tiny outfit. "All right, go ahead."

Lila nosed at the edge of the spread, then disappeared beneath it like a mole.

Charlotte tossed Lila's sweater on the dresser and turned off the electric blanket before sliding beneath the covers. The Tiffany-style lamp on her bedside table illuminated reading glasses and a copy of *Chihuahua Connection* magazine. She glanced at it, then sighed and switched off the light.

She was enjoying a floaty, almost-asleep sensation when she heard a sharp bark, ending in a sort of warble.

Charlotte sat up as Lila boiled out from beneath the covers. Even Chum raised his head. For a moment, all three of them stared, rigid, at the window.

The sound came again.

"Petey?" Charlotte whispered. Lila ran across her legs and jumped to the floor with a thump.

Charlotte slid over and groped for the step with one foot, then hurried to the window and pulled the curtains apart.

A blurred crescent moon floated behind clouds that suggested rain or snow. Black tree branches waved slightly against the cobalt sky. Directly below lay the patio, with the dark hump of a covered table and chairs. Her gaze moved farther, past Ellen's stone workshop and the dogs' agility course.

Lila whimpered at her feet.

Charlotte picked her up and kissed the top of her sleek head. "It was probably a raccoon." It couldn't have been Petey's bark. Petey had been dead for almost a year. She looked out the window again and took a sharp, quick breath.

A small, glowing shape drifted slowly across the darkened lawn, illuminating the sere grass beneath it. After a moment, it turned sideways, and Charlotte saw the pointed ears and high, domed forehead.

She put Lila down, almost dropping her, then gripped the window and tried to lift it. When it didn't budge, she fumbled for the catch.

Outside, the shape rose and floated onto the roof of the workshop, then pivoted and looked up at the window.

Charlotte grabbed the heavy wooden window again and lifted. Frigid air flowed into the room. "Petey!" she yelled toward the glowing shape.

From outside, the bark came again—warbling at the end, then fading away.

She turned, stumbling slightly as she grazed Lila's warm body, then made for the door. She hurried down the hall and descended the stairs as fast as she could, hand gripping the banister.

A door opened upstairs, but she kept going, grabbing the wall as she turned the corner into the hall that led to the kitchen and the back door.

She twisted the lock above the handle and pushed open the door. "Petey-poo!" In the backyard, autumn grass crunched under her bare feet, frigid and brittle. She took a few more steps, gazing from side to side, then saw a faint glow at the edge of the workshop. "Petey, Mommy's here!"

Charlotte made it halfway across the lawn before clouds covered the moon and she tripped on something in the dark. She went down with an "Oof!" and lay still for a moment, praying she hadn't broken anything.

The back porch light came on, illuminating her. She pushed herself up as Ivan and Cheri came out.

Cheri's silky black pajamas clung to her slender body. Without makeup, she looked about fifteen. "Grandma!" She ran forward and helped Charlotte stand. "What are you doing out here?"

"You won't believe it." Charlotte squeezed Cheri's hand, then rubbed her hip and grimaced. "I thought I heard Petey, and then I saw something out here in the yard—something that glowed."

Ellen joined them. "Where did you see it?"

"It went across the yard, then floated onto the workshop roof and disappeared," Charlotte said. "When I got out here, I thought I saw something along the ground over there." She pointed toward the workshop.

Ivan had brought a flashlight. He switched it on and walked toward the stone building, waving the light across the ground. The three women followed close behind as the flashlight's beam cast harsh shadows across the ground. "Here?" Ivan asked.

Charlotte gestured vaguely. "Somewhere around the corner."

"I see nothing," Ivan rumbled. He switched off the light.

Charlotte pointed. "Look! What's that?"

They moved in a clump, Charlotte gripping Ellen's sleeve. "Does anyone else see that?" Her voice shook as she pointed.

The downspout of a gutter ran down the side of the stone building. In the muddy earth below, a few indentations shone faintly— the glowing tracks of a very small dog.

A sound came from behind the group, and they all turned. Charlotte gave a little gasp.

Thomas Baskerville stood there, hands in the pockets of his dressing gown. "What's going on?"

The others exchanged looks.

Finally Cheri said, "Charlotte thinks she saw a ghost."

Thomas's brows rose, and a smile flickered on his thin lips. "As I said, Charlotte, I'm worried about the state of your mental health."

Two

Angus MacGregor's cell phone woke him. His futon mattress had no frame, and he groaned a little as he got to his feet. At fifty-two, a man shouldn't have to sleep on the floor.

Two steps took him to his camel-colored corduroy jacket, hanging from a hook on the back of the bedroom door. He took the phone out of its pocket and flipped it open. "Hello?" Grogginess added gravel to his Scottish accent.

"Angus, it's Pendergast. Are you busy?"

Angus hiked the waistband of his boxer shorts higher. "Not right this moment, but I can't talk long." His phrasing made it sound as though an urgent appointment were in the offing. In reality, his pay-as-you-go minutes were running low.

"Listen, I have a lead on a story, and what a story!" Pendergast spoke with an East Coaster's rapidity. "Plus, it's right here in Colorado."

It was cold in the room. As goose pimples rose on his skin, Angus pulled on his jacket one-handed and buttoned it over his chest.

"You told me *Tripping* magazine was finished. Your exact words were 'dead as a stinking halibut,' as I recall."

"We're only a month past when the last issue should have been out. I doubt the subscribers have noticed. We'll bring it back with a bang."

"What's the story?" Angus looked around for his pants.

"There's a woman in Manitou Springs, made her family's fortune selling designer clothing for small dogs. This is after her husband lost the family's previous fortune with some crummy investments. Anyway, the Chihuahua who started it all, Petey, has been dead for a year, but get this—last night, *his ghost* appeared to her. To put a frickin' cherry on it, the family's last name is Baskerville!"

"Who else has covered it?"

"No one! Charlotte Baskerville and my wife, Carol, are cousins. Charlotte called Carol this morning, wanting to talk to someone sympathetic. I listened in on the extension."

Angus put the phone on speaker and set it on the floor before pulling on his pants. "I need my first two weeks' pay in advance. And I want a photographer."

"I've got one all lined up—used to work for *National Geographic*."

"You're kidding." Angus paused with a sock in his hand. "When? In 1940?"

"No, she's young. She got fired over some little question of ethics, but it doesn't apply here. I've also lined up a writer-slash-graphic designer."

Angus picked up the phone and took it off speaker. "Why do we need another writer?"

"Writer-slash-*graphic designer*. He has some great ideas for layout, and he works fast. We want this issue to hit the stands before anyone scoops us. Anyway, it's too much work for you to write everything. Michael's a novelist."

"A graphic-designing novelist?"

"Is there any other kind? Speaking of which, where do you want me to send your check?"

"I'll give you my bank-account number and you can deposit it directly. End of today?"

"End of tomorrow. I've got four sets of braces to put on today, and one of them has a mouth that looks like a broken Chrysler grille. I'll e-mail directions to the Baskerville house and you can take it from there."

"Right." Angus hung up. He had sold Len Pendergast his first Lexus two years ago. Angus's obvious Scottishness led to talk of the Loch Ness monster, and the two men found they had a common interest. *Tripping,* a travel magazine for aficionados of the paranormal, was the result.

Funded by Len and written and edited by Angus, *Tripping* had enjoyed some local success in the New Age community of Boulder, Colorado, but sagging sales caused Len Pendergast to abandon his expensive hobby. Now they were apparently back in business.

Filled with new purpose, Angus slipped on his loafers and squared his shoulders before stepping out of his bedroom.

In the kitchen, the three college students who rented the other bedrooms in the house sat around the table, eating cereal. They looked up as he entered, and Christine snickered. "Is it laundry day, or is stomach fur the new thing?"

Angus resisted the urge to look down at his shirtless chest beneath the jacket. "I had no idea young people were so prudish." He headed back to his room.

Three

Angus asked his new staff members to meet him at a local tea place. Retail products filled the shelves, while tea drinkers sat at small tables.

Angus took a moment to order a pot of tea with three cups and looked around for a good place to sit.

A solitary woman sat at one of the tables. Her long legs were encased in high-heeled boots that laced to the knee, visible in the slit of a long velvet skirt. A brown leather bustier constrained a white blouse that ended in long sleeves and frothy lace cuffs.

She turned, and Angus got the full effect of her red-painted mouth, slanted eyes, and black hair, cut short beneath an improbable velvet hat. By the look of her features, she was part Asian.

"Suki Oota?" he asked as she stood to meet him.

"I hope you didn't ask me to a tea shop because of the Japanese thing." Her voice was pure Los Angeles.

"No. I thought Oota might be Dutch." He offered his hand, and she shook it. "This is a regular spot of mine. I'm a fan of the

Tung Ting oolong." He pulled out the chair opposite her, and they both sat. "I understand you worked for *National Geographic*," Angus said. "Did you bring a portfolio?"

She raised delicate eyebrows at him. "Do I *need* a portfolio, having worked at *National Geographic*?"

"Perhaps you only photographed insects. I need someone with wide scope."

Suki bent and rummaged through a carpet-bag purse. "You can look at the pictures I've taken this week." She handed him a bulky digital camera. "Use that button to scroll."

The waitress brought the tea while Angus clicked through the pictures. Suki's shots included candid portraits, swallows flying above Boulder Creek, and some night shots of the CU campus, all outstanding.

Angus handed the camera back. "You're very good."

"I am." She shrugged. "I don't actually need to work. Not that you shouldn't pay me, but be aware that I can walk at any time."

"What happened at *National Geographic*?" Angus asked, pouring tea for both of them. "So I can do my best to avoid losing you."

She sighed. "Sexual impropriety on the staff's part."

"Ah." Angus nodded solemnly. "Objectively speaking, you are quite attractive."

"So was he, in a dark, loinclothed kind of way." She frowned. "No one told me there was a hands-off policy with the natives. I guess you're just supposed to *know*. Honestly, it was so clubby there."

"Well, Ms. Oota, carnal temptations are rare in the world of paranormal travel, so I think you'll do fine." Angus looked past her as someone approached the table. "And this must be our writer-slash–graphic designer."

The newcomer was a lean man in his late twenties with a worn messenger bag slung over the shoulder of his black leather jacket. Dark, shaggy hair touched the top of gold-wire glasses perched on his narrow face. He didn't smile as he came over. "Angus Mac-Gregor?"

"A pleasure." Angus stood and offered his hand. "And this is Suki Oota, our staff photographer."

Pendergast had told him Michael's last name was Abernathy. Angus had looked forward to having another Scot on staff, even if he wasn't native. But judging by Michael Abernathy's olive-skinned good looks, the Scottish part of him was on one side only. *French,* Angus thought. *Or Jewish.*

Michael looked Suki up and down as they shook hands. "Nice outfit. Steampunk?"

"For the moment," she said.

They sat, and Angus turned to Michael. "I understand you're a novelist."

Michael shook his head. "Writer. You don't call yourself a novelist until you publish a book. I do sell a fair amount of magazine articles. They're good for the résumé." He took a battered laptop out of his bag and set it on the table. "Len said you need someone for layout, too."

"That would be helpful, although we have a template that I use without any problems."

"If it's anything like the Web site, it needs updating."

"Oolong tea?" Angus picked up the Yixing clay pot.

Michael didn't look up from his computer. "Only if it's Formosa."

"What else?" said Angus, who had no idea. He went by smell and taste. He poured into the small, handleless cup.

Michael turned his laptop toward Angus. "This is my proposed look and feel for the Web site and cover design, using stock photos. My research showed that the most active paranormal groups revolve around UFOs, Bigfoot, and ghosts. I threw Stonehenge in there because it's a well-known tourist destination and you're working the travel angle." He picked up his cup and inhaled deeply before sipping. After a moment he swallowed. "A little thin on the back note. Probably not spring pick."

Angus used the laptop's down arrow to scroll through the proposed site. "I like the blue."

"I used blue because most of your readers are male, and men like blue."

"They also like red," Suki said.

"Blue is more calming. Good for when you're asking someone to spend money."

"But red incites action, so they hit that BUY button." She smiled slowly, her red lips curving.

Michael stared at her a moment. "Maybe."

Angus turned the computer back toward Michael. "I think we have a good team. Manitou Springs is a two-hour drive, and as you know, Len told Mrs. Baskerville to expect us after lunch. We'll take my car."

Michael took one sip of the coffee Angus brought on the trip before sticking the plastic thermos cup out the car window and dumping it.

"You can wash that off the fender when we stop for gas, lad." Angus stepped on the pedal of his Mitsubishi Eclipse as he merged onto I-25.

"Happy to," Michael muttered, turning sideways in the backseat. "You should always ask to smell the coffee before they fill the bag, to make sure it's fresh."

"I'll keep that in mind," said Angus, who bought all his coffee at the Dollar Store. "Now let's talk about Manitou Springs. It's a perfect vacation spot for paranormal fans, close to cliff dwellings and a couple of ghost towns. They have a haunted cemetery, a haunted stately home—Miramont Castle—and of course, the Emma Crawford Coffin Race."

"Who is Emma Crawford, and why did she like fast coffins?" Michael asked.

"She didn't. The poor girl died of tuberculosis in 1891. She had just gotten engaged."

"That was wishful thinking."

"She hoped Manitou's healthful waters would cure her, but when it became clear she was dying, she asked her fiancé to bury her at the top of Red Mountain, which wasn't an official cemetery by any means. A dozen men, headed by the heartbroken beau, carried the coffin to the peak and buried her there."

"So it's a race to see who can get to the top of the mountain first?" Suki asked.

"Not exactly. As I said, it wasn't an official grave site, and her coffin was moved once to make way for the railroad. After a few years, a rainy spell unearthed Emma and sent her remains hurtling down the side of the mountain on a tide of mud. So every year, folks build coffin-shaped vehicles, someone dresses as Emma and gets inside, and they push her as fast as possible down Manitou's main street, as a way to remember Miss Crawford."

"Well, that *is* touching," Michael said.

"So you see, Manitou is perfect for *Tripping*. Pendergast is lining up advertisers as we speak. We'll mention places to stay—"

"Where are we staying?" Suki asked.

"The Manitou Arms, which fits the budget of most of our readers.

But we'll tour the full spectrum—the bed and breakfasts, deluxe. We'll need to list places to eat, as well. There's a haunted restaurant, the Regency."

From the backseat, Michael asked, "Do you actually believe in ghost dogs?"

Angus glanced in the rearview mirror and frowned. "If you don't, for God's sake keep it to yourself."

Michael tapped Suki's shoulder. "You on board with astral Airedales and ectoplasmic Afghans?"

She lifted one shoulder. "Eh. Who knows?"

"Michael, I hope your personal beliefs won't interfere with your professionalism," Angus said. "We want to be very respectful of Mrs. Baskerville's experience."

"Don't worry about me. It's just the lack of real coffee talking."

"I hope so. Suki, ghosts are notoriously hard to photograph, but at the very least, get some atmospheric shots of the yard and house." He hesitated. "Reflective surfaces look nice in pictures."

"I brought a fog filter that does some cool stuff," she said.

Angus smiled. "There's a good lass."

Four

The Baskervilles lived in a large Victorian house on a corner lot, not far from the main street of Manitou Avenue.

Ellen Froehlich opened the door. "Can I help you?"

Angus smiled graciously. "We're with *Tripping,* ma'am."

"Excuse me?" She smiled nervously. "I'll lend you my cell phone if someone's had an overdose, but you can't come in the house."

Michael looked at Angus. "We really need to change the magazine's name."

"If we did that, we'd lose existing readers."

Suki caught Ellen's eye and lifted the camera around her neck. "We're here about the ghost dog."

"Oh, the magazine people!" Ellen's expression lightened, and she opened the door wider. "Charlotte's expecting you. Come on in."

They followed her into the foyer.

"Um . . ." She peeked into the front parlor. "You can wait in here for a minute. I'll get Charlotte for you."

As Ellen's footsteps pattered up the stairs, Suki took a few photos of the room. "Nice clock. It'd be spookier without the stuffed pooch."

Michael took out a notebook and scribbled a few notes as he looked at the framed photos of costumed dogs. "Do you suppose they put on doggy fashion shows, and if so, do they use a catwalk?"

Angus wandered over to a bookshelf. "I don't know, but if Charlotte Baskerville likes the article, she'll mention our magazine to everyone on her client list, and her business is worth three hundred thousand a year."

Michael looked up from taking notes. "Are you serious?"

"Toy breeds are on the rise." Angus angled his head to see a book title better. "Small dogs are cheaper to keep, and outfits from Petey's Closet start at under twenty dollars. It's inexpensive entertainment to take your dressed-up pup for a walk." He turned as a door opened in the back wall of the room.

Thomas Baskerville took two steps before coming to a halt. His gaze took in the newcomers and stopped on Suki. "Who are you people?"

Angus stepped forward and offered his hand. "Angus MacGregor. *Tripping.*"

Thomas took a step back. "Damn hippies."

"*Tripping* magazine," Suki said. "We're here about the ghost."

Thomas's mouth turned up in a sneer. "I suppose you're here to capitalize on my wife's increasing instability."

Angus's smile disappeared. "We're here to report on a legitimate phenomenon. Fifty percent of Americans believe in hauntings."

"Which means half don't—the sane half."

Angus regained his smile. "Let's talk about Petey's Closet. Presumably you have no objection to promoting the family business."

"It's nothing to do with me, and I wouldn't dignify it with the name *business*. Just a club of crazy women who think their dogs are babies." Thomas went back into his room. The door closed behind him with a sharp click.

"*Well,*" Angus said. "So much for Mr. Baskerville."

Michael shook his head in disbelief. "Talk about dirty laundry. Why is Charlotte Baskerville's husband trying to sabotage her?"

Angus shook his head. "We're not here to unearth family skeletons. We'll write up the ghost and the town—that's it."

They turned as Charlotte Baskerville entered the room, followed by Ellen. Lila trotted at their heels.

Angus strode forward and engulfed Charlotte's small hand in both of his. "Angus MacGregor," he said, his Scottish accent thickening. "It's a pleasure to meet such an accomplished lady."

Charlotte's smile strengthened. "Thank you, Mr. MacGregor. I'm so glad you could come."

"It must be very exciting to have seen your beloved Petey."

She let go of his hand and sat rather suddenly. "I've never given ghosts any thought, but not only did I see something, I *heard* Petey. He had a very distinctive bark, with a little yodel at the end." She looked up at Ellen, who stood beside her. "You remember."

Ellen smiled. "We used to call him our little coyote."

"I'm sorry," Angus said to Ellen, "but I didn't get your name."

"Ellen Froehlich. I design the clothes for Petey's Closet."

"Then compliments are in order. I particularly like the sweater with the leather elbow patches. It's something I might wear myself."

She flushed slightly. "Thank you. I was one of the first designers to use patches. They're actually Ultrasuede, so the dog's joints aren't restricted."

Angus nodded. "It's all in the details." He looked down at Lila, who stood at the bottom of Charlotte's chair, wearing a periwinkle blue jacket with white piping. "This must be someone important."

"Lila, sit," Charlotte said. The dog's rump went down smartly. "Now be pretty."

Lila cocked her head at Angus and raised one paw.

Angus chuckled. "Very sweet."

"She'll stay that way until you shake hands," Charlotte said.

Angus squatted and gently clasped the tiny black paw. "Pleasure," he said solemnly. He stood and gestured to Michael and Suki. "This is my staff, Michael Abernathy, writer, and Suki Oota, photographer. Perhaps we could have a look at where the apparition appeared?"

"Of course." Charlotte pushed herself to her feet and led the way out of the parlor, down the hall, and into the kitchen. "There's always a pot of coffee on the counter, and cookies in the jar. Please feel free to help yourself." She passed a large kitchen table and opened the door to the backyard.

Lila rushed to the edge of the yard and began a circuit of the wooden fence, sniffing as she went.

The rest of them walked across the flagstone patio. A weak autumn sun shone through the bare branches of an ash on the east side of the yard. The other side was taken up with an extensive agility course, complete with tube, ladder, and jumps.

The stone workshop sat near the back of the lot. A man squatted next to the corner of the building, staring at the ground.

Angus narrowed his eyes. "Is that someone from another publication?"

"No, that's Ivan Blotski, the dogs' trainer," Charlotte said.

Ivan stood as they neared him. He wasn't tall, but the black pullover sweater he wore accentuated powerful shoulders and gave the illusion of stature, as did his heeled Italian boots. He looked to be in his mid-thirties, though deep lines ran on either side of his mouth. A ponytail held his thick black hair away from his face.

"Ivan, these are the people from *Tripping* magazine," Charlotte said. She introduced each of them.

When introduced to Suki, Ivan smiled, revealing yellowed teeth, one of them broken. "You look like Mongol princess."

"Not really, but thanks. Can I take your picture?"

"Please. I could use new head shot." He closed his mouth and looked moodily into the distance.

"Are you an entertainer?" Suki snapped the picture and lowered the camera.

"Not yet, but I will have TV show soon." He shot a glance at Charlotte. "It will be excellent for Petey's Closet to sponsor it."

Michael lifted his notebook. "What's the show's name?"

Charlotte smiled a little wearily. "There's no show. I'd love to help Ivan, but I have too much on my plate to get involved with a new project." She looked at the ground Ivan had been examining. "Oh, you've put stakes around the tracks—what a good idea."

He glowered at her. "All Ivan's ideas are excellent."

Charlotte pushed him gently to one side. "See the little paw prints? They glow in the dark."

"Could you all stand back a little?" Suki came forward and shot a series of pictures from overhead.

Michael took a small device from his pocket.

"Is that ghost meter?" Ivan asked.

"No, it's a digital recorder. Ms. Baskerville, is it all right if I record our conversations?"

"Of course, dear," Charlotte said.

Michael switched on the machine. "Do you have to shine a light on the tracks for them to glow?"

Angus chuckled, but there was an edge to the sound. "Perhaps you think Petey carried his own flashlight."

"I'm sorry," Charlotte said. "I don't understand."

"What I mean is, do they work like commercial glow-in-the-dark paint or chalk, which needs to be charged with light?" Michael asked.

"Oh, I see." Charlotte smiled. "I don't think so. They were glowing when I came out here, and it was night."

Michael nodded. "Sure, but if someone charged the paint somewhere else—say, the workshop—it would glow for a while. I see your dogs run around in the yard."

"Yes."

"So the glowing tracks could be their tracks that were simply rubbed with—"

Angus cleared his throat loudly. "None of that explains a spectral dog that can float onto a ten-foot roof, of course."

Michael looked at the workshop. "Its only six feet at the edge."

Ivan chortled. "Americans—always looking for the complicated explanation. Is simple. Is ghost. We had two ghosts follow us through the countryside in Siberia, till we laid a trail of dried peas." He frowned. "Peas might not stop ghost dog. Trail of raw liver, maybe."

Suki looked up from her camera. "That would certainly stop me."

"What's on the other side of the workshop?" Michael asked. He headed that way, and the others followed.

The fence at the back of the yard was older and shorter than the privacy fence that surrounded the rest of the backyard. In the middle, a decrepit gate sagged on its hinges.

Michael jotted a note. "Did you look in the workshop after you saw the ghost?"

"We didn't." Charlotte looked from Ivan to Ellen. "There didn't seem to be a reason."

"Can we go in there now?" Michael asked.

"I really don't think—," Angus began.

"No, it's fine," Charlotte said. "Ellen, do you have your key with you? Mine is in the house."

"Um, let me think. Oh, it's all right, I have it." She patted her pants pockets, then pulled out a key.

They followed her to the other side, where a modern door looked incongruous in the rough stone wall.

"Why doesn't the workshop face the back of the house?" Michael asked.

Charlotte answered. "The workshop is the original house, dating from 1867. They built it to face the other street of this corner lot. You don't make structural changes lightly when it comes to stone."

Ellen opened the door. The rest of them followed her inside, except for Ivan. He waved a box of cigarettes and said, "I will stay here," before closing the door.

The workshop's long interior was surprisingly modern, with white walls and track lighting. Tables and shelves lined the walls, and long bolts of fabric hung from a rack in a corner.

"This is a nice space," Suki said, raising her camera.

"No pictures." Ellen spoke sharply, then looked apologetic. "It's just that we have to protect the designs."

"Of course." Angus wandered over to one of the tables. "I've never seen a sewing machine with a computer screen in the side." He picked up a scrap of dark blue fabric. "Little embroidered bones! Where do you find something like that?"

"The machine sews them, along with about sixty other things." Ellen smiled at her employer. "Charlotte insisted on getting the best."

Charlotte squeezed her arm. "You needed something to distract you."

"Distract her from what?" Michael asked.

Ellen looked at the floor. "I was going through a rough time, personally."

"I see." When she didn't say anything more, Michael pointed toward two file cabinets on the far wall. "Aren't you worried someone will break in here one night and steal your design records?"

Charlotte shook her head. "Anyone who wants previous patterns could just look in our back catalogs. It's the current work that needs to be kept under wraps, but the workshop has a good lock, and we can look out the window from the house and see it."

Suki scanned the worktables, which were almost clear. "What are you working on?"

Ellen bit her lip.

"Nothing, at the moment," Charlotte answered brightly. "I guess all artists need some time to percolate. Shall we go back to the house? The heater's not on in here, and I'm getting cold."

Outside, Ivan ground out the stub of his cigarette and followed them as they returned to the house.

"Mr. MacGregor, would you like to set up headquarters in the upstairs parlor?" Charlotte smiled at Michael. "We can come out tonight after it's dark and see if the tracks glow before we shine a light on them."

"That's very thoughtful, Mrs. Baskerville," Angus said. "Would it also be possible to interview the members of your staff? We'll try not to take too much of their time, but it sounds as though Ivan here has some previous experiences with the supernatural."

"That is true," Ivan said. "When you are ready, I will go first."

"We'll probably interview Mrs. Baskerville first," Angus said.

"It's up to each of them," Charlotte said, "but as far as I'm concerned, you can interview anyone. And please, call me Charlotte."

As they neared the house, Ellen lagged behind. "I think I'll turn on the heater in the workshop. Get some stuff done."

"That's a wonderful idea, dear."

The back door opened, and a petite young woman stood there, one hand over the mouthpiece of a portable phone. "Grandma? It's for you." Her mouth turned down, giving her a bored, sulky look.

"Thank you, dear." Charlotte took the phone from her. "Cheri, these are the people from *Tripping* magazine." To Angus, she said, "This is my granddaughter, Cheri Baskerville. She's helping with the photography for Petey's Closet. I need to take this call, but I'll find you afterward and we'll talk."

"Whatever's most convenient for you."

Charlotte turned toward the workshop. "Ellen! Could you show Mr. MacGregor and his staff the upstairs parlor and help them get settled?"

Ellen had just reached the door to the workshop. Her shoulders slumped. "Coming." She turned back to join them.

Charlotte was already speaking into the phone. "Barbara? Did you get the corrected copy I sent you?" She disappeared into the house.

Cheri Baskerville wore sexy jeans and a dark blue blouse that showed the tops of her small breasts. Her brunette hair, cut in wispy layers, accentuated her long neck and large, dark eyes. The scent of strawberry perfume wafted around her.

Angus smiled benignly at her. "You must be very talented, to already be working on the catalog. Are you taking photography in high school?"

"I'm twenty."

Angus's face fell. "I'm so sorry. Young people look younger every year to someone my age."

Cheri smiled suddenly, dispelling the image of a sullen teen. "That's okay. It happens a lot. You're here about Petey, right?"

Angus beamed at her. "We are. Have you had any paranormal experiences?"

She nodded. "We had a poltergeist when I was little."

Michael raised his notebook. "Was that in this house?"

"No." Cheri's gaze traveled to Suki, who stood slightly behind the others. "Oh, my God. Where did you get that jacket?"

Suki adjusted the turned-up sleeves of her leather jacket, which was lined in wine-colored satin. "Paris, I think. Or Amsterdam. That whole trip is kind of a blur."

Ellen patted Cheri on the shoulder. "You'll get a chance to talk to them later. They'll be interviewing everyone."

Cheri's full mouth twisted slightly. "Sorry. Didn't know I was hogging them."

"I didn't mean—," Ellen began.

"Don't worry about it." Cheri turned, coming chest to chest with Ivan before going inside.

Ellen turned back to the others. "If you'll come this way, please?"

She led them upstairs and waved a hand at the doors on either side of the hallway. "These are mostly staff bedrooms, so please don't go into those rooms." She pushed open the second door on the left. "This is my bathroom, but guests can use it, too."

"How many of you live here?" Michael asked.

"In addition to Charlotte and Thomas? Me, Ivan, and Cheri."

"How long have you been here?"

"And have you ever seen a ghost?" Angus added, giving Michael a pointed look.

"I've worked with Charlotte for seven years—almost since the beginning of the business. And I've never seen a ghost." Ellen walked to the second-to-last door on the left, which was open. "Here's the upstairs parlor. You can use this room to work in. I hope it has enough outlets."

They entered a pretty room decorated with Victorian antiques. Upholstery and drapes in shades of rose and pastel blue gave it a feminine look.

Angus pointed to a door between two bookcases. "I assume we should keep that closed?"

Ellen nodded. "That door leads to Charlotte's bedroom, and she usually keeps it locked. This room is really part of her suite, but she lets anyone use it." She edged toward the hall. "Do you want me to send Ivan up for an interview?"

"Thank you, but I think we'll bring some equipment up first," Angus said. "We'll find him."

"All right. I'll be in the workshop if you need me."

They went down to Angus's car and were unloading the rest of Suki's equipment when the tinny sound of a cell phone made Angus reach for his pocket.

"Michael Jackson's 'Thriller' is your ring tone?" Michael snorted.

Angus looked at the screen. "It's Pendergast." He flipped open the phone. "Len? We're all here, so I'm going to put you on speaker." He walked away from the Baskerville house, gesturing for the others to follow him.

"How's it going?" Pendergast asked.

"It's certainly an interesting household." Angus reached the sidewalk on the other side of the narrow, quiet street.

"Interesting is right," Len said. "And how 'bout that town? They say you can't take a midnight piss in Manitou without running into a ghost."

Michael pulled his notebook from his pocket and leaned toward the phone. "Who says that?"

"I do, but it's good, don't you think? Use it in the article."

"Len . . ." Angus dropped his voice and held the phone closer to his mouth. "You didn't mention the fox in the henhouse."

"They have hens?"

"Thomas Baskerville. I thought he was going to kick us out, and he doesn't seem happy about his wife's business."

"Oh. Right. My wife is a little worried about Charlotte, if you want to know the truth. Apparently Thomas is making noises about having the old girl put away."

"Charlotte seemed smart as a whip to me," Angus said. "What possible grounds could he have for saying she's incapable?"

"On the grounds of seeing a ghost and dressing up dogs."

Angus shook his head. "He's got an uphill battle."

"I don't think he has a chance in hell, but it's an exciting story, isn't it? Cute little old lady married to an asshole. Stay away from anything libelous, of course, but you can get the idea across without using the word *asshole,* right?"

Angus rolled his eyes. "We'll see what we can do."

"That's great. Well, I just wanted to check in. Go work your magic, big guy."

Five

Charlotte was still on the phone when the staff of *Tripping* was ready to begin interviewing, so Angus decided to talk to Ivan first.

He and Michael took their places on a settee in the upstairs parlor. Across from them, Ivan straightened one leg, achieving a negligent he-man look despite the fussy Victorian chair in which he sat.

Michael started his recorder, then set it on the low table between them before nodding to Angus.

"Full name?" Angus prompted. "And may I ask where your accent is from?"

"Ivan Blotski. I am from Russia. Siberia."

Angus nodded. "Why do you think Petey's ghost appeared?"

Ivan stroked his upper lip with two fingers. "Ghosts appear for two reasons—to harm or to warn. Petey would not harm Charlotte, so maybe she needs checkup at doctor or is considering bad investment." He grinned. "Maybe Petey warns her not to pass up chance of working with super successful Russian TV star."

"You train Mrs. Baskerville's dogs," Angus said. "Have you always worked with Chihuahuas?"

Ivan chortled and stood. "Let me show you something."

Angus and Michael followed him into the hall, Michael carrying his recorder.

Ivan pushed open the door of his room and stood aside to let the two men enter. "This is what Ivan was."

Unlike the pastel tones in the rest of the Baskerville house, rich color saturated this room, along with the odor of stale cigarette smoke. A garnet velvet bedspread looked positively opulent against gold-figured wallpaper, but what really caught the eye were the posters on the walls, their leaping forms depicted in strong, inky strokes.

"Good Lord," Angus said. "You worked with *wolves?*"

"Six years, I toured with the Trans-Siberian Circus." Ivan pointed to the one poster that wasn't covered in Cyrillic characters. "That one you can read. Is from engagement in London."

Angus stepped closer. " 'Ivan Blotski and His Wonder Wolves.' " He peered at the drawing of a man down on one knee, a wolf jumping between his upstretched arms. "You had a beard then, I see."

Ivan rubbed his clean-shaven chin. "It was required, because they did not change poster art, only performer's name. I wore the same costume as the man before me, and kohl around my eyes."

"And this television show you want," Angus said. "Would that involve wolves?"

"Possibly." Ivan's languor disappeared. "It will be a dog-training show like no other. It will be huge."

"What makes it like no other?" Michael asked.

"*Me.* I am exotic, being Russian, and I have trained wolves. It is a . . . no-brainer, but Charlotte will not make up her mind."

"What would Charlotte have to do with it?" Michael asked.

Ivan rubbed his fingers together in the gesture for money. "I need to get teeth fixed, have media training, make demo." He gripped the back of a worn leather chair. "Cesar Millan and his pit bulls . . . *Tcha!* You don't know fear until wolf has his jaws around your neck." He turned his head to the side and touched a patch of scarred skin below one ear.

Angus gave a low whistle. "What happened?"

Ivan shrugged. "The oldest wolf challenged me for leadership of the pack. I submitted rather than die, but when he let me go, I got my gun. I shot him, making sure the others saw." He sighed. "For five years I considered that wolf a friend, but what could I do? It was my livelihood."

Angus shook his head in awe. "Man, that's one hell of a story."

"I have many stories. You want to hear about ghosts?" Ivan's eyelids lowered, and his voice became more guttural. "For thirteen days after I shot wolf, I woke to this sound each night at midnight." He panted huskily, then gave a rising growl that ended in a sudden, vicious snarl.

Michael raised a hand to smooth the fine hairs on the back of his neck. "Very authentic."

"When visiting foreign country, it helps to know the language."

"How did you become Charlotte Baskerville's trainer?" Angus asked.

"I came to this country for better opportunities. Got work at a wolf sanctuary." Ivan frowned. "Sanctuary went away when someone poisoned all the wolves. One thing about Chihuahuas—people don't think they kill cows." He smiled wryly. "After wolf sanctuary, I set up dog-training Web site, and Charlotte found me. Her dogs were"—he laughed—"not well behaved. I train them not only to stop barking, but also to hold poses for camera. So she asks me to stay. Sometimes we do tours, events, and I help with those, too."

"What would you do if you saw Petey's ghost?" Angus asked.

Ivan stepped forward and clapped him on the shoulder. "If I see ghost, I will tell it to *stay,* so you can take pictures. All dogs obey Ivan, even dead ones." He went to the door. "I need cigarette, which means I have to go outside. You want one?"

"No thank you. I'm an ex-smoker," Angus said, as he and Michael followed Ivan into the hall. "I do want Suki to get a picture of you with that poster at some point."

Ivan gave a sharp nod. "Is no problem." He closed the door to his room and strolled toward the stairs.

Angus and Michael returned to the parlor.

"I hope your recorder got all that, Michael," Angus said. "What a story!"

Michael pressed a button and listened for a moment. "Got it. Just remember, that's probably exactly what it is—a story. He's not the first Russian I've met. Let's just say they're prone to exaggeration."

"Michael," Angus chided. "Don't tell me you're a bigot as well as a cynic?"

"All right, forget that he's Russian. But remember, part of every circus performer's job is to mislead."

"What about the pretty girls on white horses?" Angus asked. "They're not trying to fool anyone."

"They want you to think they're prettier and younger than they are. Also, those horses are whitewashed."

Angus shook his head sadly. "Jesus, Michael, I'd hate to be you."

Suki came into the room, carrying a camera on a tripod and

followed by Cheri, who looked remarkably old-fashioned in a long
black coat worn over a white cotton dress.

"I got some great shots of Cheri standing in front of the workshop," Suki said. "I think I'll make them sepia, to bring out the
texture of the stone."

Cheri took off her coat and smiled shyly at Suki. "If you need
any more, just tell me. I don't have much to do until we start the
next catalog."

Suki removed the camera from the tripod. "If you're serious
about photography, now's a good time to experiment with different
backdrops and lighting, or practice your candids and action shots."
She placed the tripod next to the wall.

Cheri lifted one shoulder. "I guess." She hugged the coat to her
chest. "I should probably put something else on. It's cold in here."

Angus, who had been jotting some notes, looked up sharply.
"Regular cold or *ghost cold*?"

Cheri's eyes widened. "Oh, my God. Do you think there's a
presence in here *right now*?"

"Oh, please," Michael muttered.

"Shhh . . ." Angus held a finger to his lips. In the ensuing quiet,
a slight noise could be heard.

Angus raised his head slowly and studied the ornate light fixture that hung from the ceiling. "It almost sounds like screws
unscrewing."

Suki looked up from fiddling with her camera. "Why's everyone so quiet all of a sudden?"

"That noise," Cheri whispered. She looked around wildly. "It's
stopped now."

Suki lifted the camera she held and rotated the lens. It squeaked
and came off in her hand. "You mean this?"

Michael sighed. "Cheri, after you change into something warmer, would you like to come back here for your interview?"

"Okay." She went out the door.

Angus gave the light fixture a disappointed look before turning to Suki. "What was Cheri wearing? She looked like something from an old photograph."

"I put her in one of Charlotte's nightgowns." Suki brought the camera over and showed Angus the screen. "We have this Victorian house and a lot of antique furniture, so I thought I'd go for an old-fashioned look. I don't know if the kid has any talent as a photographer, but she's a natural in front of the camera."

Angus clicked through the photos and gave a low whistle. "Brilliant." He looked at Michael. "If your writing is half as good as these pictures, this article could see *Tripping* really take off."

"Don't worry about my writing," Michael said.

Angus handed the camera back to Suki. "Ivan should be back from his smoke break. I'd like you to get a picture of him beside a poster he has in his room. He'll show it to you." He looked at Michael. "Could a Chihuahua jump between a man's arms like that?"

"I think you might have to toss it."

"All right, scratch that. It was just an idea."

Cheri knocked on the door frame as she came in. "Are you ready for me?"

"Absolutely," Angus said. "Have a seat. Michael can show me his interview technique."

Cheri wore her regular clothes again, but had put little sparkly clips in her hair. She sat next to Michael on the settee and looked at him through her eyelashes. "Ask whatever you want."

"Do you mind if I record our conversation?"

"Feel free."

The recorder sat on the coffee table in front of them. Michael leaned forward to switch it on, scooting slightly away from Cheri as he did so. "You said something about a poltergeist."

She clasped her hands. "When I was fifteen, strange things started happening around the house. The windows opened during the night, which drove my dad nuts, and all the stuff in our cabinets would be rearranged in the morning."

"Sounds like a prowler," he said.

She shook her head. "Nothing was missing."

"Maybe it was one of your brothers or sisters."

"I'm an only child." She stared at him a moment. "And I didn't do it."

"I didn't say you did. How long did this go on?"

"A little over two years. When I left home for school, it petered out, so we think I was the focus."

"Did you have any incidents at school?"

"Once, in the dorm. My roommate and I woke up because we heard drawers opening and closing. I said, really loud, 'I'm sick of this and I want you to get out!' After that, it never came back."

"Well done," Angus said. "That's pretty much what a professional would do."

"A professional what?" Michael asked.

"Ghostbuster." Angus leaned forward. "Cheri, why do you think Petey appeared to your grandmother?"

She looked at her hands for a few moments. "I don't know. Maybe because she's lonely."

"She has a houseful of people," Angus said gently.

"I know, but Thomas . . . Well, Petey was really special. When he was younger, he used to jump into her arms."

"It's handy she's so short," Michael said.

She smiled. "And when Petey was old and couldn't jump, he used to put his front paws on her leg and sort of hop until Charlotte picked him up. I know she misses him."

The sound of raised voices filtered up from downstairs. Michael turned toward the doorway. "What is going on down there?"

"It's probably Grandpa," Cheri said bitterly. "He's always yelling about something."

Angus and Michael went to the doorway and listened. Across the hallway, Suki appeared in the door to Ivan's room and did the same.

The wooden staircase made an admirable conduit for Thomas Baskerville's thunderous tones. "Don't pander to her, Bob! She's taking advantage of you—can't you see that?"

Another man's voice said, "I know you feel strongly about this, Thomas, but if we're going to work with Charlotte, we need to stay professional."

Charlotte's voice wasn't raised much, but she sounded harried. "Bob is just a good deal more polite than you, Thomas."

Michael looked at Angus as Thomas went into another tirade, which included the words *selfish old bitch*. "Should we go down?" he said quietly.

"I think that's a fine idea," Angus said, looking grim. "Mrs. Baskerville would probably like to be interviewed about now." He glanced behind. "Cheri, we'll be back in a bit."

Michael and Suki followed Angus as he strode into the hall and went downstairs, making no effort to be quiet.

Thomas and Charlotte stood at the base of the stairs with a much shorter, tubby man, who carried a plastic bucket by the handle. He looked to be in his forties, and wore cotton slacks and an oxford shirt. Wire-framed glasses and a beard gave him the look of a professor.

By the time the *Tripping* crew reached the bottom of the stairs, Thomas Baskerville had fallen silent. His face, already red with anger, flushed darker when he saw the camera in Suki's hand.

In contrast to Thomas's mottled skin, Charlotte's complexion was very pale. She held Lila in her arms, a hand wrapped around the dog's muzzle. Lila trembled inside her yellow polka-dotted dress, but her eyes glared at Thomas Baskerville.

The stranger nodded in a friendly manner and raised the bucket he held. "I'll just drop off this batch of the new formula." It appeared to be full of dog kibble.

"Thank you, Bob." Charlotte's voice shook only slightly.

Angus touched her back in a light, comforting gesture. "I believe it's time for your interview, isn't it?"

She looked up at him gratefully. "That's right. I'm sorry if I kept you waiting."

"Oh, are these the magazine people?" Bob asked. He put down the bucket and offered his hand. "Bob Hume. I'm developing a line of dog food using the açaí berry. Are you familiar with the açaí berry?"

"I have a hat made of açaí leaves," Suki said. "Don't the berries have antioxidants or something?"

Bob Hume beamed at her. "My goodness, you're beautiful. That's right, the açaí berry contains high levels of antioxidants, which are known to fight cancer. That's what killed Petey, you know." He turned to Thomas. "I thought we might call the food Petey's Pride. Branding is all about telling a story."

Thomas shook his head angrily. "Get your damn bucket and let's go. You're wasting your time talking to these people."

"It's never a waste of time talking to people, especially members of the press," Bob said, turning back to them. "Do any of you have dogs?"

They shook their heads.

"Well, you might someday, and then a high-quality food is a good investment. What you spend on good food, you save on vet bills, and then some."

Charlotte moved toward the stairs. "If you'll excuse us, Bob, we need to get going." She put Lila on the floor. The little dog had calmed during Bob's lecture.

"It was good to see you, Charlotte," Bob said.

Angus moved aside to let the others go upstairs first, and wound up standing between Thomas and Bob.

At their feet, Lila sniffed the bucket of kibble and turned away. As she passed in front of Thomas, he drew back his foot as if to kick her.

Angus leaned sideways and bumped Thomas's shoulder, making him reach for the banister to steady himself. "Sorry, did I nudge you? I can be very clumsy sometimes. It's a real hazard." He smiled pleasantly and followed the dog upstairs.

In the upstairs parlor, Suki rummaged through one of her camera bags while Charlotte moved around the room, plumping pillows with quick nervous gestures.

Angus sat next to Michael, on the settee. "Where's Cheri?"

Michael shrugged. "She was gone when we got here."

Charlotte finally settled in the chair Ivan had used. Two spots of pink burned in her cheeks. "I'm so sorry you had to see that." Lila jumped on her lap, and she stroked the dog. "Bob is an old friend of the family's. He and Thomas want to start a dog-food business together, and they want me to fund it. Len Pendergast is a relative of mine by marriage, so he may have filled you in a little."

"He was very discreet," Angus said smoothly.

Charlotte sighed. "Thomas wasn't always like this, but his family is very proud and . . . He didn't have very many challenges growing up." She smiled. "Whereas I was the daughter of an alterations tailor."

"How did you and Thomas meet?" Angus asked.

"We were both in community theater, in New York. Thomas painted sets. He was a bit of an artist and rebel back then, very strong-willed, but then I am, too. For a long time we wanted the same things, so it didn't matter."

"What changed?"

"Money." She smiled slightly. "It all started with a little bug. The Baskerville fortune was in lumber. For a long time Thomas did very well as the head of the company, until the pine-bark beetle destroyed most of the timber. Thomas, trying to diversify, made some investments that didn't pan out. Then there was a hostile takeover bid. Instead of bowing to the inevitable, he sold many of the family assets, trying to buy enough stock to keep the takeover from happening. But it did, because another family stockholder decided to sell."

"Ouch," Michael said.

"I had this house as a bequest from one of Thomas's aunts who had taken a shine to me. So we moved here to live out our lives on a limited income."

Angus looked at Lila, in her perky outfit. "But that didn't happen."

"No." Charlotte chucked Lila under the chin, and the dog nosed her fingers. "Shortly after we moved here, Thomas fell into a depression. When he took a double dose of his medications and wound up in the hospital, he swore it was an accident, but I wondered. I bought Petey hoping to cheer him up." She put Lila down and went to a drop-front desk, where she took a small photo album from the drawer. She handed it to Angus and resumed her seat.

Angus flipped open the cover. "Aww . . . Look at the wee mite."

"Wow, Chihuahua puppies are really small!" Michael said, looking at a photo. In it, a smiling Thomas held Petey cupped in one large hand.

Suki came over. "Can I get a shot of you with that picture, Charlotte? It's all right if you look sad." She took a few pictures. "Thanks."

Charlotte handed the album back to Angus. "Petey was irresistible. Thomas taught him to sit and lie down—all the things that made him such a good photography subject later on."

Angus turned a few pages, then held up a picture that showed Petey wearing a plaid raincoat. "Is this the first outfit you made?"

"No, I bought that one." She took the book and flipped the pages, then held it out. "This was the first, and I had no idea of selling it."

The photo showed Petey, grown up and wearing a tuxedo dickey, complete with bow tie. Other dogs and their owners surrounded him, and many of the humans wore party hats. "Thomas was happier after I got Petey," Charlotte said, "but we had missed our initial opportunity to make friends in the community. I'd spent all my time trying to cheer him up, and people thought of us as a couple who didn't like to socialize."

"So you threw a party," Michael said, looking at the photo.

"A birthday party for Petey. I invited the few people I did know—other dog owners I'd met while out walking. When I brought Petey out in his tuxedo, he was an instant hit. I got a few informal orders that night."

"How long ago was that?" Angus asked.

"About ten years. I built up a small business on eBay and sent out a funny little newsletter. Still, it was nothing that gave me more than some extra spending money and a hobby. Then came the movie that changed my life. *Hollywood Chihuahua*. Before that, canine fashion was the province of dotty old ladies, like me." Charlotte smiled. "Turns out, I'd built up a big Web presence mostly by accident. When the media looked around for someone to interview on canine fashion, there I was." She patted Lila. "Business boomed."

"But your husband wasn't happy about your success?" Angus asked.

Charlotte shook her head sadly. "He might have been, but in one of the first magazine articles about me, the reporter had the bad taste to imply that Thomas would be remembered for almost bankrupting the Baskervilles, while I was on my way to restoring the family fortune. The morning after that article appeared, Petey climbed across the bed to say good morning to each of us, as he always did." She pressed her lips together for a moment. "Thomas pushed him away. I still remember the expression on Petey's little face—confused and hurt, wondering what he'd done wrong."

A brief silence ensued, which was broken by a knock on the door.

"Come in," Charlotte called.

Cheri opened the door and put her head around the corner. "Did you need me for anything more? It's just that I have a date."

Angus looked at his watch. "I didn't realize it was so late."

Charlotte stood. "I should eat something. I'd ask you to stay for dinner, but we've fallen into the habit of fending for ourselves."

"That's fine." Angus handed her the photo album. "We need to scout the local restaurants anyway." He caught sight of Cheri's expression. "Don't worry, lass. We're not going to invite ourselves on your date."

She smiled. "But you'll be here tomorrow?"

He nodded. "Through Saturday. We're staying for the Emma Crawford Race."

"Cool. And if you're looking for a restaurant, I like the Happy Mountaineer." She pointed toward the front of the house. "Go to Manitou Avenue and head west. You can't miss it."

"Can we walk?" Suki asked. "I'm jonesing for some exercise."

"You can walk to anything in Manitou." Cheri sounded a little depressed by the fact. She left, closing the door behind her.

"How about you?" Angus asked Charlotte. "Any recommendations on places to eat?"

She stood and put the album back in the desk drawer. "Manitou Springs is too small for a bad restaurant to survive. Wherever you go will be fine." She put a hand on his sleeve as he turned to go. "While I'm telling you all the family secrets, there's one other thing you should know."

Angus raised his eyebrows.

"It's fine if you take Cheri out to interview her, but don't buy her a drink."

"I wouldn't anyway, seeing as how she's underage."

"Thank you." Charlotte looked at the floor. "Some people are more casual about the law than that, but Cheri is a recovering alcoholic. It's not that I don't trust her—I just don't want temptation put in her way. You know."

"I do know," Angus said. "The question is, does her date?"

"That would be Jay, and he's basically a good boy. The fact is, I can't put Cheri on a leash." She picked up Lila and smiled. "Or even dress her up. You'll be back later this evening?"

Angus nodded. "To see if Petey walks again."

Six

A painted mountain scene decorated the front of the Happy Mountaineer, and the door handle was fashioned of braided climbing rope.

Angus peered through the door. "It's not my usual kind of place."

Michael shrugged. "It looks like a typical college-kid hangout. They probably have good burgers. Hey, there's a jukebox!"

Angus turned away. "We don't have to decide this moment. Let's get a feel for the town."

They walked the roughly two miles of main street, pausing frequently for Suki to take pictures.

About halfway through their walk, they stopped and looked down at a sunken courtyard with a small decorative building in its center. Water poured from a spigot mounted on the side.

Angus consulted his tourist map. "This is the Shoshone Spring."

Suki took a picture and lowered her camera. "Is this why it's called Manitou Springs? I thought there'd be hot springs."

Angus shook his head. "It's named for these natural drinking fountains—about a dozen of them, each with an individual flavor from the various minerals. Can you believe they paved over a lot of them in the sixties? I call that outrageous."

When the commercial buildings petered out, they crossed the street and went back on the other side. Finally they wound up in front of a restaurant called Rhumbalicious. "This looks more my style," Angus said.

Inside, the atmosphere was festive, with bright colors and lighted flower garlands. A hostess led them to the back of the large main room.

"Would you look at the size of those daiquiris?" Suki pointed to a glass the size of the drinker's head. "Anyone want to split one?"

"I don't know if they'd pour it into two glasses," Michael said.

"Alcohol kills the cooties, Michael. How about you, Angus?"

"Not for me, thanks, and you'll have to pay for it yourself. Liquor doesn't go on the expense account." He nudged Michael and tilted his head toward a table where a lone woman sat, wearing glasses and reading a thick book. "There's the girl of your dreams."

"Would you shut up?" Michael hissed.

"Ach, she can't hear me over this din."

"What if your hearing is going and you're louder than you think?" Michael asked.

Angus looked taken aback. "Am I loud?"

"No, but it's something to think about."

Angus put an arm around his shoulder. "It's good I have you to remind me of old age and decrepitude. You're like the son I never wanted."

They sat. Suki put in her order for one of the enormous daiquiris before studying the menu. "I'm ready," she said after a while, slapping the laminated pages down. "Hey, there's Thomas Baskerville." She tipped her head toward the front door.

Angus watched Thomas and another man thread their way between tables. "Out for a relaxing evening with a friend, assuming he has such a thing," he murmured. "You'd certainly never know it by his face."

Thomas Baskerville looked as dour as ever, his mouth turned down in lines of discontent. He wore a button-down shirt above his slacks, and carried a coat. His companion appeared to be in his thirties, and was dressed more casually in jeans and a sweater beneath a leather jacket.

The waitress returned to the table. "Do you know what you'd like?"

"Almost," Angus said absently. "Do you see those two men?" He pointed, keeping the gesture behind the menu. "Isn't the younger one Christopher Peters, the actor?"

She peered for a moment. "No. That's Martin Carson."

"The doctor?" Angus asked.

She shook her head. "Lawyer."

"Of course." Angus looked at his menu. "I'd like the two-fish combo, and iced tea to drink."

The waitress scribbled it down and turned to Michael. "How 'bout you?"

"Curry from Hell."

While the waitress took Suki's order for jerk chicken, Angus watched Thomas Baskerville. After a moment, Thomas looked around the restaurant and caught sight of him.

Angus nodded slightly while Thomas glared back at him.

Martin Carson looked up as Thomas slid out of the booth. Thomas said a few words. Carson seemed to argue for a moment, then sighed and stood. The hostess watched them leave and changed a mark on her seating chart.

"I'll be right back with your drink," the waitress said to Suki.

Michael turned from watching Thomas and Carson walk out the front door. "A lawyer, huh? If Pendergast is right about Thomas wanting to have Charlotte committed, do you think Thomas faked the ghost? Or"—he held up his wrapped silverware—"maybe the ghost will tell her to shut down Petey's Closet and start making açaí-berry dog food."

Angus chose a plantain chip from the basket. "I think it would take more than a ghost to make Charlotte Baskerville give up her business. And there's no reason to believe the ghost is fake."

Suki leaned back in her chair. "If it comes to faking ghosts, my money's on Ivan."

"Why?" Angus asked.

"He *really* likes attention."

"Is that the only reason?" Michael said.

"There doesn't need to be more. Take it from someone who likes to be noticed—and I'm not trying to get on TV."

The waitress came back and carefully set an enormous daiquiri by Suki's plate.

"Oh, yeah," Suki murmured, and took a healthy swig.

Angus rested his clasped hands on the table. "As I said, there's no reason to think the ghost is fake. But if there were, you're both missing the most obvious candidate."

"Who?" Michael asked.

"Ellen. She's the one most likely to whip up a ghost costume."

Suki shook her head. "What has she got to gain? Anyway, a costume is so low-tech. If I were going to fake a ghost, I'd use some sort of projector."

Michael unwrapped his flatware. "I could see where you could project it against the workshop wall, but what about when it floated onto the roof?"

"Smoked glass, or even a sheet of plastic."

Angus squeezed lemon into his tea. "It's all moot, because as far as we're concerned, this is a real ghost, and if we're lucky, it'll make an appearance tonight." He turned and looked out the front windows of the restaurant. "Looks like it's already dark."

As it turned out, some of the darkness was due to weather. By the time Angus and his crew finished their meal, a heavy rain was falling. They stood just inside the restaurant's door, staring out at the deluge.

"So much for seeing if those paw prints glow without light," Michael said bitterly. "They'll be completely washed away by now."

A man and woman in their fifties came up next to them, shrugging on coats. "Good thing we parked right outside," the man said conversationally. "You folks might want to wait a little if you're not parked close."

"Actually, we walked," Angus said. "I don't suppose Manitou Springs has a cab service."

"I think it'd have to come from Colorado Springs, which would cost you a mint. Where do you need to go? We could give you a ride."

"That's very kind of you. We're practically around the corner," Angus said.

By the time the man and his wife dropped them off in front of the Baskerville house, the pounding rain had become the barest sprinkle.

Someone hailed them as they trotted up the walk to the house. Looking around, Angus spotted Thomas's dog-food partner waving from the second-floor deck of the neighboring house.

"Hellooo, magazine people! It's Bob Hume!"

"Oh, hello, Bob," Angus called back, without enthusiasm. He turned to Michael and Suki and muttered, "You two go in. I'll get rid of him."

They hustled inside the front door with no argument.

"Stay there, Mr. MacGregor, and I'll come down," Bob called. "I have something to show you."

Angus stepped onto the front porch. "I'm sorry, Mr. Hume, but I'm in a bit of a hurry. Have to set up for the ghost watching, you know, and it's already dark."

Bob had started toward the door that led inside his house, but now he came back onto the deck and leaned over the railing. "But this is completely pertinent to that. I was looking through some old photos of Petey that I have, and I think I've spotted a spectral face in one of them!"

Angus hesitated. Spectral faces were always good. "Is it a spectral *dog's* face?" he shouted.

"No, it's much better! I'll be right there!"

Angus sighed and stayed where he was.

Bob emerged from the front door of his house moments later and ran over to join Angus on the porch. "Take a look at this." He reached inside his coat and took out a photograph.

Angus took the photo and angled it toward the porch light.

Bob, panting slightly, bent down and adjusted his slip-on shoes, the backs of which were folded under his heels.

"Where's this face?" Angus asked.

"Let's go inside where it's dry and the light's better," Bob said, straightening. He led the way inside and glanced around the empty foyer. "Where's the rest of your crew? They should see this, too."

"I'd rather not interrupt their preparations." Angus went into the parlor and felt for the switch of a floor lamp with a stained-glass shade. "That's better." He held the picture under the bright light.

Bob pointed. "That's Petey. He was a nice little dog. Charlotte had him on the kitchen table to dress him." In the photo, Charlotte appeared to be fastening the closure of a hooded red sweater under Petey's belly. "Now look in the kitchen window behind them."

Angus did. It was a flash photo, and light shone off the window in a smudgy glare. "Is it this?" He pointed. "You said it was a face, but that looks like someone's hand."

"It does a little. No, it's a woman's face. See, here's her nose and there's the chin, and she's wearing a sort of bonnet. Victorian, I think."

Angus squinted. "Now I see it." His mind kept trying to make it a hand, but he persevered. "Who do you think it is?"

"Charlotte's aunt," Bob whispered. "The one who gave her this house. Perhaps she's been trying to tell Charlotte something all this time, but they didn't have a strong enough connection. Now that Petey is dead, she's trying to send a message through him."

Angus looked at the little man with admiration. "Have you ever thought of writing, Mr. Hume? Just one minor detail—the Victorian era ended around 1900. The house may be that old, but Charlotte's aunt was probably an adult in . . ." He did some quick math. "Oh, somewhere around 1920. They did wear hats of various sorts then."

"But not bonnets?"

"Not so much, no."

Bob studied the picture. "It could be a spectral shower cap."

Angus revised his view of Bob as a regular contributor to *Tripping*. "Regardless, it's an intriguing photo. Was it you who took the photograph?"

"Yes."

"We'll give you a photo credit. And I know it was some time ago, but do you remember feeling anything odd when you took it?"

Bob looked at him blankly.

"A sense of unease? Possibly a drop in temperature?"

"Oh, *right*. Um, I heard a voice, whispering. At the time, I thought it was the radio."

"Excellent." Angus gestured with the photo. "I'll keep this for now, if it's all right with you. We'll get it back to you as soon as possible." He headed toward the stairs, then realized Bob was following him and turned back. "I'm sorry, but you'll have to excuse me while we set up. Trade secrets, you know."

"Oh, sure." Bob nodded. "Can the photo credit mention Petey's Pride dog food as well as my name?"

"That's a bit long for a credit. We'll try to get it in the article, shall we?"

Bob's face lit up. "Great! Thanks!"

Angus started up the stairs, then realized he hadn't heard Bob use the front door. He turned.

Bob was gazing toward the kitchen.

"Perhaps you should see if you can find any more photos of Petey," Angus said, gesturing toward the door.

"Okay." Bob left.

Angus went upstairs to the shared parlor and closed the door behind him.

Suki looked up from attaching one of her cameras to a tripod. "What took you so long?"

Angus held up the picture. "Yet because of his importunity, he will rise and give him a photo credit."

"Huh?" Michael said.

"I'm quoting a biblical parable, about nagging."

"And is God for nagging or against it?" Michael asked.

"For, as is Bob Hume, but we got a nice photo of Petey with a spectral form behind him."

They crowded around him, and he pointed to the shape.

"Is that a guy on a snowboard?" Suki asked. "They don't die as often as you'd think."

"No, it's a woman's face. There's her chin and there's her mouth, and she has something on her head."

Michael squinted at it. "A dead Chihuahua, maybe."

Angus handed him the picture. "Poke fun if you want, but he says it's Charlotte Baskerville's deceased aunt trying to get in touch with her through Petey's ghost."

Michael raised his eyebrows. "Not bad."

"I'm glad you recognize good material when you hear it."

Suki picked up a nylon bag from the floor and hung it from her shoulder. "Where do you want to set up tonight, Angus? Ideally, the ghost would appear where I can shoot him with the tripod, but I'm prepared to go with video and take a still from that."

"I'd say the back patio, but if our ghost is shy, we might be better shooting out a window." He held up a hand. "Listen."

From out in the hall, they heard voices and the sound of footfalls on the wooden floor.

"*Now* what?" Michael muttered, as Thomas Baskerville's hectoring voice became recognizable.

"No!" This was shouted by Charlotte Baskerville, and was followed by the sound of a door slamming.

Angus opened the door and strode into the hall.

At the end of the corridor, Thomas Baskerville banged on his wife's closed door.

A nervous-looking man in a suit stood next to him. As Thomas paused, the man glanced back at Angus and said, "Mr. Baskerville, I'm not sure I—"

"Charlotte!" Thomas shouted through the door. "If you're fine, then why won't you talk to the man?"

"What seems to be the problem?" Angus said, coming up to them.

The door opened and Charlotte stood there, clutching Lila. She stabbed a finger at her husband. "If you think I'm going to talk to your hired psychiatrist, Thomas, then *you're* the one who's crazy."

Thomas smiled ingratiatingly. "It's not me who sees things, dear."

"Have I ever struck you as a stupid woman?" Charlotte patted Lila nervously. "If I get therapy, which I probably need from living with you, it won't be with some shrink you've paid to show I'm incapable."

The man in the suit raised his hands in apology. "I'm very sorry to have approached you this way, ma'am. Mr. Baskerville told me you had agreed to a consultation."

"You heard her say she needs therapy, right?" Thomas demanded.

The suited man took a step back. "I'll be going now."

"Just a moment," Angus said, moving between him and the stairs. "I think you should give Mrs. Baskerville your card, in case she needs another witness to her husband's harassment."

The man groaned and reached into a pocket.

"Don't listen to them!" Thomas raged. "The house is full of moochers, living off my wife's money! These people are probably telling her the spirits want her to write them a big check."

Angus shook his head sadly. "What a thing to say, and after you had dinner with a lawyer, too. Do you not know the meaning of slander, Mr. Baskerville?"

"I said *probably*. You can't get me on that." He jerked his head at the psychiatrist. "Let's go. You're no help at all." Thomas walked quickly down the hallway, but the other man beat him and clattered down the stairs first.

Charlotte let out a breath that was almost a sob. "I just want you to know that I would *never* have married a man who acted this way. It's as though he got into the habit of being angry and now he can't stop."

"Not to be too personal, but I hope the Petey's Closet finances are separate from your joint accounts," Angus said.

She nodded. "I set them up that way from the first, so I wouldn't be tempted to take money from the household budget." She sighed, then turned in the doorway and looked behind her. "*Listen.* Did you hear something?"

Followed by Angus, Charlotte tiptoed toward the window, then stopped at the sound of a faint howl, coming from somewhere outside. It ended in a tremulous warble. "That's him," she whispered. "That's Petey!"

Angus turned toward Suki and Michael, who stood just outside the bedroom door. "Get out there," he said, jerking his head toward the stairs. "Quietly."

Michael and Suki ran back into the parlor to collect their gear. Michael found his recorder in the pocket of his jacket, then saw that Suki was already out the door.

He ran into the hallway after her, pulling his arms through the jacket's sleeves and wishing his shoes made less noise. Suki was almost silent as they ran down the stairs, and he saw that what he'd taken for dressy shoes actually had flat, soft soles. "Is that the still or video camera?" he asked.

"Both," she whispered back. When they got to the bottom, she turned toward the front door.

Michael grabbed her shoulder. "What are you doing? It's in the back!"

"The kitchen light's on, and all those windows make that room like a goldfish bowl. Whatever's out there, it'll see us coming if we go that way."

"We could turn out the light," Michael suggested.

"That's just as obvious." She opened the front door and slipped outside.

Michael followed as Suki ran lightly across the wet front yard, holding the camera tripod at the halfway mark. The bark came again, louder this time, still warbling at the end.

Michael switched on his recorder and held it in front of him. The little machine was designed to be spoken into, but maybe it would pick up something.

A nearby streetlight gave enough illumination to show the end of a narrow sidewalk that led to the backyard. It was darker between the houses, and they walked more slowly.

Michael saw Suki step over something and hesitated until he

could make out a coiled garden hose on the path. They reached the privacy fence. Luckily, the gate stood open.

The bark came again. *It sounds the same as the last time,* Michael thought. *As though it's a recording.*

Suki stood close to the house and gently eased the tripod legs open. Then she walked a few steps forward onto the patio and set it carefully in front of her.

Michael was close enough to hear the soft noise of the camera powering on. He expected to see the tiny blink of a status light, but nothing happened. Maybe she had it disabled. He looked down at his recorder and covered the red power light with his thumb before moving quietly forward.

Rowf . . . OohooOOoo . . .

The now-familiar sound floated through the air. When it ended, Michael heard a solitary car drive by, maybe a block away. After that, the deep silence of a small town descended, broken only by the occasional drip of rainwater from branches.

Still, they weren't the only people out here. Slits of light interrupted the dark walls of Ellen's stone workshop, from behind lowered shades.

Michael stepped carefully to Suki's side and put his mouth close enough to feel her hair on his lips. His voice no more than a breath, he said, "What if it's just Ellen, putting a video of Petey on the Web site or something?"

The bark came again, but this time the wavering howl at the end grew longer, louder, the final note oscillating until it sounded like words spoken in a high, quavering voice.

Woourtuhvohsss . . . Tuhvortahmahhhhhzzz . . . Duhvohhh-hzzzz . . . Tihbohrahnowwww . . . The sound died away.

Michael, still with his head next to Suki's, whispered, "Or maybe not."

They waited, but the night remained silent. The voice had apparently gone. Michael was just switching off his recorder when Angus's loud whisper came from above.

"Hey, you lot. Are you down there?"

Michael and Suki walked forward into the yard and looked up and back, to where Angus and Charlotte could be seen at the open second-floor window.

"We're here!" Suki said, just loud enough to be heard. "I didn't see anything, did you?"

"No."

"I had my recorder going," Michael said, in a more normal voice. "But it's not designed for distance. I don't know if it picked up anything."

"My camera has a microphone that's for more general stuff," Suki added. "It might have gotten something."

"I'm coming down," Angus called. He disappeared from the window.

"I'm going to check the workshop," Michael said. Followed by Suki, he walked over to the stone building and knocked on the door.

After a moment, Ellen opened it. "Yes?" Classical music played in the background, the romantic swell of violins overlying the whir of an electric heater that stood in one corner of the room.

"Did you hear the howling outside?" Michael asked her.

"When?"

"Just now."

She looked from one to the other of them. "I didn't hear a thing. These stone walls block most sound, plus, we had storm windows put on." She opened the door wider. "Do you want to come in?"

Angus joined them. "What's going on?"

"Can I try a brief experiment in here?" Michael asked Ellen.

"Go ahead."

Inside, the workshop tables were bare except for papers. Several file drawers stood open.

Michael walked over to a small boom box and turned the music up to about three times the volume. "Sorry, but this will just take a second." He gestured to Suki and Angus. "Could you two go outside and listen?"

The other two went outside, and Michael closed the door behind them. Then he opened it. "Is the music about the same volume as the dog noise?"

"Crank it up maybe twenty-five percent," Suki said.

Angus hunched deeper into his jacket and blew out a breath. "This is a waste of time."

Michael went inside again. The music played, and they stood in the chill air. Then the sound dropped and disappeared, and Michael opened the door.

Ellen appeared beside him, looking angry. "I wasn't playing dog sounds from in here."

"Of course not," Angus soothed.

Michael stepped outside and folded his arms. "Recorded violins heard through a stone building might conceivably sound like a dog howling."

Suki shook her head doubtfully. "This is Bach, not Stravinsky."

"If you'll excuse me," Ellen said, "I'm going back to work." She closed the door.

"Where's Charlotte?" Suki asked.

"Lying down," Angus said. "She feels a bit rattled, as you might expect after hearing a ghost. Not to mention her husband suggesting she's crazy."

"Speaking of Mr. Charm," Michael said, "where is Thomas Baskerville?"

"I suppose we ought to make sure he's not playing tricks," Angus said.

They went back inside and trooped through the house to the downstairs parlor, where Angus rapped on the door to Thomas's room. No one answered.

"Anyone notice what kind of car he drives?" Angus asked.

"I saw a silver Corolla parked outside," Suki said. "That might be his."

They went outside and looked up and down the street. There was no Corolla, and the closest car was two houses away. "Hmm . . . ," Angus said. "I don't like the idea of Charlotte being at home alone if he comes back."

"Ellen's here," Michael pointed out.

"In that stone hut where she can't hear a damn thing."

At that moment, a battered Ford Explorer pulled up, bass speakers thumping through the closed windows. The engine and music shut off, and Cheri opened the passenger door. Her fur-trimmed suede jacket hung open, showing a silvery, low-necked top. "Hey," she said to them. "Did you go to the Happy Mountaineer?"

"We went to Rhumbalicious," Angus said.

A young man appeared around the other side of the car. His jet black hair was shiny and short, and led into long sideburns. He wore black jeans and a long fitted coat, and held his arms away from his body as he walked toward them.

"Hey," he said, his glance taking them all in before coming to rest on Suki.

"Guys, this is Jay," Cheri said. "Jay, these are the people from the magazine."

"You missed all the excitement," Angus said.

"Did you see something?" Cheri asked eagerly.

"We heard something," Angus said. "If we're lucky, either Michael or Suki will have caught it on tape."

"Digital, actually," Michael said.

The sound of a sliding-glass door preceded Bob Hume's voice. "Are you having a party? I have some dip." Light silhouetted his rounded figure as he stood on the upstairs deck of the neighboring house.

Jay muttered something too quiet to hear.

"I'll come over," Bob called.

Angus raised his hands to his mouth. "It's not neces—" He broke off as the sliding door thumped shut.

"You gotta be quick," Jay said quietly.

In moments, Bob was pattering up the sidewalk, holding a bowl in both hands.

Angus reluctantly held open the door to the Baskerville house. "We're not having a party."

"That's all right. Dip is good anytime. This one has celery and Tabasco added to regular onion dip."

"I'll see if Charlotte is up to joining us." Angus said, his hand on the banister. "Why don't the rest of you go into the kitchen?"

"I have to get my laptop." Suki went up the stairs past him, carrying her camera on its tripod.

Bob followed Michael, Cheri, and Jay toward the kitchen, chattering as he went. "The only thing is, I don't have chips. I was going to buy chips tomorrow. Maybe we could eat this on toast. Is Charlotte all right?"

"She's fine." Michael sat at the kitchen table and fiddled with his recorder.

Cheri opened a cupboard and took out a bag of corn chips, which she put on the table. "So you heard the ghost. What did it sound like?"

"Like a dog that was trying to talk," Michael said.

"Whoa." Jay took off his black coat and folded it carefully over the back of his chair before sitting.

Angus and Charlotte came in. Suki followed, carrying her laptop, her video camera, and a handful of other equipment.

They settled around the table, Charlotte at the head, her hands clasped tightly. "I've never heard anything so frightening." Her voice was barely audible over the crackling of the chip bag as Bob opened it.

"Michael, did your machine get anything?" Angus asked.

Michael turned the volume all the way up on his recorder and held it to his ear. "You can tell there's a sound, but that's about it."

"We might be able to jack into my car stereo," Jay said.

Suki plugged a set of small cube speakers into her laptop. "Let's see what we get with this."

On the laptop screen, the video frame showed a foggy square of charcoal. They heard the gentle crunch of a leaf under someone's foot, remarkably clear. And then the sound of Petey's distinctive bark.

Charlotte wrapped her arms around herself.

"I think it's the next one where he talks," Suki said.

They sat, tense and listening. Soft white noise came through, and then a slight breathy sound.

"Oh, you have got to be kidding me," Michael said. "Is that it?"

Suki raised a hand. "That's *you,* whispering."

"Oh."

Rowf . . . OohooOOoo . . . Woourtuhvohsss . . . Tuhvortahmahh-hhhzzz . . . Duhvohhhhzzzz . . . Tihbohrahnowwww . . .

"Oh, my *God*," Cheri whispered.

"That is seriously weird." Jay shook his head solemnly, then put a loaded chip in his mouth.

Bob bounced in his chair. "It sounds like words, doesn't it? Can we hear it again?"

"Just a sec." Suki pulled the laptop toward her. "I have a video-editing program on this. I'll cut the talking part out and put it on loop. It'll be quicker in the long run."

After a few minutes, she clicked on the touchpad and sat back. The weirdly modulated words played through once, then started over. "Hold on. Let me see if I can screen out the fuzz." She made an adjustment. "That's better."

Charlotte leaned forward on the table. "That almost sounded like 'Thomas.'"

"Try making it faster," Michael suggested.

Their lips moved as they tried to make sense of the syllables.

"That last word kind of sounds like *tiburón*," Suki said.

"It does," Bob agreed. "*Tiburón* means *shark* in Spanish. Maybe it's a warning."

Angus gave him a wry look. "I think we're pretty safe from sharks, here in the center of the country."

Woourtuhvohsss . . . Tuhvortahmahhhhhzzz . . . Duhvohhh-hzzzz . . . Tihbohrahnowwww . . .

"Tuhvor, duhvohz . . . ," Michael muttered.

Cheri squinted at the speakers. "I don't think that first word starts with *T*. I think they all began with *D*."

"Maybe." Michael frowned in concentration. "Duhvohz, duhvor—"

"Divorce," Charlotte whispered, hands clutching her upper arms.

They stared at her.

"Divorce Thomas," she said.

Seven

Half an hour later, Angus paced the floor of the upstairs parlor as Suki put her equipment away. "I don't like the idea of Charlotte being here alone except for that girl," he grumbled.

"Charlotte said she wasn't going to tell Thomas tonight," Suki said. "And Ellen is here, although she's not in the house."

"Apparently she sometimes spends half the night in that hut. She wouldn't hear a thing if Thomas decided to throw his wife out a window." Angus sat on the settee and drummed his fingers on his knees.

Michael came in and closed the door softly behind him. "Jay's gone home. I talked to Cheri and she says this is one of Ivan's evenings to go to the casinos in Silver City. He has dinner there and then gambles. There's no telling when he'll be back."

"That's it." Angus pushed himself to his feet. "I'm going to ask Charlotte if I can stay the night." He went into the hall.

Michael sighed and sat down in a chair. "So much for the distance between a reporter and his subject."

Suki looked up. "That's exactly what they said at *National Geographic*."

The room at the Manitou Arms had two double beds and a small table with two chairs. Michael, wearing flannel pajama bottoms and a T-shirt, sat on the bed, studying back issues of *Tripping*. As far as he could tell, Angus had written every article. The style was florid and the layout needed a lot of work.

He tossed aside the issue featuring mystery cats, pulled his laptop onto his thighs, and typed some possible headlines for the Baskerville story. Faithful Unto Death, and Beyond? Phantom Pup Stalks Manitou Springs. The Curious Incident of the Chihuahua in the Nighttime. He smiled and shook his head at the last one but kept typing. When he had twenty possible titles, he stopped and considered a first line. *Charlotte Baskerville's dog refuses to leave her side, even though he's dead.* That was a grabber, and short enough that even the most ADD reader shouldn't lose interest halfway through.

Michael spent the next couple of hours transcribing notes from his recorder and writing. Finally he backed up his work and closed the document before opening the file for his own book—his baby.

> *Sonia knelt and rested her hot forehead against Don Juan Conejo's cooler silken one, until his ruby eyes blurred into the surrounding white fur, like blood on melting snow.*
> "You shore do love that rabbit, don't you?" Earl drawled.

Michael studied the screen. Then he added *li'l* before *rabbit*. Then he took it out. Don Juan Conejo weighed seven pounds, after all. Some rabbits were much smaller. But would Earl Buckhalter know that? He chewed his lip.

An hour later, he put the computer away and lay on his back, arms crossed behind his head. Was Earl's accent too thick? Would Sonia, a woman who had grown up listening to Bizet's *Carmen* over and over, seriously consider marrying a man who said *shore*? Wouldn't pride keep her from loving him?

Pride had certainly destroyed the Baskervilles' relationship. Charlotte and Thomas had raised a son, weathered financial loss, and fussed over a dog together, but now Thomas seemed determined to undermine his wife's success, even if it meant ruining a business that benefited him.

Looked at that way, anyone who profited from Petey's Closet would want Charlotte to divorce Thomas. Presumably she wouldn't have listened to Ellen, Cheri, or Ivan, but she was certainly listening to Petey.

Michael wondered how Angus was doing at the Baskerville house.

Angus rolled over carefully. The cot Charlotte had provided was not big, but at least it had a thin pad. Still, whichever shoulder he lay on ached after a while.

Angus had couched his offer to spend the night in terms of ghost watching, and Charlotte Baskerville had accepted eagerly. He even had his little digital camera, in case the ghost decided to show itself.

After a quick trip to the motel, he'd returned with the essentials: toothbrush and paste, razor, and a change of clothes. Now he lay on the cot in plaid boxers and a white T-shirt, wide awake.

He had managed to sleep for a little while, but had woken when he heard heavy, irregular footsteps in the hall. He opened his door a crack. The hall light was off, but he could still see Ivan walk carefully to his room, one hand on the wall.

That had been shortly after one o'clock. No sooner had he gone back to his cot than he'd heard a door open somewhere in the hall, and then the sound of someone quietly knocking on a door. Peeking out again, he saw Cheri standing outside Ivan's room, a robe wrapped around her.

She tapped again, and the door opened. Cheri murmured something and slipped inside Ivan's room with a giggle. Angus waited until it became obvious that Cheri wasn't coming out immediately. Then he tiptoed quietly into the hall and put his ear to Ivan's door.

He heard the sound of voices—Ivan's low and ponderous, Cheri's light, with lots of laughing. Was that the clink of bottle and glass? He pressed his ear closer but the heavy wood let no more sound out.

Finally he went back to his room and lay on his back for a change. He was just starting to get drowsy when he heard a door open again. He rose quickly, took two large steps across the room, and went into the hall.

Cheri closed Ivan's door carefully, then turned and saw Angus. "What are you doing up?" she asked, her expression pouty.

"Bathroom." He took a few steps toward Charlotte's end of the hall. It was the opposite direction from the guest bathroom, but put him directly in Cheri's path to her bedroom. She took a few steps toward him. Was she weaving?

"Other way," she whispered, pointing back toward the stairs.

"Sorry, what?" Angus whispered. He put a hand to one ear and bent over.

She obligingly stepped closer. "You're going the *wrong way*. It's there." She pointed again.

Angus sniffed. "That's quite the strawberry breath you have." Was it covering something, like vodka?

"It's my toothpaste. Good night, Mr. Ghost Man." She giggled.

"Good night." He walked the correct way down the hall, glancing back briefly. Cheri opened her door with no sign of difficulty, and her steps didn't seem unsteady.

With a sigh, Angus went into the bathroom, switched on the light, and closed the door. One side of the counter held someone's personal toiletries, and he remembered that the guest bathroom was also Ellen's.

As he took a leak, he thought about mousy Ellen. She seemed to be lowest on the totem pole, always opening doors and showing people around, yet Petey's Closet was built on her designs.

That wasn't strictly true. It was built on Ellen's designs plus Charlotte's networking, marketing know-how, and money. Presumably they were partners. Ellen was simply the kind of person who opened doors and fetched things, whereas Charlotte was not.

Angus flushed the toilet, then opened the door and checked the distance to his room before turning off the light. Second door along.

He switched off the bathroom light, then paused as something caught his eye.

A small green dot shone up from the floor where the bathroom threshold met the wood floor of the hall. In shape, it resembled nothing so much as a paint drip.

Angus squatted and ran his finger over it. It felt dry. He looked at his fingertip and thought he saw a faint glow there, as well. It was difficult to tell, as his eyes struggled with shades of darkness.

Angus stood and flipped the bathroom light back on, then dampened some toilet paper under the tap and squeezed it out. He turned the light back out and rubbed at the spot, using his thumbnail behind the paper.

When he was finished, only the tiniest glow remained from where the stuff had run into a crack in the wood. Someone would have to really look to spot it.

Angus flushed the wad of damp toilet paper down the toilet, washed his hands, and went back to his cot.

Eight

The next morning, Angus called Suki and Michael and told them to meet him at a local breakfast place at ten.

They took their seats, and Michael studied Angus's face. "Everything quiet last night? You look a little tired."

"There was some to-ing and fro-ing during the night, but Thomas and the ghost stayed away." Angus leaned forward and whispered, "The granddaughter may be drinking. She may also be sleeping with Ivan."

"Interesting," Michael murmured.

"Not something we can write about, however."

"Well, we *could*," Michael countered.

"But we're not going to." Angus took the menu the waitress handed him.

"The special today is cherry French toast," she said.

They all ordered the special. When the waitress had left, Suki pointed to the front window, awash in sunshine. "A beautiful day like this is great for detail and color but not so good for spooky. Do you have anything particular in mind?"

Angus shrugged. "We've never tried for atmosphere in the travel-oriented photos."

"I could go for odd angles and framing," Suki said. "Shoot from down low, catch the sides and backs of people passing. That's more interesting than standard shots, but doesn't sacrifice information."

"It sounds a great deal more effective than my little snapshots," Angus said. "I leave it in your capable hands."

Their food came shortly afterward. Michael looked at his plate. The triangles of French toast were red with cherry preserves, making them look like a smiling mouth, and two circles of whipped cream had been squirted above them to look like eyes. "This is disturbing."

Angus squeezed lemon into his cup of tea. "Too cynical to enjoy a bit of innocent whimsy, Michael?"

"You guys should shut up and eat," Suki said. "This is the best thing I've had in my mouth for a month."

Michael took a bite of food. "Mmmm! Uhmum mmph."

"Told you," Suki said.

They ate in silence for a while, pausing only to nod in appreciation when the waitress asked how everything was.

"So what's the plan?" Michael asked, after scraping his plate clean.

Angus took a sip of tea. "At some point, I'd like more information from Charlotte as to what her ghost experience was like. But I suppose we should stay out of her hair today and focus on the town, seeing as how she might be asking her husband for a divorce."

"I wouldn't mind a few more photos at the Baskerville house," Suki said, "but I can make do with what I have."

Angus nodded. "We'll see how it goes. In the meantime, Michael, I want you to go to Miramont Castle and ask about their ghosts. Officially it's too late to get tickets to Emma Crawford's wake, but tell them you're a reporter and see what they'll do for you."

"So this is a different event than the race," Michael said. "Emma's corpse isn't really in the coffin, is it?"

"No," Angus assured him. "It's one of the local girls, very much alive. They serve a buffet dinner, and there's a history lesson by people dressed as notables who visited or lived in Manitou Springs at the time. They have photos online that they'll probably let us use, but do you have a camera?"

"Yeah, but where's Suki going to be?"

Angus turned to her. "Suki, I'd like you to go to the Regency. It's supposed to be one of the most haunted restaurants in America. I set things up so they know you're coming. There should be a packet of materials waiting for you."

Suki nodded. "So all you need from me is pictures?"

"Yes, but I hope you'll feel free to ask questions and take notes," Angus said.

Michael wiped his mouth with his napkin. "And where are you going, Angus?"

"I'm going to talk to the Chamber of Commerce and see who might want to advertise in *Tripping*. I also think Manitou Springs is just the kind of place that might be interested in a festival to honor Petey."

Michael walked from the restaurant to Miramont Castle, taking notes as he went. Manitou Springs' downtown appeared to be thriving. He passed several of the natural springs. A well-muscled man in his sixties rode his bicycle up to one, leaned against the wall without dismounting, and filled up a bottle before riding on.

Miramont Castle lay on a side street off Ruxton Avenue. It wasn't a castle in the fortress style, but rather a three-storied, many-chimneyed mansion made of red stone. It did have one crenellated section. In fact, the general effect was of five or so imposing houses squeezed into one.

Before going inside, Michael waited until a thin cloud covered the sun, and then squatted to take a picture of the castle's face. The result looked properly imposing. "Not bad," he murmured, pocketing the camera and trotting up the stairs to the entrance.

A pretty brunette sat at the wooden reception desk, wearing a blazer over a purple satin blouse. "May I help you?"

"I'm Michael Abernathy, from *Tripping* magazine. We write about travel destinations with paranormal aspects. I understand you have some ghosts?"

The woman's face lit up. "We certainly do!" She opened one of the desk drawers. "I'm Phoebe. You know, I don't show these pictures to everyone." She came around the desk with a small stack of photos in her hand.

"Do you mind if I record our conversation, for the article?"

"Go right ahead!"

The first photo was grainy and looked as though it had been shot in a dark room with a flash. Two pale spots floated in the middle. They had been circled with a ballpoint pen.

"Do you know what those are?" Phoebe asked, pointing to them.

To Michael, the spots looked like they might be caused by water spots on the emulsion. He stopped himself from saying so. "What?"

"Orbs. Energetic spirits." She flipped to another photo. "There's one hovering over one of the dolls in our collection. You have to wonder if it's the spirit of the little girl who owned the doll, and she can't bear to leave it."

Michael wondered if Mattel had heard about this, and if the company was working on a Dear Departed Barbie. "What about Emma Crawford? You have a wake for her here, right? Does her ghost ever appear?"

"Emma died before the castle was completed, but the ghosts of other Victorian ladies and gentlemen have been seen." She put the top photo behind the others. "Which brings me to this."

Michael looked at the new photo. "What?"

"In the mirror. Do you see it? It's a figure in a black dress, floating beside that dress mannequin. Only the dress is *not there*."

Michael took the photo from her hand and squinted at it, trying to make sense of the arrangement of items. The unoccupied black dress did appear to float in midair, and he could see a chair through it. "That's quite a picture. Do you think I could get a copy?"

"This one is on our Web site," she said.

"Great." He handed the photo back. "Listen, my magazine is happy to pay admission, but we don't have reservations for the Emma Crawford wake. Would it be possible to just stand in a corner? We'd really love to do a write-up on the event for our magazine."

"I think we can fit you in, as members of the press. You won't be able to have dinner, is all. Is it just you?"

"Me, a photographer, and the general editor."

"Do you have a card, so I can tell the organizer that you're coming?"

Michael reached into his coat pocket and pulled out a business card. Pendergast hadn't printed any in time, so he'd made his own. "If there's any problem, give me a call." He looked around. "I suppose I should tour the castle now."

She handed him a piece of paper. "Here's the self-guided tour. That door leads to the doll collection, or you can go that way to start your tour of the castle. Have fun!"

Michael decided to skip the doll collection and walked slowly up the stairs instead, reading the handout as he went. The builder of Miramont, Father Francolon, came from a wealthy French family. Sent to Manitou Springs in 1892, he decided to build a house for himself and his aged mother.

After he and his mother died, nuns took over the house and ran it as a hospital. Afterward, it stood derelict for a while before the people of Manitou Springs restored it through volunteer labor, turning it into a tourist attraction.

The self-guided tour pointed out some original wallpaper that used arsenic as a coloring agent. Moving on, Michael looked out the window at a parapet with no railing and reflected that there were a lot of ways to die in old houses.

Finally he reached the solarium. A full wall of multipaned glass looked out on the surrounding peaks. After soaking in the panoramic view of sun-washed slopes and cerulean sky, Michael looked down at the neighborhood below.

His gaze picked out a small stone building in the backyard of one of the homes, and he realized it was the workshop behind the Baskerville house. As he watched, a pickup truck pulled into the driveway of the house next door—Bob Hume's place.

The driver's door opened and a man got out. It looked like Bob, although the distance was too great to tell for sure. Whoever it was went to the rear of the truck and opened the tailgate.

The passenger-side door opened and someone wearing a coat with the hood pulled up got out. Noting the coat's hot pink color, Michael decided it was probably a woman.

She joined Bob for a moment, then cut across Bob's yard diagonally, away from the Baskerville place, and walked briskly down the sidewalk.

Bob slid a box out of the truck and put it on the ground as though it were fairly heavy. After closing the truck's tailgate, he opened the garage and took the box inside.

Michael turned away. He'd been curious as to whether Bob had a girlfriend, but it didn't look that way—probably someone to whom he'd given a lift.

Michael moved on to Father Francolon's library and spent a jealous few minutes admiring the tall bookcases and equally tall windows before remembering what he was there for. He should ask Phoebe whether the place had any secret passageways.

Returning to the solarium for a final look at the view, he saw that the small figure in pink had gone right around the block. As Michael peered downward, she went up the walk to the Baskerville house and disappeared inside.

"That's weird," he muttered.

Suki parked Angus's car at the Regency. The sun was shining brightly, giving the rosy bricks a glow that looked anything but macabre. Luckily, it cast the shadow of a large tree across the face of the house.

Carrying her camera on its tripod, she walked to and fro across the graveled drive until she found a spot where the tree's shadow appeared to be flowing out of the front door like a plague of locusts. *Nice.*

Finally she went up to the entrance. It felt strange to go in without knocking, but it was a restaurant, after all.

The foyer, a symphony of cream upholstery and dark wood, was deserted. She took a few photos of the fireplace, staircase, and molded-tin ceiling.

"Hello?" Suki called. "Anybody here?" She wandered down a hall and into yet another graceful room, with a bar on one side. "Hello?"

The temperature suddenly dropped, and she heard a sucking sound behind her. Her camera came up automatically as she turned.

"Sorry to make you wait." The woman approaching Suki wore jeans and a flannel shirt. "I was in the wine cooler and didn't hear you." In the alcove behind her, a glass door closed, the gasket making a suction noise. The flow of cold air died away.

"No problem." Suki introduced herself. "I'm here to take pictures of the manor for *Tripping* magazine."

"Right. I'm Barb Metcalf." Barb had a sweet, round face topped by curly blond hair. She looked admiringly at Suki's clothes. "I love your outfit. I wish I could be super fashionable like that."

"Like any hobby, it can be a real money sink," Suki said.

Barb smiled at her. "Do you want to take the tour first, or look at the stuff I put together for you? There's not a lot, because you can get pretty much anything you need off the Web site."

"Let's do the tour."

"Okay, we'll start with the basement. That's not something most people get to see." She led the way into a huge light-filled room, windowed on two sides. "Your magazine has such an interesting concept—paranormal and travel, I mean," she said, threading her way through tables set with linens and china.

"Yeah. Can you hold up a minute? I want to get a shot of the dining room."

"Sure. This is the largest of the dining rooms." Barb came back and waited while Suki took several photos. "Is your article about haunted restaurants?"

"No, it's about a local family being haunted by one of their dead pets."

"I know who that is! The Baskervilles, right? My son, Jay, dates their granddaughter, and he told me about it." Barb led Suki into the brightly lit kitchen. A few men were already prepping vegetables and laboring over a steaming pot of soup.

"If you're a friend of the family, maybe Michael or Angus should interview you," Suki said.

"Oh, I don't know Charlotte or Thomas that well. But I am friends with Ellen Froehlich."

Suki nodded, mentally contrasting chatty Barb with quiet Ellen. Ellen must be the listener in that relationship. "I guess Ellen is really a big part of the company."

"Not as big as she should be, that's for sure. On the other hand, Charlotte saw Ellen through a really tough time."

"Yeah?" As they went past a series of industrial refrigerators, Suki wondered how to encourage Barb to gossip, but it appeared encouragement wasn't needed.

"Ellen lived with a man for twelve years," Barb said. "The guy was very against marriage—talked about it being a tool of the state. Then one day, he comes home and tells Ellen he's met someone and is hot to marry *her*. Can you believe it?"

"That's pretty bad."

"*And* he took their dogs. They'd been his to begin with, I guess. Anyway, Ellen was so depressed, she quit her job and was living off savings in some poky apartment, because of course the house was his and she'd been spending her extra money to keep up with him on vacations."

"How did Charlotte come to know Ellen?" Suki asked.

"From dog walking. Charlotte asked her to help fill orders for Petey's Closet. I don't know if she really needed the help, but it gave Ellen something new to think about, which was a good thing."

"Was Ellen into sewing before she started working with Charlotte?"

"She knew the basics. Charlotte taught her more, and pretty soon Ellen was coming up with designs on her own. Charlotte likes to say it was the dog movie that made business take off, but it was around that same time that the first catalog came out with all of Ellen's designs."

"And now Ellen lives with Charlotte, as well," Suki said. "That's a lot of togetherness."

"Uh-huh." Barb opened a door. "These steps are really steep, so hang on to the rail."

Suki wondered if Ellen paid rent to Charlotte. She waited to see if Barb would dish on that, but they had reached the cellar and the conversation turned.

"We used to keep more supplies down here, but it's not handy for the kitchen. Now we only use it for overstock—you know, like if we get a super good deal on canned tomatoes or something." Barb shivered. "Feel how cold it is? I brought you down here first because it's where something happened to me."

"Can I take your picture while you tell me?" Suki asked, putting the tripod in place.

Barb looked flattered. "Okay. It was about two years ago, and I came down here to get some stock."

"Chicken?" Suki lowered the camera a tad, so the flash would throw slight shadows up onto Barb's face.

"I think it was cannellini beans. Anyway, I was getting the beans when the light suddenly flickered and went out. And then, from somewhere behind me, *I heard a can fall off the shelves.*"

"That must have freaked you out." Suki took a couple of shots and wished Barb were wearing something without a plaid pattern. Plaid wasn't scary, except in a cheesy *Blair Witch Project* kind of way.

"You bet it scared me!" Barb said. "I let out a bloodcurdling scream and started feeling my way toward the stairs, but I think I would have had a heart attack if José hadn't been passing by and turned on the light." She held up a hand. "And to those people who say José turned it off to play a trick—first of all, he swore on a Bible that he didn't, and second, that doesn't explain the can that fell off the shelf."

At that moment, the overhead lights flickered and went out.

Barb let out a scream that made Suki's ears ring.

The light came back on. "Sorry!" a man's voice called from the stairwell. "Didn't know anyone was down there."

Barb stood with her hand pressed against her chest, eyes bulging and mouth open as she took panting breaths.

Suki took her picture and smiled with satisfaction. "Perfect."

Angus took his time walking to the Chamber of Commerce. The city had a ton of quirky charm. Because it lay in a fairly narrow canyon, there wasn't room for businesses that didn't fill a strong need.

In fact, Manitou Springs brought to mind one of those miniature villages people put under Christmas trees. It even had a small train—the Pikes Peak Cog Railway. No wonder Charlotte Baskerville did so well with her line of tiny clothing.

He pushed open the door to the Chamber of Commerce.

A grizzled man with a beard and wire-rimmed glasses sat behind the front desk. "Hello," he said. "Help you?"

"I'm Angus MacGregor, from *Tripping* magazine. We're doing a story on the ghost of Petey."

"*Tripping* magazine? What drugs do you have to take to see this Petey?"

"No, *Tripping* is a travel magazine about paranormal destinations."

"Oh." The man looked thoughtful. "Petey . . . I know a lot of local ghosts, but that one's new to me."

"Petey was Mrs. Charlotte Baskerville's Chihuahua."

The man gave a bemused nod. "We'll add him to the list." He stood and stuck out a hand. "Shermont Lester."

Angus shook it. "You have a list of ghosts?"

"And one mummy. Tom O'Neal."

"What's his story?" Angus asked.

"Died in a saloon brawl in the late 1800s. No family came to claim the body, so Doc Davis, a man with a scientific bent in addition to being county coroner, decided to turn Tom into a mummy. It worked real well. When the doc died, his family buried Tom O'Neal, but grave robbers took the mummy. It wound up in a traveling sideshow, tricked out with a wig and tomahawk and billed as a petrified Indian found in the caverns around here."

Angus smiled. "I hadn't heard that story, but apparently there was a spate of sideshow mummies with similar backgrounds during that time."

Shermont nodded. "Those wacky Victorians."

Angus laughed and handed Shermont a card. "Would it be possible to e-mail me a copy of your ghost list, for our article?"

Shermont took the card. "Will do."

Angus leaned on the counter. "I understand Manitou Springs has several yearly festivals."

"*Several* doesn't begin to cut it. There's the Emma Crawford Coffin Festival, the Great Fruitcake Toss, the Buffalo BBQ, Huck Finn Day, the Mumbo Jumbo Gumbo Cook-off, Mardi Gras Carnivale Parade—"

"That last must be a little chilly, during February in Colorado."

"There'll be no bare breasts, I can tell you that. Even if a woman wanted to show something, the parade would be long past by the time she got it out from under four layers. We've got a couple of art and music festivals, a wine festival, the historic speaker series, and Author Fest of the Rockies. Lotta creative types in this town."

"One thing you don't seem to have is a pet-oriented festival."

Shermont pursed his lips thoughtfully. "You got me there. What'd you have in mind?"

"Pet costume parades are popular," Angus said. "And you have a designer of dog clothing right here in town."

"Puppy paraphernalia. Proceeds to go to an animal charity. Would your magazine want to sponsor it?"

"I was thinking more of Charlotte Baskerville. It would be a good promotional opportunity for her. Of course, she's going through a rough time right now, what with being haunted and all, but I thought

I'd mention the idea, to make sure you hadn't tried it and struck it from the list, for some reason."

"Not to my knowledge."

"You know," Angus said, "I'm a little surprised that Bob Hume hasn't already suggested this."

"Bob Hume?" Shermont gave a dismissive grunt. "This isn't something he's involved with, is it?"

"No. Is there something I should know about him?" Angus asked.

"Sorry. I only gossip about people after they're dead."

Nine

After conferring by cell phone, Angus, Suki, and Michael met for dinner at the Happy Mountaineer restaurant. A young woman showed them to a booth beneath a Halloween decoration of a large spider with blinking eyes.

"I thought this wasn't your usual kind of place," Suki said to Angus.

"I feel like having fish-and-chips. Also, this is one of the least expensive places to eat, unless we want a hot dog down at the arcade."

"I saw the arcade. It's a pretty interesting place, isn't it?" Michael observed. "It's like they picked up a tiny chunk of Coney Island and plopped it in the middle of Manitou Avenue. You'd think the rent would be too high for something like that."

"Every town should have a place for the kids to hang out," Angus said, "and the middle of town is ideal. You can see 'em better there."

The server came back. Suki and Michael ordered burgers, and Angus asked for fish-and-chips.

"You know they're French fries, right?" the server asked.

"I figured."

When she left, Michael stood and stuck his hand in his pocket. "I'm going to play something on the jukebox."

"I doubt you'll find any Thelonius Monk on it, if that's what you're after," Angus said.

"Don't be ridiculous. You have to play Johnny Cash or Patsy Cline on a jukebox. It's the rule." Michael went over and pushed buttons for a while, then sauntered back in rhythm to Cline's "Walkin' After Midnight."

"Nice strut," Suki said.

"So what did you come up with today?" Angus asked her.

"Charlotte Baskerville pulled Ellen Froehlich out of a deep depression over a man," Suki said.

"Hah. That's paltry," Michael scoffed. "I saw Bob Hume give a ride to a woman who then sneaked all the way around the block to go inside the Baskerville house."

"That's weird," Suki said. "If she didn't want to be seen with him, why not have him drop her half a block away?"

"Maybe Bob wouldn't do it," Michael suggested.

"Or maybe she just wanted the exercise," Suki countered.

"I *meant*," Angus said loudly, "what did you come up with in the way of material for our article?"

"Oh." Suki stared into space for a moment. "Possible ghost in the cellar of the Regency restaurant, and the lights went out while we were there."

"Did they indeed?" Angus asked.

"Turned out to be a prep cook who's keen on saving energy. Still, that Barb Metcalf has a pair of lungs on her."

"Is that a euphemism?" Michael asked.

"No, I'm talking about actual lungs. Judging by the scream she let out, she must have the aerobic capacity of a triathlete. I got a great picture of her looking terrified. At first she didn't want to sign a release, but I told her it made her look like Jodie Foster."

"Good work, Suki." Angus gave Michael a pointed look.

"I did stuff," Michael said. "I took a tour of Miramont Castle and saw some pictures of ghosts and orbs—little circles of light."

"You get those when the flash reflects off particles in the air," Suki said.

"I figured it was something like that," Michael said. "Anyway, Phoebe said that since we're press, we can come to the wake for free. We just don't get to eat. Oh, and on the way here, I got some man-on-the-street interviews about the ghosts of pets—people who feel their cat jump up on the bed at night, even though Fluffy is buried in a box in the backyard."

Angus nodded. "That's good, relatable material."

"It's a hypnagogic hallucination is what it is," Michael said.

"What's that?" Suki asked.

"It's—," Michael began.

Angus cut him off. "Hypnagogia is the state between being awake and being asleep. During it, people sometimes hear, see, or feel things."

"Like something jumping on the bed," Michael finished. "Or spiders crawling across the ceiling. That's very popular for some reason."

"Here's a question for you, Michael," Angus said. "If you hear a loud bang, do you assume that it's a gunshot?"

"No. It's more likely to be a car backfiring."

"It could also be caused by someone dropping a stack of boards, or any number of things. My point is, different events can be responsible for the same result—a loud noise. So why does hypnagogia have to be the *only* explanation for feeling that your cat is jumping on the bed?"

"Because you can spot the signs of hypnagogia on an EEG, but to my knowledge, people aren't reliably spotting ghosts. In real life, you don't get to choose what makes the loud noise."

Angus held up a finger. "Ah, but ghosts aren't real life. They're outside life, and can't be measured."

"Then why do ghost hunters run around measuring drops in temperature?" Michael asked triumphantly.

As the waitress brought their food to the table, Angus shook out his napkin. "Let's get something straight. While you're working for *Tripping,* strange noises are caused by spirit activity and orbs are . . ." He looked at Suki pointedly. "What?"

She paused with a fry halfway to her mouth. "Ghost cats jumping on the bed?"

"Floating entities."

"You're the boss." Suki wiped her fingers on her napkin. "Do you think Charlotte has kicked Thomas out yet?"

Michael unwrapped his flatware from its paper napkin. "Is she really going to ask for a divorce, based on a ghostly voice?"

"I think it's based on the fact that he's an asshole," Suki said. "The voice was just the kicker."

"There's no asking about it," Angus said. "She's telling him they're getting a divorce." He dipped a fry in ketchup. "Perhaps we should call first instead of showing up unannounced."

The sky had clouded over and it was near dark when they reached the Baskerville house.

Charlotte opened the door to them. She had dark circles under her eyes but looked happier than they'd seen her last. "You won't believe the change in Thomas," she whispered. "I should have threatened to divorce him years ago."

"So you're not going to do it?" Angus whispered.

"We'll see, but he's apologized and promised to see a therapist about his anger."

Angus squeezed her shoulder. "That's good news."

"And to think that Petey was the catalyst." She took Angus's hands and gripped them. "He's still looking out for me from beyond the grave." She gave his hands a final squeeze and turned toward the interior of the house. "If you want to go into the kitchen, there's a fresh pot of decaf. I'm going to put on something warmer, and then I'll join you to finish the interview."

They went into the kitchen as her footsteps pattered up the stairs.

Angus sat on one of the kitchen chairs, looking pleased. "This has just turned into one hell of a story. *Dog's ghost reconciles beloved owners. It was the one thing he had to do before his spirit could rest.*"

Michael picked up the coffeepot and sniffed it before filling a mug with a picture of a Chihuahua on it. "That's assuming Charlotte Baskerville wants her personal life put in a magazine."

"We needn't go into details." Angus straightened a plaid place mat with an appliquéd Chihuahua. "We'll say something like, *Their busy lives kept them apart—until Petey's ghost reminded them of what they meant to each other.*"

Suki laughed. "Thomas's busy life consisting of trying to get his wife committed."

"Shh . . ." Angus held up a hand and looked toward the doorway.

A moment later, Thomas Baskerville entered, neck thrust forward and hands in his pockets. He saw them and stopped, frowning. Then he straightened and smiled, though the smile didn't reach his eyes. "Come to tie up some loose ends before you go?"

"Something like that," Angus said.

"Good, good." Thomas went over to the coffeemaker. His hand hovered over the upturned mugs on the draining rack before picking one that pictured a Chihuahua in a clown costume and filling it. "I won't intrude," he said, turning to leave.

Charlotte appeared in the doorway, wearing a rose-colored cardigan with a ruffled scarf tied around her neck. She held out both hands to her husband. "Don't go, Thomas. We're going to talk about Petey. You can help me remember some of the funny things he used to do."

As they found seats, Michael looked at Suki and mouthed, *Awkward.* Then he took his recorder out of his pocket and raised it. "Do you mind if I turn this on?"

"Of course not," Charlotte said. "Do you, Thomas?"

Thomas shook his head and stared glassily out the window.

Angus took out a notepad. "Charlotte, I'd like to start with your experience of seeing Petey's ghost the first time. Did you feel any kind of intent from him?"

She thought for a moment. "No, I can't say that I did. I just remember thinking it couldn't be real—I must be dreaming."

"Maybe you were dreaming," Thomas put in. His hands tightened on the mug he held.

Charlotte patted his wrist. "No, dear. I think getting the window up would have woken me. It took a bit of work, and it was so cold outside. Plus, Lila and Chum both heard him."

"You might have dreamed that, too."

"I don't think so." Her tone held a little asperity. She turned back to Angus. "Anyway, all I remember is the sense of disbelief. I was a little afraid, too. Have you ever seen a ghost?"

Angus hesitated. "No."

Her penciled brows rose. "Really?"

He shrugged. "Can you describe the ghost's appearance?"

Charlotte stared into space. "Vague and floaty. It didn't look exactly like Petey, but it was definitely Chihuahua-shaped. And it moved so lightly, like a soap bubble on the air." Her gaze returned to Angus. "I knew it was Petey, because of his voice."

As if on cue, the yodeling bark of a dog came from outside. Charlotte gasped.

Michael turned toward the back door. "So much for Petey's spirit being able to rest."

Suki went to her camera bag and unzipped it. "Maybe he's doing one last check."

The bark came again, and Charlotte pushed back her chair.

Thomas put a hand on her shoulder. "Charlotte, do not go out there."

"But it's Petey!" She braced herself on the table and squirmed from under his grip.

"Charlotte, don't be an idiot!" He stood and struggled to keep her in her chair. "There's no such thing as ghosts!"

She bent and lunged forward, managing to stand but hitting the corner of the table as she did so. "Ow!" She trotted toward the door, one hand pressed to her hip.

Thomas's long stride took him there before her. "It's not Petey! I'll show you." He wrenched open the door. A gust of cold air flowed in, and the howl came again, sounding closer. Leaving the door open, he ran into the backyard. "Where are you, you bastard?!"

The rest of them followed, Suki holding up her video camera.

Thomas stood on the patio like an angry bull, swinging his head back and forth.

AhoooahooooooooooooOOooOO!

"It's around front!" Michael whispered loudly, holding his recorder aloft. He took a few quiet steps in that direction.

Thomas ran past him, but instead of heading toward the narrow corridor between the Baskerville house and Bob Hume's place, he ran toward the side yard that ran along the street. The rest of them gave up on stealth and pelted after him, Michael in the lead.

Thomas stopped in the front yard, breathing hard. The others came to a halt behind him.

Angus felt a drop of wetness on his cheek and looked up. Sparse flakes of snow fell through the light of a streetlamp. Suki cupped a hand over the top of her camera lens.

As they peered into the dark, a tiny glowing shape seemed to materialize in front of the dark hump of a bush. The head turned toward them, showing large, triangular ears.

Thomas lunged forward. "I'll get you!" he roared, breaking into a run.

"Thomas, don't!" Charlotte cried.

The glowing shape moved rapidly away, its legs seeming to drift above the ground. It hesitated briefly, then made a beeline for the street that curved around the house.

It all happened very quickly.

The glowing shape, looking more like a ball now, ran into the street as a car rounded the corner. Thomas Baskerville, pursuing, reached the road and windmilled his arms to stop his trajectory. Instead, he slipped on the wet asphalt and went down, out of sight.

"No!" Charlotte screamed, and her voice seemed to echo in a high-pitched wail.

The car hit something—*thud, thump*—and stopped with a screech of brakes.

Ten

Charlotte Baskerville and the *Tripping* crew stood as if frozen for a moment. Then they heard the sound of a car door opening, and it was as if the world rushed forward.

"Oh, no. No!" The man's voice came from the road.

Charlotte turned to Angus and clutched his arm, her face anguished. Then her other hand went to her chest, and her grip on him slackened.

He caught her as she slumped. "Call 911." The snow thickened, spiraling down onto Charlotte Baskerville's still face.

"I'll do it." Suki put her camera under her arm. "Michael, give me your cell phone and help him get her inside." She took the phone he held out and ran across the lawn toward the street and the sound of a woman's hysterical crying.

Michael and Angus lifted Charlotte and walked toward the front door.

It opened as they reached it.

Ellen Froehlich stood in the doorway. "What happened? Oh,

my God, Charlotte!" She stood aside to let them in, then ran into the parlor ahead of them and plucked a throw off the chaise. "Put her down here. Do we need to call 911? I'll find Thomas."

"Suki's calling. I'm pretty sure Thomas has been hit by a car out there." As Angus lowered Charlotte's shoulders onto the worn velvet, he heard the clicking of claws behind him. He looked down and saw Lila, dressed in a wedding-dress costume. Sequins glinted on the fabric, and the short train hung over her rump, threads trailing from the unfinished seams.

"Thomas was hit . . ." Ellen sat down suddenly. "Do I need to go outside?"

He took the throw from her limp hands and tossed it to Michael before squatting next to Ellen's chair. "No. Suki's out there. Do you know if Charlotte has a heart condition? Is there anything particular we should do for her?"

"She takes medication for arthritis and hypertension, but I don't know of anything more serious." She half rose, then sat back and gripped her knees. "Is Thomas . . . ?" Her eyes filled with tears.

"I don't know." Angus looked over his shoulder, to where Michael was tucking the throw around Charlotte's feet. One of her arms had fallen off the love seat, and Lila nosed at her curled fingers.

Michael looked down at Charlotte. "She's breathing, anyway."

The wail of a siren made them turn toward the front door. Lila let out a sharp bark.

"Should I go tell them she's in here?" Ellen asked.

Angus shook his head. "Stay with Charlotte. We'll let them know."

Outside, an EMT met them on the porch.

"First room on the right," Angus said, jerking a thumb over his shoulder. The man nodded and went inside.

The ambulance stood in the middle of the street, lights flashing. Its headlights illuminated the nose of the other car and a dark shape on the ground in front of it.

A man and woman stood near the side of the car, the man with his arm around the woman, who cried in a helpless way.

Across the street, the doors to several neighboring houses stood open, their owners silhouetted against the lights from inside.

As Angus and Michael walked across the yard toward the ambulance, a truck came down the street from the other direction and pulled into Bob Hume's driveway. Bob Hume got out and trotted down the sidewalk toward them, hands stuck in the pockets of his coat.

"What's happening?" he asked breathlessly. "Has there been an accident?"

"Thomas Baskerville's been hit by a car." Angus put a restraining hand on Bob's shoulder. "Don't go over there. You'll just be in the way."

"*You* were going over there."

"That's because we saw it happen," Michael said. "They might need to ask us something."

"Why did the emergency people go inside?" Bob asked.

"Charlotte needs help, too," Angus answered. "She may have had a heart attack."

Bob seemed stunned. "They're not both dead, are they?"

"I think Charlotte will be okay," Michael said. "But it doesn't look good for Thomas." He followed Angus toward the street, leaving Bob standing there.

When they reached the ambulance, Suki stood watching as the EMT zipped Thomas's body into a long plastic bag. The man finished his task and stepped back, avoiding a slick of something dark on the road.

Next to the ambulance, the driver of the car looked away, and the woman hid her face against his chest. The snow fell more heavily, melting into droplets on the body bag.

The driver of the car saw Angus and Michael approach. "There was nothing I could do! He ran right out in front of me."

"I know. We saw it," Angus said. He crossed his arms over his chest, feeling the chill.

They watched the EMT load Thomas's body into the ambulance. Across the street, several of the neighbors' front doors closed quietly.

Suki came over to join the others. "Dead before they got here," she announced.

The woman gave a wail.

"Hey, if it helps any, he wasn't a very nice man," Suki said.

Michael gave a nervous laugh.

Angus pushed them both toward the house. "Go make yourselves useful. See that Ellen gives Charlotte's medications to the EMT." He turned to the man and woman. "Do you live around here?"

The woman shook her head. "We were coming back from vacation," she gulped.

"My wife and I have relatives in Breckenridge," the man said. "We were on our way back to Colorado Springs to stay the night. Our plane leaves early tomorrow."

"He ran right in front of us," the woman said, shaking her head and sniffling.

The man squeezed her close. "I'm Sean, and this is my wife, Julie. Are you related to the, uh . . ."

"No. Just an acquaintance of the family," Angus said.

"What was he doing, running like that after dark?" Sean asked.

Angus thought for a moment before answering. On one hand, Charlotte might not want the details of her husband's death to come out. On the other hand, he already had permission to do the story. Plus, Thomas's death had a sense of fate about it, and these poor people could stand to feel less responsible. "He was chasing a ghost."

They stared at him, openmouthed.

If there was a third hand, Angus thought, as he reached in his pants pocket for a business card, it was that word of mouth was always good for the magazine.

The *Tripping* crew received a call from the police, asking them to come to the hospital.

When they reached Charlotte's room, they found her sitting upright on the adjustable bed, a flowered hospital gown around her and sensors taped to her arm. Her eyes were red, but also snapped with anger.

A policewoman sat in the chair by the bed. Her curly black hair was pulled into a ponytail, and a multitude of bobby pins fastened any wayward strands to the sides of her head. She vacated the chair when Angus and the others entered the room.

"Are you all right?" Angus asked Charlotte, taking the chair.

She gripped the arm of his coat. "Petey would *never* have harmed someone. I don't believe it was his ghost after all."

Angus glanced at the police officer.

"I'm Officer Deloit," she said. "My partner is checking out the accident scene. Perhaps you'd like to tell me what you saw." She took out a pen and pad.

"I can show you video, if you want," Suki said.

Charlotte put her face in her hands. "Please, no."

Officer Deloit turned to Suki. "Later."

It took awhile to explain everything, including their presence and the purpose of the magazine, which Officer Deloit seemed to have trouble understanding. "Leaving aside the name for the moment, why would people want to go to places where bad things happen?"

"No one has ever died before," Angus protested.

"If they haven't died, then how can there be ghosts?"

"The ghosts are from a long time ago, in most cases," Angus clarified. "And the magazine doesn't deal exclusively with ghosts. We also cover things like Bigfoot and thunderbirds."

"Those old cars?" Officer Deloit made a note on her pad.

"Supernatural birds," Angus said. "Really big ones."

Charlotte replaced her water glass on the bedside tray. "None of that matters now, because this couldn't have been Petey's ghost. I think someone purposefully set out to kill Thomas."

"With a fake ghost designed to lure him into the street?" Officer Deloit asked.

Charlotte nodded emphatically. "Exactly."

Officer Deloit tapped the end of her pen on the pad. "There are a few problems with that theory. First of all, how could they know he would chase it? Had he ever chased a ghost before?"

"No, but he was a very aggressive person." Charlotte smoothed the blanket over her lap. "Anyone who knew him could have predicted his behavior."

"Then there's the timing," Officer Deloit continued. "The driver of the car is from Indiana, has no priors, and no connection with your family. How could someone predict that his car would come along at that moment?"

Charlotte bit her lip.

"Finally, there's the ghost itself," Deloit went on. "If someone did rig something to run across the street, wouldn't a passing car have disabled the mechanism?"

Charlotte held up a finger. "I've been thinking about that, and I don't think it was a mechanism. I think it was an animal, painted to glow."

Officer Deloit tilted her head skeptically. "In that case, you're suggesting that someone trained an animal to run through the yard and into the street at a particular moment. Don't you think it's more likely that some random animal ran through the yard—a white cat perhaps—and your husband, prepped by these ghost stories"—she paused to give Angus a reproving look—"ran after it and was hit by accident?"

"But what about Petey's bark?" Charlotte demanded, her voice rising. "We all heard him!"

Officer Deloit checked her notebook. "Petey is your dead dog?"

"Yes!"

"As for that, ma'am, raccoons make a lot of different noises. I really think we're looking at a series of coincidences. It happens."

Charlotte looked at her lap and muttered something.

"All right," Officer Deloit said. "For the sake of argument, let's assume you're right."

Charlotte looked up. "Yes?"

"Can you think of anyone with a reason to kill your husband?"

Charlotte plucked at the blanket, looking from side to side as if an answer might present itself. "No."

Michael caught Angus's glance and raised his brows.

Angus shrugged slightly. The person with the best motive to kill Thomas Baskerville was his wife.

The door opened to Charlotte's hospital room, and Ellen Froehlich came in, clutching her purse and a cosmetics case printed with little Chihuahuas. "How are you feeling? What did the doctors say?"

Charlotte held out her arms. "They want to do more tests and keep me for the night, to make sure it was just shock."

Ellen put the cosmetics bag on the nightstand and sat on the bed to hug Charlotte.

Officer Deloit looked at Suki. "Let's go into the hall. Bring your camera."

They went outside, followed by Angus and Michael. Angus closed the door quietly behind them.

Suki powered up the camera, then flipped open the screen and touched it several times. "Do you want to see the whole video, or just the ghost part?"

"Everything, please," Officer Deloit said.

Suki handed her the camera, and they crowded around to watch the night's tragic events play out on the little screen.

When a glowing spot appeared on the screen, Officer Deloit touched the pause icon at the bottom of the screen. "That's the ghost, right?"

"Yeah."

The police officer squinted at the screen. "Can we zoom in on it?"

"Not on the camera, but once it's loaded onto a computer you can grab a still and zoom in on that."

Officer Deloit handed the camera to Suki and took out a business card. "Send me a copy of the video." She took the camera back and started the video again, watched it to the end, then replayed it from the beginning. "I have to admit, that looks like the ghost of a Chihuahua." She handed the camera back to Suki.

Angus sighed. "Unfortunately, it may not be." When they all looked at him, he said, "I found a spot of glow-in-the-dark paint in one of the upstairs bathrooms at the Baskerville house."

"And you didn't tell us?" Michael said.

Officer Deloit took out her notepad. "Who uses that bathroom?"

"Guests to the house, but it's also Ellen Froehlich's personal bathroom."

Officer Deloit pointed toward Charlotte's room with her pen. "The woman in there, right? She lives at the house?"

"A lot of people live at that house." Angus held up one hand and counted on his fingers. "Charlotte and her husband. Their grand-daughter, Cheri. Ivan Blotski, who trains the dogs. Ellen Froehlich, who designs the clothes for Petey's Closet, and two Chihuahuas." He frowned. "At the time of the accident, Ellen had one of the dogs in a white wedding dress. I wish I'd thought to check and see if the dress was wet. It was snowing outside."

Officer Deloit scribbled frantically. "Do you think Ms. Froehlich had anything to do with this? Did she have any reason to dislike Thomas Baskerville?"

"Everybody did," Suki said. "He was a real son of a bitch."

"But would she have wanted him dead?" Officer Deloit clarified. "Were there any bad feelings between them?"

Suki shrugged and looked at the other two.

"Thomas generated bad feelings wherever he went," Michael offered. "But it occurs to me that he may not have been the target."

"What do you mean?" Deloit asked.

Michael held up two fingers. "This is the second sighting of the ghost, and it was Charlotte who ran after it the first time."

"That's true," Angus said heavily. "Thomas tried to stop her from following it tonight."

"Just a second. I need to get all this down." Officer Deloit wrote quickly, then flipped through her notes. "Okay. Assuming Thomas wasn't the target, did Ellen Froehlich have a reason to hurt Charlotte Baskerville? They look pretty friendly."

"I talked to a friend of Ellen's today," Suki said. "Apparently Ellen was broken up after some guy dumped her, and Charlotte helped her through that. But I also get the impression that Ellen ought to be a partner in the company, instead of a paid employee."

Officer Deloit stared into space for a moment. "As it stands now, the company would cease to exist if Charlotte Baskerville died, right? It wouldn't make sense for Ms. Froehlich to kill her employer." She held up a hand. "Not that sense always comes into it."

"Presumably Charlotte has a will," Angus said, "but I don't know anything about it. Maybe she leaves the company to Ellen."

Officer Deloit made a note before asking, "Have you seen this glow paint anywhere else in the house, or heard anyone talking about it?"

They looked at each other, heads shaking.

Officer Deloit waggled the pen between her fingers. "I think we'll have a chat with Ms. Froehlich. Anything else?"

Michael spoke. "I think someone is using a recording of Petey's voice. Last night, the voice told Charlotte to divorce Thomas."

She stared at him a moment, then sighed and flipped to a new page in her notebook. "All right, tell me about the talking ghost dog."

Angus looked at his watch: nine thirty at night. "I can't think of anything else, Officer." They still stood in the hallway outside Charlotte's room.

Officer Deloit waved a finger between Michael and Suki. "How about you two? No?" She clipped the notebook to her belt. "Then let's go back inside."

Ellen had moved to the chair beside Charlotte's bed. Both women looked up as the others trooped into the room.

"You've been gone a long time," Charlotte said. "I forgot to ask, was Thomas the only one hit?" She swallowed. "You didn't find a dog, did you?"

Officer Deloit took out her cell phone and tapped on the keypad. She watched the screen for a moment. "Nope. No dog." Looking up, she said, "Ms. Froehlich, I'd like you to come to the station with me. Given Ms. Baskerville's concerns about the death of her husband, we need someone to fill us in on the household, and I don't want to tire her out."

Ellen looked startled. "Now?"

"If you don't mind, that would be best for us." Officer Deloit's lips turned up in a brief smile.

Ellen picked up her purse and stood. "Okay." She turned back toward Charlotte. "I'll call tomorrow morning and pick you up, all right?"

Charlotte nodded. "Thank you, dear. Feel free to tell the police whatever they want to know." She waved Ellen out of the room, then sank back into her pillows.

"We should be going," Angus said.

Charlotte smiled sadly. "I suppose you think I've spoiled your article, now that I don't think this was Petey's ghost."

Angus made a dismissive gesture. "*Tripping* magazine encourages informed discussion."

"I'm sure you do. The thing is, ghosts are good publicity," Charlotte said, "whereas murder and family troubles are not." She gave a half smile. "Ladies who buy outfits for their dogs are not big fans of gritty reality."

"Does that mean you're still willing to be quoted as believing there's a ghost?" Angus asked.

"Yes. And after all, the verdict is still out. Perhaps it is a ghost, but not Petey's ghost." She reached out to Angus. "Will you do me a favor?"

He stepped forward so she could take his hand. "If I can."

"Will you tell Cheri that Thomas is dead?" Charlotte Baskerville's face crumpled, and she covered it with her fingers.

Angus patted her shoulder while she sobbed for a few moments.

Finally Charlotte wiped her cheeks and took several deep breaths. "Cheri hasn't answered her phone, so she's probably still out with Jay. She shouldn't hear news like this over the phone, regardless." Charlotte shook her head despairingly. "Cheri's father, my son, also died in a car accident. Cheri and Thomas haven't been close for a while, but still . . ."

"It's bound to be hard on the lass," Angus said sympathetically. "This isn't my business, but is her father's death the reason she lives with you?"

"Sort of. Cheri's mother remarried last year, and Cheri and her stepfather don't get along. Cheri started drinking again. I told her she could live with me and help with Petey's Closet as long as she stayed sober."

"That was very kind of you," Angus said, patting her again. "Are you sure it wouldn't be better for someone closer to Cheri to tell her about Thomas? How long has Bob Hume been a friend of the family's?"

"Ages. He met Cheri's father in college. But Bob is not a person you want to hear bad news from," Charlotte said dismissively. "He has all the emotional warmth of an infomercial. I'd have Ellen tell her, but Cheri and Ellen don't get along that well. As for Ivan, he may not be back until tomorrow. I think he has a lady friend somewhere."

"So Cheri may come home to an empty house," Angus said.

"Exactly." She looked up at him pleadingly. "Stay there tonight. I'll leave a message for Ellen that you can use whatever rooms you like. Mine, Thomas's." She pressed her lips together and closed her eyes. "The police gave me his keys. They're in that drawer, if you'll get them out."

Angus opened the drawer of the hospital nightstand and took out the bunch of keys. "What about the dogs? If Ellen and Ivan aren't back, should we do anything special for them?"

"There's a piece of paper on the refrigerator door that has all their information." She smiled tremulously at him. "I know this is a lot to ask, but anyone could blurt out the news to Cheri. You know how people are. I don't want her to hear her grandfather is dead and then go home to find no one around."

A nurse came into the room. "Mrs. Baskerville, you need to get some rest." He looked at the monitor with Charlotte's vital signs. "I'm going to bring you something to help you sleep, and then you'll be done with visitors for the night."

Eleven

Angus drove them back to the Baskerville house.

Traffic lights made red and green reflections on the wet asphalt, but the snow had stopped. The tires hissed on the pavement, and Angus put the wipers on intermittent when they got behind another car.

Michael shifted in the backseat. "I'm surprised you told the police about the glow paint, Angus." His tone was bitter.

"I wasn't going to withhold what might be evidence," Angus said primly.

"You withheld it from us."

"Temporarily."

"*Temporarily* can mean anything. *Temporarily* could mean years."

Angus sighed. "Well, now you know, so in this case *temporarily* meant only a day."

After a moment, Michael said, "Still, the paint suggests that this is a hoax and Ellen is the most likely candidate. I mean, really, did it seem like a ghost to you? It wasn't particularly frightening."

Angus lifted one shoulder. "There are as many descriptions of ghosts as there are people who see them. I've often wondered if the same ghost looks different to different people. And there are a lot of reasons Ellen might have glow paint. She is a costume designer, after all." He turned onto Manitou Avenue. The streets were quiet aside from people leaving the few restaurants that were still open.

"What we saw tonight didn't match how Charlotte described the first ghost," Suki said.

"In what way?" Angus asked. "It glowed, and it looked like a Chihuahua."

"Yeah, but it didn't float like a bubble on the air. It ran like a bat out of hell."

Angus nodded. "Perhaps Charlotte is right, and it was a different ghost."

Michael groaned. "And I suppose it locked Petey in some astral basement while it led Thomas Baskerville to his death."

They drove past the arcade. A young couple in hooded sweatshirts stood under the snack bar's awning, looking cold.

"That could be why the ghost put in another appearance," Angus said thoughtfully. "Thomas came to heel, and Charlotte decided to give him another chance. But Petey still wanted her to divorce him."

"*Someone* certainly did," Michael said. "Let's talk about why Ellen might want Charlotte to divorce her husband. She might worry that Thomas would convince Charlotte to switch to dog food. Then Ellen wouldn't be needed."

"Charlotte didn't seem like she was going to change businesses," Angus said.

"Okay . . . Ellen might worry that Charlotte would die and leave the business to Thomas instead of her."

Angus turned left on Ruxton Avenue. "I think anyone who lives in that house would want to see Charlotte give Thomas the boot. He was like a big, black cloud."

"I don't imagine that bothered Ivan much," Michael said. "He seems hard as nails."

"Ivan spends a lot of time away from the house," Suki pointed out. "Maybe to get away from Thomas. And don't forget Cheri. She's young, has a drinking problem, and wound up with her grandmother. There must be a lot of stress there."

"Hoaxing is often a young person's game," Michael agreed. "They get a kick out of fooling authority figures. She wouldn't want to kill her own grandfather, though, would she?"

"I sincerely hope not," Angus said. "If this was a hoax, I think divorce was the goal, and Thomas's death was an accident." He parked on the street in front of the Baskerville house.

All three of them looked toward the side street where Thomas Baskerville's body had lain. A few dead leaves fell, to shine wetly against the pavement. Only the silver Corolla stood in the driveway, but a few lights burned inside the house. They got out and closed the car doors.

Michael stuck his hands in his coat pockets. "Who's going to tell Cheri?"

"I'll tell her if you want," Suki offered.

"*I'll* tell her," Angus said.

"I think that's best," Michael agreed. "You have that comforting thing going on." He looked up at the house as they approached. "Both the father and the son died the same way. It's like the Baskerville men are cursed." He shook his head. "I can't believe I just said that."

The door was unlocked. They had barely stepped inside when steps sounded along the upstairs hallway.

Cheri clattered downstairs in high-heeled boots, stopping on the last stair. "Oh, it's you." Her eyes were red-rimmed, her face blotchy.

Angus took off his coat. "I see you've heard. I'm so sorry, Cheri. Charlotte's been trying to call you."

"What are you talking about?" Cheri's hand moved restlessly on the wooden banister. "Where *is* everyone?"

Angus paused in the act of hanging his coat on the bronze rack. "Why have you been crying, Cheri?"

She sat down on a step. "Not that it's any of your business, but Jay and I broke up tonight. I turned my cell off so he couldn't call me."

"Oh, Lord." Angus came over and squatted in front of Cheri. "I'm sorry to add to your troubles, but I have very bad news. Your grandfather was hit by a car and did not survive. Charlotte is in the hospital—"

"Grandpa and Grandma?" Cheri's voice sounded very childlike. Tears spilled from her eyes.

Angus raised a reassuring hand. "Charlotte should recover completely. They think it was just shock. But I'm so sorry about your grandfather."

Cheri bent and hid her face against her knees.

Angus rested his hand on the back of her head for a moment. "Charlotte has asked us to stay the night here. I'm not sure when Ellen will be back." He got to his feet.

Cheri looked up at him and gulped down a sob. "Will you take me to the hospital to see Grandma?"

"I would, but the doctors have given her a sedative and said she can't have any more visitors tonight. Ellen hopes to bring her home tomorrow morning. Is there anything else we can do for you?"

"Nooo," Cheri said, collapsing forward again.

Someone knocked on the front door.

"I'll get it." Michael went to the door and opened it.

Bob Hume walked inside immediately. "Did Charlotte have a heart attack? Is she going to be okay?" He saw Cheri and stopped. "I'm sorry about your grandfather."

Cheri covered the back of her bent head with her arms. "Thanks," she said, her voice breaking.

Bob raised his eyebrows at Angus and mouthed, *Charlotte?*

"Charlotte's in the hospital, recovering," Angus said.

Bob nodded. "Good. I don't know what everyone would do without her."

Cheri looked up. Her eyes were almost swelled shut. "But she'll be gone someday!"

Bob looked uncomfortable. "You have other people. There's Ellen, and Jay . . ."

"Jay and Cheri broke up tonight," Suki offered.

Someone knocked on the door.

"Oh, God," Cheri moaned. "Who is it *now*?"

While Michael opened the door a second time, Bob patted Cheri's shoulder awkwardly.

A uniformed policeman stood outside, notebook in hand. "I'm looking for Angus MacGregor."

Angus raised a hand. "That's me."

"Officer Boyd. May I come in?"

Angus looked back at Cheri. "It's not actually my house."

Cheri stood and gripped the banister. "What is it? Is it my grandmother?"

"Are you Cheri Baskerville?" He took out a notepad. "Where were you around seven thirty this evening?"

Cheri began to cry in earnest, arms wrapped around herself. "I can't believe you would ask me that! I was out with Jay Metcalf!"

"Do you have his phone number?"

Cheri collapsed, sobbing, against Bob Hume. "I can't take this right now!"

Bob raised his arms and held her, a little tentatively.

"We can look him up," Officer Boyd said. "That's M-E-T, *calf* like the cow?"

"That's right," Bob answered. He patted Cheri's back. "Cheri, why don't you come over to my house? I'll make you some açaí-berry tea. Warm beverages are very good for stress."

She nodded, head still against his shoulder.

"She'll be right next door if you need her," Bob said. "Come on, Cheri. You don't even have to wait for anything to boil. I have an on-demand hot-water heater. I don't know why everyone doesn't have one."

Officer Boyd stood aside to let them out, then closed the door and put his hands on his hips. "I'm supposed to look at some glow paint?"

"Right," Angus said, nodding. "It's very faint, but I'll see if I can find it for you." He pointed to a switch on the foyer wall. "Michael, could you turn that light off? It'll need to be pretty dark."

The upstairs hall light was still on. Angus led the way to the second floor and switched on the light in Ellen's bathroom. "We'll give the paint a moment to charge while I turn off the hall light. Just a sec." When he returned, he pointed to the threshold. "Watch this area." He switched off the bathroom light.

They stood in the darkness.

"I don't see anything," Officer Boyd said.

"I think I do," Suki said. "Turn the light back on, Angus."

When he had, she squatted and put her finger on the crack between two boards. "It's right about here. You might have to get down close to see it."

Officer Boyd knelt, and Michael squatted next to him.

Angus switched off the light.

After a moment, Boyd said, "Okay, I see it."

"It's pretty faint, though," Michael said. "Were you crawling around on the floor for some reason, Angus?"

"I must have been looking at the right place, or maybe it was darker that night." Angus turned the light back on. "Do you want to take a sample?"

Boyd got to his feet. "Not necessary. We already know the source of the paint."

"You do?" Angus asked.

"Does that mean someone purposely tried to kill Thomas Baskerville?" Michael added. "Who is it?"

"This is not a murder case, although there is the possibility of reckless endangerment, which is a crime. At this point in time, we do not know who, if anyone, created the ghost." He gave them all a stern look.

"But you *are* questioning Ellen Froehlich," Angus said.

"To help rule things out. Ms. Froehlich is being very helpful."

"Did you look for signs of a mechanism or anything suspicious on the street?" Michael asked.

"Yes, and I questioned the neighbors. We'll send someone over to look at the scene during the day tomorrow, to make sure we haven't missed anything."

Angus nodded. "Well, it sounds as though you've been thorough."

Officer Boyd went to the head of the stairs and switched on the hall light before leading the way downstairs. "I'd like to get all of your contact information before I leave."

They stood in the foyer while he wrote down their names, addresses, and phone numbers. Finally he handed each of them a card. "If you think of anything important, give me a call."

Angus closed the door behind him. "So they've found out who had the paint, but they still don't know anything about a hoax."

"That'd be good in the article." Suki made a frame with her hands. *"Police baffled by strange goings-on."*

"It has to be Ellen who had the paint," Michael said. "She's the only one they've talked to."

"That makes the most sense," Angus agreed. "But if she had the paint and didn't make the ghost, it could still be real." He rubbed his hands together.

"Or she lied, or someone else made a ghost costume," Michael said drily. "I don't imagine that glow paint is hard to get hold of."

"You can buy it at any craft store," Suki offered. "What's that whole list of things cops look for? Starts with *M*."

"Means, motive, and opportunity," Michael said. "Means would be access to something that makes a ghost, which we're assuming is glow paint."

"Or the ability to call up spirits from beyond," Angus said mildly.

"You're joking, right?" Michael asked.

"Just throwing out possibilities."

Michael rolled his eyes. "After Thomas was hit, there were a lot of people standing around, and then the police came, so it would have been difficult to get rid of any kind of mechanism. Let's say the ghost was some kind of animal."

"That suggests Ivan, in terms of means," Suki pointed out. "He's most likely to be able to train a dog to do something."

"Maybe, except that supposedly he wasn't around, which leads us to opportunity," Michael said. "Ivan was gone, but we don't know where. Maybe the police do. Cheri and Jay are each other's alibis, but we all know how that goes. Ellen was inside the house, which puts her at the scene." He looked at Angus. "Did you notice that when we carried Charlotte to the house, Ellen opened the door without us knocking?"

"I assumed it was because she heard Charlotte scream for Thomas to stop," Angus said. "The people in the car were also carrying on a bit."

"All right, what about this . . . Why was Ellen working on Lila's outfit in the house rather than in the workshop?"

Angus shrugged. "You could ask Charlotte if that's unusual. You'd need to be a bit delicate about it."

Suki leaned against the wall. "Speaking of delicate, this story is going to be difficult to write without talking about Thomas's death, isn't it?"

"Why would we not talk about that?" Angus asked.

"Our demographic is going to eat this up," Michael added. " 'Killer spook disposes of horrible husband.' Of course, that's assuming we don't find out it's a hoax first."

Suki looked from one to the other of them. "But didn't Charlotte say something about not wanting her family troubles in the article?"

Michael rested a hand on her shoulder. "Charlotte is a lovely woman, but she doesn't pay our salaries. First rule of journalism."

Angus nodded. "Anyway, thanks to the Internet and our video of the ghost, Petey's Closet will become the most famous dog couturier ever. That should go some way toward mending Charlotte's heart."

"Assuming it's broken," Michael said.

"In that case," Suki said, "I wonder when she'll hold Thomas's funeral. You can get awesome reflections off those shiny casket lids."

Michael zipped up his leather jacket. "If we're going to stay here tonight, I want to get some stuff from the motel."

"Good idea." Angus took his coat off the rack and opened the front door.

As they walked down the sidewalk to the street, Michael said, "You know, if we're talking about getting rid of Thomas, Charlotte had means, motive, and opportunity."

Angus unlocked the car with a click of the remote. "I still say Thomas's death couldn't have been planned, and I don't see why Charlotte would fake a ghost to tell herself to get a divorce."

"Maybe so Thomas would get angry at Petey instead of her," Suki suggested.

Michael opened his door. "If Charlotte did fake a ghost as an excuse to dump Thomas, it must have worked way better than she thought it would."

When they returned from the motel, they found the door to the Baskerville house locked. Angus knocked loudly.

Ellen Froehlich opened it, wearing a bathrobe. Her expression darkened when she saw who it was. "What do *you* want?"

Angus shifted his duffel bag from one hand to the other. "I realize this is awkward, but Charlotte asked us to inform Cheri of her grandfather's death and then spend the night here."

Ellen stepped away from the door. "Better you than me, but I don't think Cheri's here. I don't know where she is."

"Probably still at Bob's," Suki said. "And we already told her about Thomas." She put her luggage, a leather satchel with buckles, at the foot of the stairs. Michael and Angus put their bags next to it.

"Cheri is at Bob's?" Ellen said. "Why?"

"No sooner did I tell her about Thomas's death than the police came." Angus said. "She was feeling too fragile to talk to them, so Bob asked her over to drink some tea."

Ellen wandered down the hall toward the kitchen. The others followed. A cup sat on the kitchen table. Ellen slumped into the chair by it and took a sip. "I suppose the police told you I had the glow paint."

Angus glanced at the others before pulling out a chair for himself. "They didn't, actually. They only said you were being helpful."

"I wish I could have denied having it, but my lawyer recommended against that, and he knows what's at stake."

Michael sat next to her. "What is at stake?"

"Partnership in Petey's Closet. I have an idea for a new line of glowing costumes, but my contract specifies that any designs I make automatically belong to Charlotte. So I'm not going to make them until she makes me a partner. It's my bargaining chip." She put the cup down and pushed it away from her. "Do you know how hard it is to demand things from the woman who turned your life around?"

"It must be very difficult," Angus murmured.

"Of course I'm grateful, but *I* created her best-selling designs," Ellen went on. "Yes, she taught me a lot about sewing, but *I'm* the one who steered her away from baby-doll dresses and into contemporary fashion. And do I get any royalties? Profit sharing? Nooo. I'm a salaried employee who doubles as personal assistant. I should have my own assistant."

"Does Charlotte know you feel this way?" Angus asked.

She sighed and stretched her arms along the table, palms down. "I'm sure she knows I'm unhappy. Charlotte's a generous woman in a lot of ways, but she doesn't miss a trick when it comes to business." She gave a bitter laugh. "I couldn't ask for a better teacher."

"If you can't make the new costumes yet, why did you have glow paint?" Michael asked.

"I can't make sketches or mock-ups, but I can still play around with materials. So I picked up some paint at the craft store, to see how it worked on fabric. I opened the plastic bottle in my bedroom and the stuff burped all over my hand."

Michael nodded. "It was packed at a lower altitude."

"Anyway, I went to the bathroom to wash it off, my hands dripping the whole way. I thought I'd cleaned everything, but I must have missed a spot. It was the clear kind of paint—not easy to see until it's glowing."

Angus nodded. "I hope you understand that I had to report it to the police."

She shrugged dismissively. "It's okay. Maybe better than okay, since it's going to force me to confront Charlotte. I've been dragging my feet. Of course, doing this when her husband's just died isn't the best timing." She rolled her eyes to the ceiling.

Angus stood and patted her shoulder. "I'm sorry." He looked at his watch. "Do you think we should go to Bob's house and check on Cheri?"

Ellen shook her head. "I'll leave the front door unlocked. She'll come back when she's ready. Did Charlotte tell you what rooms to use?"

He nodded. "Michael, why don't you and I bunk in Thomas's room, and Suki, you can stay in Charlotte's? Oh, and we were supposed to check on the dogs, but I assume Cheri or you did that."

Ellen shoved her chair back. "Oh, my God, I haven't seen Lila since I got home." A few steps took her to the back door, which she opened. Lila pranced in. Her wedding dress hung crooked and low on her hips, the white fabric muddy around the edges.

"Thank goodness she's okay." Ellen reached under the dog's belly and unfastened the costume with a *scritch* of Velcro. Leaving the costume on the floor, she scooped up Lila and kissed her sleek head. "She must have sneaked out when the paramedics were loading Charlotte onto the stretcher. If a mountain lion or coyote had gotten her . . ."

"Isn't there another dog?" Suki asked.

"Chum. He doesn't really leave Charlotte's room. I'll go check and make sure he has new pee pads."

"Oh, boy." Suki glanced at Angus and Michael. "You guys sure you don't want to sleep in Charlotte's room?"

Twelve

Thomas Baskerville's downstairs bedroom was locked. Angus took out the keys Charlotte had given him. The second of the larger ones unlocked the door, and he pushed it open.

The room's furnishings consisted of a double bed with matching nightstand in dark, carved wood, a veneer desk with a leather-upholstered chair pulled up to it, an oak wardrobe, and a four-drawer file cabinet in black metal.

Dust and hair had collected at the edge of the worn carpet in the middle of the floor, and more clumps could be seen beneath the edges of the bed, which had boxes stored under it. Heavy drapes in blue velvet covered the two windows.

Michael put his messenger bag by the foot of the bed and looked around. "I guess he didn't let anyone in to give it a good cleaning."

Angus pulled one of the drapes aside and shaded the glass with his hand so he could see into the darkness beyond. "Looks right out onto where he was hit." He let the fabric fall and waved away the resulting dust.

Michael stood at the wall on the far side of the wardrobe. "There's a door back here." He rattled the handle. "It's locked."

Angus retrieved the keys from the desk. "Let's see. This one, maybe." He twisted it in the lock a few times and it opened. "Partial bath, with toilet and sink." He ducked under the slanted ceiling and opened a door on the far wall. "Here's the hall to the kitchen. I never noticed this door. It's right under the stairway."

"Probably storage space at one time," Michael said, peering around the door frame from the bedroom. "At least the bathroom looks like it's been cleaned." He turned around and regarded the bed. "I hope the sheets aren't too gross."

"You weren't planning on sleeping in the nude, were you, what with us sharing a bed?" Angus closed the back door of the bathroom and came out, ducking to avoid the low ceiling.

"Of course I was," Michael said. "Didn't you know that about my generation?"

"Ha-ha." Angus crossed to the file cabinet and pulled on a drawer. When it didn't open, he flipped through the keys on the ring.

Michael looked up from unpacking his bag. "What are you doing?"

"Exercising my reporter's prerogative." Angus fitted a key in the lock and swiveled it, then pulled open the top drawer.

"You can't snoop through his files!" Michael whispered.

Angus pulled a folder out and opened it. "Apparently I can. And oh, my, would you look at this . . ."

"What?" Michael put down his bag and came over to see.

"Private detective's report on Charlotte. Shut the door to the rest of the house, will you?"

Michael quickly closed the door, then came back.

Angus flipped the top page over and studied the one beneath. "Looks as though Thomas thought Charlotte might be cheating on him."

"At her age?"

Angus gave him a wry look. "You'd be surprised what the old folks get up to, laddie." He went back to reading. "Correction, Thomas *hoped* his wife was cheating on him. It says here, *Look for any actionable behavior.* Sounds as though he would have been happy to divorce her, but only on his terms."

"Nice guy." Michael knelt and pulled open the bottom file drawer. "I take it he didn't find anything actionable?"

"Not that I can see." Angus looked down. "I thought you were dead set against snooping?"

"You're already doing it. I could put my fingers in my ears and hum, but I'd feel silly." He rifled through the folders. "Bank statements and some very old investments." He pulled out a sheet and looked at the summary figure. "Ouch. Not worth much now."

"Watch your head." Angus closed the top drawer and opened the second one. "What's this? *More* detective reports?"

"Maybe he thought the first guy wasn't any good."

Angus scanned the letters. "This is the same detective, but these reports are from twenty years ago." He flipped to the last page. "Oh, I don't believe this."

"What?" Michael rose up, banging his head slightly on the bottom of the file drawer. "I'm okay."

"Glad to hear it." Angus took the file to the desk and pushed aside a stapler and a dirty mug so he could lay it flat. "Take a look at these."

Michael came over and paged through the papers. "Why would anyone name their kid Betsy Baskerville?"

"That's the married name of Charlotte and Thomas's daughter-in-law." Angus pointed to a relevant paragraph. "Her maiden name was Elizabeth Widmer, until she married their son, Randolph Baskerville. Betsy Baskerville is Cheri's mother."

"'Betsy Baskerville, patterns of behavior March through April,' blah, blah," Michael read. He flipped to the next page and his eyes widened. "Paternity test?"

Angus nodded. "Apparently our Thomas has been a paranoid bastard for a long time. He suspected Cheri wasn't really his granddaughter."

"And is she?" Michael scanned the page. "According to the test, she is. This report doesn't say if they found out whether Betsy Baskerville was sleeping around."

Angus slid out the next set of stapled sheets. "Says here that evidence of extramarital activity is 'inconclusive.' The detective didn't start work until Betsy was already pregnant." He scanned the rest of the page. "Reading between the lines, Randolph suspected his wife might be cheating on him, but he didn't follow up on it until Thomas insisted. The detective says that often a woman will give up an illicit liaison when she finds out she's going to be a mother."

"So she might have been fooling around before they hired the detective, or it might have all been in these two charmers' heads," Michael said.

"That's about the size of it." Angus shuffled through the papers to make sure he hadn't missed anything. "What I want to know is how Thomas could afford to pay for all this snooping and legal work."

"The paternity test was twenty years ago. He still had his lumber business then, right?"

"I'm thinking of the more recent investigation, on his own wife. Surely Charlotte wouldn't foot the bill for him to have her followed."

Michael closed the second file drawer and opened the bottom one again. "We've got bank statements right here."

Angus smiled benignly. "I can see you're getting the hang of this."

Michael pulled out a folder and brought it over to the desk. "See if you can find the most recent bills for the lawyer and detective."

After a moment, Angus said, "There are bills from the detective for the last two months, totaling three thousand dollars. Looks like Thomas has the lawyer on retainer. He gets eight hundred a month, due on the fifteenth."

Michael frowned. "I don't see any checks written for amounts that large." He pointed to the statement. "This is the joint account for Thomas and Charlotte, with two automatic deposits every month."

Angus looked. "Probably Social Security. The amounts are too odd to be an allowance."

Michael nodded. "They add up to a nice chunk of change when you don't have to pay room or board, but it's not enough to cover the lawyer and detective."

"Could Thomas have had some other source of cash?" Angus wondered.

"From what? Selling drugs? Walking the streets? Seems unlikely. There's another option, of course."

"What?"

"Someone else paid the bills for him. A partner."

Angus thought for a moment. "Bob Hume?"

Michael nodded. "Maybe the açaí-berry business is better than we thought."

⋯

In Charlotte's room, Suki unzipped her calf-high boots and stripped off her velvet leggings. The waist cincher she wore looked complicated, but had a hidden zipper on the side. Free of that and her long-sleeved white shirt, she stretched to one side and then the other. Finally she shimmied out of her La Perla bra and panties and donned a black silk robe with red dragons.

After getting ready for bed, she lounged in a chair and stayed up until past midnight, answering e-mails and surfing the Internet. Eventually she yawned, got up, and draped the robe over the chair's back. Suki hadn't slept in anything since she was five, and wasn't about to start now. Charlotte looked plenty clean.

As she walked across the room, Lila came out from under the bed, bounded up the little wooden stairs, and pranced onto the bedspread.

"That side," Suki said, pointing.

Lila obeyed.

Chum lifted his gray muzzle from where he lay in the exact center of the bed.

"You, too. Up." Suki patted the spot where she wanted him to be.

Chum heaved himself to his feet, went over to Lila, and flopped down with a sigh.

Suki lifted the covers and got in. Making dogs obey wasn't particularly hard, in her experience. You just had to know who was boss, at your very core. She switched off the bedside lamp and began her presleep Kegel exercises. Around thirty-four, the sound of intermittent creaking in the hall outside reached her.

She slid out of bed. Lila showed signs of following, but Suki held up her hand, palm out, and the dog subsided.

The crack under the door showed no light from the hallway outside. Suki listened intently before opening the door and looking outside. She slipped into the deserted hallway, still naked, then closed the bedroom door noiselessly and stood in the dark.

Downstairs, the front door opened and closed quietly.

Suki ran lightly downstairs and pulled the curtain aside from the window.

Ellen Froehlich walked quickly down the driveway, wearing her coat and carrying a shoe box in addition to her purse. She unlocked her car, got in, and drove away.

Suki watched a moment longer. Then she went back upstairs and tried the door to Ellen's room. It opened.

Moonlight from two windows showed that Ellen was a tidy woman. The quilt on the four-poster bed lay unrumpled, and the small desk under the windows had a minimum of clutter—an engagement calendar, a work light, and a pencil cup, which also held two pairs of scissors and a seam ripper.

Suki closed the curtains before switching on the small lamp and looking at the contents of the desk's two drawers. Aside from the usual jumble of pens, envelopes, and tape, they contained sewing supplies and catalogs for thread, trim, and fabric.

Closing the drawers, Suki wondered if she would hear Ellen's return if she searched inside the closet. Probably not. She turned off the desk lamp and wondered what to do next.

Areas of the desk glowed faintly where spilled paint had been imperfectly cleaned from the wood's grain. Her gaze wandered and came to rest on the pencil cup. Standing, she could see almost to the bottom, where something shone faintly.

Suki turned the light back on. Using the largest scissors like a tweezer, she pulled out a small V of fabric, perhaps a third of an inch square. A seam ran down the center. She turned off the light.

The fabric glowed.

Thirteen

Michael woke to the sound of a knock on the bedroom door. Beside him, Angus lay on his back, mouth open, snoring gently. Early-morning light shone through the curtains.

Michael got out of bed, not bothering to be quiet, and took a quick look around to make sure they had returned all the files to their places. They had, and Thomas's keys were safely out of sight. Behind him, Angus mumbled something and rolled over.

The knock came again.

Michael pulled open the door. "Yeah?"

Ivan blinked at him. He wore dressy slacks and a shirt with an expensive sheen, but his clothes were rumpled, as though he'd been up all night.

The smell of stale cigarette smoke assaulted Michael's nose. "Can I do something for you?"

"I want to talk to Thomas." Ivan looked past him, to the lump on the bed, and his eyebrows rose considerably. "I will wait until later."

"You can wait forever, but it won't help. Haven't you heard?"

Ivan's forehead wrinkled. "Heard what?"

"Thomas ran after the ghost last night and was hit by a car. He's dead. Charlotte's in the hospital. They thought she might have had a heart attack, but it looks like it was just shock. They hope she can come home this morning."

Ivan's mouth fell open slightly.

"What did you want with Thomas?" Michael asked.

Ivan shook his head slightly, as if to clear it, then patted his trouser pocket. "He asked me to play twenty dollars for him, and it won."

"Ah."

Ivan turned. "I have to . . . uh . . ." He wandered off.

"See you later." Michael closed the door.

Angus yawned and sat up. "I think you have restless-leg syndrome. You kept kickin' me."

"I meant to kick you. You kept oozing onto my side. That was Ivan, by the way. Looks like he's been up all night."

"Did he say what he wanted?"

"Thomas gave him a twenty to play at the casino, and he won on it."

Angus grunted. "Lucky bastard."

After washing and dressing, they went into the kitchen, where they found Suki and Ellen seated at the table with cups of coffee.

"Any word on Charlotte?" Angus asked, getting a cup from the drainer on the counter.

"They said I can pick her up this morning at nine." Ellen glanced at her watch. "I was supposed to have a phone meeting with a distributor this morning."

"Couldn't Cheri pick Charlotte up?" Angus asked.

Ellen gave a humorless laugh. "She lost her license for driving drunk. I think that's the main reason she dates Jay, so he can shuttle her around."

"Maybe Cheri would like to go with you to the hospital," Angus said. "She seemed pretty eager to see her grandmother."

Ellen shook her head. "Cheri doesn't get out of bed before ten. I already went up and knocked at her room. She yelled something unintelligible and threw something at the door—probably a shoe."

"Cheri and Jay broke up last night," Suki said.

"Oh, great." Ellen pushed back her chair. "Now she'll go back to asking me for rides. Before she got Jay, I used to have to sneak out of the house." She went to the sink and ran water in her coffee cup.

"Is that why you left the house late last night?" Suki asked. "To avoid giving Cheri a ride?"

Ellen shut off the faucet with a deliberate motion and turned to face them. "I really don't appreciate your nosiness. For your information, I bought some wine yesterday. I can't keep it here, because Cheri periodically goes through our rooms looking for something to drink. By the time I remembered that I needed to take it to my friend's house, it was late, but I went anyway. Regardless of any business issues we have, my friendship with Charlotte means a lot to me."

Angus got up from the table and stood in front of her with his hands clasped. "Ms. Froehlich, we're very sorry to have made you uncomfortable. I hope you'll understand that we have Charlotte's best interests at heart."

Michael brought a cup of coffee and two cookies to the table. "Ellen, do you suppose Cheri could have gone into your room to look for liquor, seen the glow paint, and got the idea to make a ghost from that?"

"That's entirely possible," Ellen said, sounding slightly mollified.

"And while I'm sure she didn't mean to hurt anyone," Angus continued, "she does seem like a lass who enjoys drama."

"That's an understatement." Ellen reached over and took her purse off the kitchen counter. "Listen, I'm sorry I flew off the handle. It's certainly in my best interests to keep Charlotte safe. Let me know if there's anything else I can do." She looked at her watch again. "And now I have to go." She walked down the hall to the front of the house, grabbed a jacket, and left.

"Nice save, Angus," Suki said, when she heard Ellen's car start up. "Sorry about that."

"Don't give it a second thought." Angus resumed his seat and leaned toward her. "So Ellen took a little jaunt last night? Do you think she was telling the truth about the wine?"

Suki shook her head. "Who puts wine in a shoe box? Also, she could have just locked it in her car. There's more. Just a sec and I'll show you." She went down the hall toward the stairway.

"Does a wine bottle even fit in a woman's shoe box?" Michael asked Angus.

"Maybe a half bottle. I suppose it depends on the size of her foot."

Suki came back and put a scrap of fabric on the table. "I found this in the bottom of Ellen's pencil cup on her desk."

"You searched her room?" Michael asked.

Suki shrugged. "Just her desk."

"Good lass," Angus murmured. He poked at the scrap with his finger. "What is it?"

"It's a piece of fabric that glows in the dark. And remember how Ellen said she hadn't actually made a costume with the glow paint? If that's the case, why does this piece of fabric have a *seam*?"

"Interesting," Angus said.

"Wait till you hear what we found last night," Michael began.

Angus put a hand on his arm. "Not in the house. It's too easy to be overheard. We'll go out to breakfast and talk on the way." To Suki he said, "Can you put that back in Ellen's room without anyone seeing you?"

She nodded. "I could hear Cheri snoring through her door, and Ivan's shower is running." She picked up the scrap of fabric. "I'll be right back."

They went out to breakfast and filled each other in on what they had found. When they had breakfasted and were back outside, Angus led the way down Manitou Avenue.

The weather had warmed considerably. Michael unzipped his coat and said, "I could get used to eating out on someone else's dime. Are we staying just through the Emma Crawford Coffin Race?"

Angus put his hands in his pockets. "That's the plan. I wish we could stay longer, if only because I'm worried about Charlotte Baskerville. She's very vulnerable."

"Or maybe she's safer, now that Thomas isn't around to try and get her committed," Michael said. "Those detective reports should help her get over her grief faster. Thomas really was a bastard."

"I wasn't going to show her, but I suppose she'll find them eventually," Angus said. "I hate to think how she'll feel when she finds them."

"You could put them at the bottom of the drawer, underneath all the other folders," Suki suggested. "Then she wouldn't find them right away."

He heaved a sigh. "Maybe."

When they got back to the house, Ellen's car was in the drive-way.

Angus started to open the front door, then knocked instead.

In a moment, Cheri opened it, wearing a hot pink corduroy jacket. "Grandma's fine!" she announced cheerfully, waving them in. "She wants to talk to you, but she's shut up with Ellen right now, having some kind of meeting. I'm going out. You can talk to Ivan if you want."

"We'll do that," Angus said.

"He's in the backyard, working with Lila." Cheri ran back up-stairs.

Michael followed. "I'll get my recorder and meet you out there."

As Angus and Suki walked through the kitchen toward the back door, he leaned over and said, "Did you notice Cheri's pink jacket?"

Suki nodded. "No hood. Michael said it had a hood."

"Oh. Right."

They opened the back door and went outside.

Ivan, dressed in black jeans and windbreaker, stood beside the blue plastic tunnel of the agility course, which wiggled. Lila emerged from the end.

"Gate!" Ivan called, and she jumped over a small wooden fence. He saw Angus and Suki and waved for them to come over.

Lila milled about uncertainly. Ivan slapped his thigh once and she darted over to sit beside his left heel.

"Very impressive," Angus said.

"Of course." Ivan grinned at Suki, showing his crooked teeth. "Hallo, Princess."

"Hey."

He reached in his jacket pocket and took out a bedraggled envelope. "It is good you are here. I am training Lila to bring a sympathetic card to Charlotte. You will be test subject. Please to go and stand at the back door."

Angus joined Ivan while Suki crossed the patio and stood at the back door.

"Lila," Ivan said.

The little dog looked at him attentively, tail wagging.

He held the card in front of her and she took it in her mouth. "Bring," he commanded, and made a sweeping gesture toward Suki.

Lila trotted across the yard to Suki, then stood on her back legs, the envelope between her teeth.

"Cool," Suki said, taking the card from Lila. She held it between thumb and forefinger. "It's kind of spitty."

"That is practice version we have been using," Ivan said, "but Charlotte is dog owner. She is used to spit."

Michael came out the back door with his recorder and followed Suki as she rejoined the others. "What did I miss?"

"A little dog being cute," Suki said. "Ivan, will she do it for me?"

He shrugged one shoulder. "Maybe. Is new trick."

Suki gave the card to Lila, who took it carefully between her teeth. Then she waved her arm toward Ivan. "Bring," she said firmly.

Lila trotted back to Ivan and sat in front of him.

"Up," he said, snapping his fingers above her. She stood on her hind legs, completing the trick, and he gave her a treat from his pocket. "Good girl."

"How long did it take for her to learn that?" Michael asked.

"Already she knows *bring,* so it is a matter of knowing that she

should stand at the end, when she has card in her mouth. Ten minutes so far, and in another ten she will stand without being reminded." He grinned. "I have to work fast, because Lila is patient
but Ellen is not, and I first used her as the target person."

"Do you work exclusively with Charlotte's dogs?" Angus asked.

"No. I have clients all over town and also in Colorado Springs
and Denver. Everyone knows that if dog is bad or stubborn, call
Ivan. Now if dog is stupid . . ." He raised a hand and waggled it.
"There is only so much I can do. Same with stupid owner."

He reached down and fondled Lila's head where she sat at heel.
"This one is very smart. Charlotte got her from rescue place, and
she wants very much to please. Watch." He straightened and held
up a hand. "Lila . . ."

Lila watched him, vibrating slightly.

"Chute!" Ivan commanded, gesturing in that direction.

Lila took off, the plume of her black tail flying like a flag. She
entered the blue plastic tunnel with a clattering of claws.

When she emerged, Ivan said, "Over!"

Bypassing the ladder, she jumped over a small wooden gate.

"Over!"

She doubled back in a swirl of fur and went over the gate in the
other direction.

"Climb!" Ivan said.

Lila headed for the ladder.

They watched as she climbed. The slanted ladder culminated in
a plastic slide. Lila rolled once on the way down, but landed on her
feet and looked at Ivan expectantly.

"Come." He touched his thigh and she raced over to stand at
heel.

"Will she do them in any order?" Michael asked.

"Of course." Ivan took a sandwich bag from his jacket pocket and gave Lila a treat from it.

Angus looked thoughtful. "Do you have to use verbal commands? In Scotland, the sheepdogs work with a combination of gestures and the occasional whistle or shout."

Ivan looked offended. "But that is too easy. Dogs are used to body language. Is more of a challenge to teach them *our* language. I could also run around track with her, but then she would just be copying me." He took a few mincing steps.

Lila followed, looking up expectantly.

Ivan stopped and shook his head. "Following is easy. Anyway, getting dog to run around is not hard. Dogs want to run around. Getting them to stay still, that is hard. Watch this."

He picked up Lila, then squatted and set her in front of him. "Look," he said firmly.

Her vibrating stopped, and she watched him, motionless.

Ivan pressed her hindquarters down so she sat, then spread her front legs slightly and guided her head to look back over one shoulder, chin lifted. "Pose." When he removed his hands, she remained frozen in that position. He stood and walked into her eye line. "Look . . . Look . . ."

Lila's eyes tracked his as he walked from side to side.

"She will stay there until I say, but if photographer cannot do the job in a few minutes, then he is the one who needs training." Ivan got down on all fours and crawled toward Lila, teeth bared. When they were face-to-face, he snapped his jaws slightly. Lila remained motionless. "Free," he murmured.

She licked his nose.

He chortled and petted her while she danced under and around him. "Good dog."

Michael shook his head in admiration. "I think you could make it in television. Maybe you could add some custom stuff to the agility course. I assume you built it?"

"No." Ivan's expression turned sour as he got to his feet. "Bob Hume built it, to sweeten Charlotte. He is not good for much besides working with his hands."

Michael raised his eyebrows at the venom in Ivan's tone. "He seems to know a lot about the açaí berry."

"Pff . . . ," Ivan scoffed. "He can repeat things, like a parrot, but he does not want them enough, or even know for sure what he wants. He is a boy, not a man."

Angus glanced at the house next door. "He may hear you. He's usually out on his deck."

"Let him hear me," Ivan said, raising his voice. "And that is not his deck. He rents the upstairs. Right now, yes, he talks about the oh-sigh berry, but before that he thought he would sell real estate, and before that to be a vet. Thomas was a fool to deal with that man." He shoved his hands in his pockets and walked toward the house, Lila following.

"Well," Michael said, when the back door had closed with a bang. "Don't sugarcoat it, Ivan. Tell us how you really feel."

"It's hard to blame him," Angus said. "Any money Bob and Thomas managed to get from Charlotte would have made it less likely for her to help Ivan with his TV show."

Suki picked a leaf off the ground and examined it. "Ivan should be happy, then. I don't see Charlotte helping Bob with his dog-food company now that Thomas is gone."

"True." Angus tilted his head in thought. "And if anyone could train a dog to lure someone into the road, it would be Ivan. But how could anyone have foreseen that it would be Thomas who chased the ghost?"

Michael, who had been gazing at the back of the house, suddenly turned. "We're missing the obvious. We don't know how the last ghost appearance was supposed to play out. Maybe the ghost was going to lead Charlotte to a secret message or talk again, but then someone saw the chance to get Thomas in front of a car, and took it."

"You're right," Angus said, looking a little stunned. "It could have been a spur-of-the-moment decision."

Suki held up the leaf she had been playing with, so light shone through it. "I wonder what's in Charlotte's will."

"I keep forgetting that," Angus said. "I've been so focused on what Charlotte can do for people while she's alive, I haven't thought much about what she could do after she's dead."

"And you call yourself a fan of the paranormal," Michael chided.

Petey's yodeling bark wavered through the air.

"Seriously?" Michael said. "In broad daylight? Can I just say I'm heartily sick of that dog, dead or alive?"

"It's coming from around front," Angus said. "Let's walk on the side away from the street, shall we? Making sure to look where we're going."

The bark came again when they were alongside the house.

Michael put his eye to the wooden privacy fence on their right. "I think it's coming from Bob's house."

"Technically it's not Bob's," Suki reminded him.

"Whatever. Come on." Michael trotted to the front edge of the fence. It butted up against the garage, with a tall wooden gate in between. He banged his fist on the gate. "Hey, is anyone back there? Bob?"

"Just a sec!"

After a moment, the gate opened and Bob stood there, wearing a paint-splotched oxford shirt and stained jeans. "What's up?"

"We heard Petey's voice." Michael tried to peer past him. "It sounded like it was coming from over here."

"I didn't realize I had it up that loud." Bob waved them in. "I'm working on the coffin. Come see."

The others exchanged looks and followed.

"Sorry about the mess," Bob said, as they passed some broken terra-cotta pots and a rusted push mower that leaned against the side of the garage. "It used to be a lot worse. I threw most of the junk out, but I kept the pots. Don't people use broken pots in gardening? And the mower just needs to be sharpened and oiled. But there was a lot more stuff. You know how renters are."

"I thought you rented here," Angus said tentatively.

"I'm the live-in manager," Bob said. "I manage the downstairs and take care of maintenance." He turned left at the back of the garage and waved an arm. "See? There's my coffin."

The backyard was mostly dirt and weeds, but a concrete slab abutted the back of the house. In the middle of this, next to a rusty barbecue grill and some tattered lawn chairs, sat a plywood box in the shape of a lidless coffin, painted black and mounted on a wheeled platform made of metal pipe.

The pipe stuck up above each of the corners, like a four-poster bed. Mounted on top of each one was a toy Chihuahua, also black.

"Dude," Suki said.

Bob looked at her uncertainly. "It's not finished, of course."

They approached. Up close, it was plain that Bob had simply

spray-painted the plush toys. Suki scraped at one of the dog's plastic eyes with her thumbnail.

"I can take that off with some remover," Bob assured her. "You'd be surprised how hard it is to find an all-black stuffed animal. I did find some little top hats online. I'm wiring those on next, and the sides of the coffin will have swags of black tulle."

Michael looked inside. The interior was lined with black plastic trash bags, which covered a foam pad. "Please don't tell me this is your entry in the coffin race."

Bob looked surprised. "Why wouldn't it be? I borrowed the basic coffin from a friend. He came in third last year, but he's out of town for the race and said I could decorate it as a tribute to Petey. I still have to paint *Petey's Pride* on the side."

"Or maybe *Petey's Wild Ride,*" Angus murmured.

"That's cute, but the name of the dog food is Petey's Pride." Bob pulled a splinter off the side of the coffin, then made a tsking noise at the resulting wood-colored streak.

"Wait a minute," Michael said. "What about the barking? We heard the sound of Petey's bark."

"I got that off YouTube, from a video of Petey." Bob pointed to two mesh screens on the outside of the coffin. "Those are some old computer speakers." Reaching inside the vehicle, he pulled an iPod from underneath a section of padding and pressed a button. Petey's distinctive bark sounded.

"Shut that off," Angus hissed.

Bob did, looking hurt. "The more detail you have on your entry, the better the judges like it."

"Did it not occur to you that this might be in poor taste?" Angus asked. "What with Thomas chasing after Petey's voice and then dying?"

"Then this can be a tribute to both of them," Bob said.

Angus stabbed a finger at Bob. "How long have you been messing about with this recording?"

"Just since this morning. I want to add the sound of chains rattling—you know, like choke chains?"

Angus groaned. "Why couldn't you leave the toys the color they were, dress them up in some Petey's Closet outfits, and sling bowls of dog food around their necks? Then you could play a catchy jingle, or even yummy eating noises."

"*Yummy eating noises?*" Bob gave him a pitying look. "This is a *coffin* race. It's supposed to be morbid. That's why there's an Emma in the coffin."

Michael pulled his recorder out of his pocket. "All right, forget about whether this is appropriate or not. Tell us about the Emma. I'm going to record this, all right?"

Bob nodded. "The way the race works is that you have a team of five people—four pushers to get the coffin down the street and an Emma to ride inside. Everybody is dressed in costumes and the Emma is usually made up to look dead. The judges give prizes for best Emma, best coffin theme, and winner of the race. Ten thousand people came to see it last year."

"And where's the race held?" Michael asked, holding up the recorder.

"Right down Manitou Avenue. It starts at the town clock and goes to Ruxton Avenue." He gave the coffin a glum look. "You really think Charlotte will have a problem with this? It's just that there's not a lot of time before the race."

"Trust me, it would be easier all around to change your decorations," Angus said.

Bob sighed. "I may have to withdraw anyway. Two of my pushers dropped out, and the other messed up his knee skiing. And Cheri was going to be my Emma, but now she says she won't." He gave them a mulish look. "She didn't say it was because of the decorations, though."

"She probably thought she didn't have to," Angus said gently.

Bob looked at the ground. "Maybe. Is Charlotte home?"

"Yes," Angus said. "But she might appreciate some time to settle in before she has company."

"*You're* staying there."

"We spent last night there, but that was an emergency situation," Angus said. "I think we'll make ourselves scarce today—go check out some of the other supernatural aspects of the town."

"I guess I'll see you around." Bob lifted his head. "Maybe you could come over later and have some chips and dip. I have plenty of beer."

"We're going to Emma Crawford's wake tonight," Michael said quickly.

"Oh, right. I've seen it a lot, so I didn't buy a ticket. But I'm bringing the fog machine."

"Will you be one of the people jumping out at us?" Suki asked. "Because I have to warn you, I don't react well to that."

He shook his head. "It's not a haunted house."

"More of a historical re-creation," Angus added.

"Plus, there's a nice dinner," Bob said. "Charlotte was really looking forward to playing Mrs. Bell. I hope they've found someone else who can do it. She was committee head this year, so they may not have thought to."

"We'll mention it to her," Angus promised.

"I could call Peggy Filbert, just in case Charlotte is all drugged up."

"I don't think she is."

"That's good to hear. I'll call Peggy anyway, just in case." He moved as if to leave, then turned back and put a hand on the coffin. "Would you guys consider being on my race team? Suki, you could be the Emma. They'd probably mention the magazine in the newspaper."

Suki looked at Angus. "What do you think?"

"I think it would interfere with your photography of the event."

"You and Michael could do it," she said.

Angus shook his head. "I don't like to run, but if Michael wants to push a coffin and cover the story from an inside angle, that'd be all right."

Bob looked hopefully at Michael.

"Get rid of the black Chihuahuas and we'll talk," Michael said.

Fourteen

When they went back to the house, they found Charlotte sitting at the kitchen table, staring into space. Lila sat at the side of her chair, looking up at her mistress.

"Should you be up and about?" Angus asked, as they came in.

"I'm fine. The doctors adjusted my hypertension medicine." Charlotte's appearance wasn't quite as careful as usual. The turquoise cardigan she wore wasn't a good match for her pale blue slacks, and she wasn't wearing any jewelry.

"Can I get you anything?" Angus asked.

She looked at the table, which was empty. "I had a cup of coffee. Oh, there it is—on the counter."

Angus waved at her to stay seated. "I'll get it." He put the cup in front of her while the others sat. "How are you?" he asked, pulling out a chair.

"Numb. Thomas was dreadful, but I can't quite take in that he's gone." She took a sip from her cup and made a face. "I must have lost track while I was measuring the grounds."

"We were over talking to Bob," Michael said. "He wondered if you had called someone to replace you in the Emma Crawford wake."

Charlotte shook her head slowly. "Don't need to. I'll still do it, to keep my mind off things. Thomas wanted cremation and no funeral, so there's nothing to arrange." She focused on Angus. "I thought of running away somewhere—leaving the country for a while."

Suki looked intrigued. "Indonesia doesn't extradite to the U.S., if that's a consideration."

"What?" Charlotte turned to stare at her.

"Pay no attention to her," Angus said, sitting forward so that he blocked Suki from Charlotte's view. "She sometimes has an inappropriate sense of humor."

"Just trying to be helpful," Suki muttered.

"Anyway, I've decided not to go anywhere," Charlotte went on. "I have my work, and people who depend on me."

"Speaking of people who depend on you . . ." Angus clasped his hands on the table. "Charlotte, does your will give anyone a compelling reason to want you dead?"

She closed her eyes. "What cheerful, comforting things you all say."

"I'm sorry," Angus said, "but I'm very worried about you. What if the ghost was meant to lure *you* into the street, not Thomas?"

Charlotte sighed and opened her eyes. "My will does have some fairly generous bequests. Cheri is my granddaughter, so of course I want to take care of her. And even though I'm a little angry with Ellen right now, she deserves to get Petey's Closet when I'm gone. Even Ivan should have his chance. But it's not as though I noise all this around. What are you suggesting—that I cut everyone out?"

"Of course not." Angus leaned forward and lowered his voice. "Just *say* you have."

Michael sucked in his breath on a hiss. "I'm not sure that's a good idea. If someone is acting from anger rather than hope of gain, telling people they're out of the will could push this person over the edge."

"That's true." Turning to Charlotte, Angus said, "Does anyone of your acquaintance have a history of mental instability? Violence?"

Charlotte started to shake her head, but stopped. "Well . . ."

"What?" Michael asked.

Charlotte bit her lip. "Ivan has something of a past."

"We already know he shot a wolf," Michael said.

"That's true, but according to him, he also threatened to kill a woman." She glanced toward the hallway and pushed back her chair. "Why don't we go out to the workshop? I'll get my keys."

They waited as Charlotte got her purse, then followed her outside, where she unlocked the door to the stone workshop. Once inside, she turned on the lights and a couple of electric heaters, then perched on a stool. "I feel like I should start with *once upon a time.*"

Suki leaned her elbows on a worktable and cupped her face in her palms. "Go ahead."

Charlotte smiled faintly. "Some time ago, when Ivan was still touring with the Trans-Siberian Circus, he had an affair with the circus owner's wife, and she got pregnant. The circus owner fired Ivan and threw his own wife out into the snow. She begged her husband's forgiveness and offered to abort the child."

"Did he take her back?" Michael asked.

"No. And Ivan told her that if she aborted their child, he would kill her. She carried it to term thinking Ivan would stay with her, but he had come to hate her. When his son was three months old, he took the baby and came to America, where he has a cousin."

"Where is the child now?" Angus asked.

"With the cousin and his wife. They weren't able to have children, so they've raised the boy as their own. He's about eight. Ivan sees him a couple of times a year."

"Does anyone know what happened to the kid's mother?" Suki asked.

"Apparently she drank herself to death." Charlotte rubbed her arms. "It's quite a story, isn't it?"

"Have you actually met this kid?" Michael asked, his tone skeptical.

"Come on, Michael," Angus said. "Why would Ivan make something like that up? It's not very flattering."

"That's arguable, and it's just the kind of operatic backstory that would go over well on television."

"I have met the boy," Charlotte said. "He lives in Texas and seems very happy with his adopted family. He calls Ivan *Uncle Papa,* and says his mother lives with the wolves."

"Is that some sort of Russian euphemism for liver failure?" Suki asked.

"No, I think that's what they told him. Ivan swore me to secrecy."

Michael rolled his eyes. "That kid is going to need years of therapy."

Angus looked thoughtful. "Ivan may have a torrid past, but the fact remains, he didn't physically harm the woman, as far as we know. What about Ellen? Anything there?"

Charlotte shook her head. "Ellen simmers and sulks. She's not big on action. And although you're diplomatically not asking about Cheri, I will tell you that while she and her stepfather get into occasional screaming matches, she's never thrown or broken anything. Cheri certainly never hit him." Charlotte chuckled. "She did sew the bottoms of his suit pants closed before a big meeting. I shouldn't laugh, but I'm not fond of the man, either."

She slid off the stool. "This has been therapeutic, talking about other people's problems. I feel better, at least for the moment."

"That's good," Angus said. "I still think you might say something about your will."

Charlotte shook her head. "It's just too melodramatic, and completely unnecessary. I think the police are right. Thomas's death was just a series of coincidences." She bit her lip for a moment. "I dreamed about Petey last night. It was a little fuzzy, but the general message was that Thomas chose to react in anger. No one made him run into that street. He did it all on his own."

Angus nodded. "I can't argue with that."

"I can," Michael said.

"But you won't," Angus said firmly.

Charlotte gestured to the door. "I'm sorry to run you out, but I have a lot of work to do for the wake tonight."

"I thought Thomas didn't want a funeral," Michael said, leading the way outside.

"Emma Crawford's wake." Charlotte pulled the door closed and took out her keys. "I have a background in theater, you know. Tonight's show must go on, and tomorrow is the coffin race. I assume you'll be here for that as well."

"I wouldn't miss it for the world," Angus said.

She turned from the locked door and smiled. "Then I insist you all stay with me another night. There's Thomas's room, of course.

I'll have Ellen . . ." She broke off. "I'll set up a cot in the upstairs parlor for whoever wants it. After all, Petey might put in another appearance, to say good-bye." She looked at her watch. "I'll see you this evening, if not before."

"Charlotte," Michael said quickly. "Does anyone in the house have a pink coat with a hood?"

She raised her eyebrows. "Why? Did you find one?"

"Uh, yes, on the street. It must have fallen out of someone's car."

"That sounds like something Cheri would do, and I know she has at least one pink jacket. But you might also check with Ellen. I talked her into a pink parka years ago, thinking it would help cheer her up. Although to my knowledge, she never wears it." She gave a wry smile. "Maybe she was taking it to charity and it fell off the top of a box."

"Okay, thanks," Michael said.

She lifted her hand. "See you all later."

They watched her cross the yard and go into the house.

"That didn't narrow things down much," Michael said. "And what's up with the dream about Petey? Last night she seemed convinced a person was behind the whole thing, but now it sounds like she's back to believing in a ghost."

"There's probably some psychology going on," Angus mused. "After the initial shock of Thomas's death, Charlotte must be feeling quite relieved. That's easier to justify if she can mark his death down to fate."

"In the form of a ghostly toy breed." Michael shook his head. "Harbingers of death seem kind of cut-rate these days. What ever happened to banshees and fire-breathing horses?"

"It's hard to get good help nowadays." Angus put his hands in his pockets and started toward the house. "Since we're spending our last night here, we might as well get all our things from the motel."

"At least staying here will let us keep an eye on Charlotte," Michael said, following him.

"And maybe Petey will stop by to bid us all farewell."

They spent the afternoon at the Crystal Valley Cemetery, site of Emma Crawford's eventual resting place.

Michael read the gravestone's inscription into his recorder. " 'In Memoriam. Emma L. Crawford. Passed To The Higher Life December 4th 1891. There Was That In Her Life Here Which Knew Not Death Nor Feared Its Shaft; A Tranquil Trust. A Faith in the Infinite Unknown—The Spirit Life. She Will Not Be Forgotten.' "

"Very nice," Angus said solemnly.

Michael clicked off his recorder. "Hey, can I use the phrase *peripatetic corpse* when I write about Emma? Will our readers know what that means?"

"If they don't, they can look it up." Angus waved a small branch with silk leaves at Suki. "Are you ready for this yet?"

"Sure." She squinted into the bright sky. "Okay, stand here." She positioned Angus and raised his arm. "Angle the branch this way. A little higher. There."

The tombstone, a slab of irregular flagstone with a black-and-white photo of Emma Crawford, looked pleasantly ordinary in full sun. With the fake branch casting dappled shade across Emma's name, it looked mysterious and moody.

"Damn, you're good," Michael said. "What if local people write in and complain that there aren't any nearby trees, so it isn't accurate?"

"Then we'll know someone is reading the magazine," Angus said. "How long do I have to hold this?"

"Just a few seconds." Suki moved the tripod and took a few more shots. "Okay. What's next?"

Angus took a printout from his pocket and consulted it. "I believe Theresa M. Kenny's mausoleum is over there." He pointed.

"Is it supposed to be haunted?" Michael asked.

"Not that I know of. Maybe we'll be the first to see something." Angus led the way through the grassy cemetery. As they walked, he said, "Ms. Kenny was an Austrian immigrant who bought her grave site fourteen years prior to her death. She built her own mausoleum, except for the roof, which she hired out. She was so enamored with what she called her 'little house' that she brought a rocking chair and sat in front of it on nice days. When she died, they put the rocking chair inside. I'm hoping we can get a nice picture." He looked around. "Ah, there's the place."

They walked around the mausoleum, but there was no way to see the chair inside.

"I guess her masonry skills didn't extend to windows," Michael said.

Suki took a few pictures. "Nice texture on the walls, though."

"She did that with a kitchen spoon." Angus bent and put his ear to the wall. "I believe I hear the chair rocking inside. Write that down."

Michael did so. "Is it a soft sound, like it's muffled by the dust of centuries?"

Suki pointed to the plaque. "She only died in 1943."

"You can say it creaks a little, if you like," Angus said. "Creaking is always good."

Michael scribbled on his pad. "Faint, rhythmic creaking, as of old wood on stone . . ." He finished and put the pen behind his ear. "Got it."

Fifteen

When they returned to the Baskerville house, Ivan opened the door to them. He had Lila tucked under one arm. Behind him, Ellen pounded up the stairs, several garments draped over her arm.

"I assume Charlotte is getting ready for the wake?" Angus asked, as they came in.

Ivan nodded. "Cheri, too. The girl who was to play Emma is sick, and Cheri will now be the body in the coffin."

Michael blew out a breath. "Really? You'd think it would be a little too close to home, what with Thomas's death and all."

Ivan shrugged. "She is a natural actress." Lila squirmed in his grip, and he made a hushing noise. "I am playing dog nanny, so this one does not get stepped on."

"Can't you just put her outside?" Suki asked.

Ivan shook his head. "Too many pets go missing for her to be out alone. She would be tasty snack for coyote, mountain lion, even a hawk."

"If you like, we'll keep her in our room for a while," Angus offered.

Ivan handed Lila over willingly. "If she scratches at door, it means she needs to go out to pee. You have to go with her."

Angus looked into Lila's face. "We'll fend off the beasties for you."

Ivan lifted a hand in thanks, then reached into his pocket and took out a pack of cigarettes before heading for the front door.

Michael headed up the stairs, but Angus pulled him back by his shirtsleeve. When the front door closed behind Ivan, he said, "Come on. I want to try something."

Michael and Suki followed him into the downstairs parlor, where he handed the dog to Michael and unlocked the door to Thomas's room.

"What's going on?" Michael whispered, as they went inside.

Angus pulled the drapes back. Outside, the sky was overcast. "Not bright enough," he muttered, switching on the overhead light. He took Lila from Michael and held her up to the ceiling, turning her this way and that under the light fixture. She looked down at him, little forehead wrinkled.

"I get it." Michael picked up the keys from where Angus had dropped them on the desk and unlocked the door to the small bathroom. "This ought to work. Come in here, Suki."

"Whatever you say, big boy."

Angus joined them in the small room and closed the door. Light came from under both doors, allowing them to see each other. Lila gave a questioning whine.

"Not dark enough," Angus said.

"Move over there," Suki said. She edged past him and squatted in the confined space, then shoved the bathroom rug across the bottom of the door into the hallway. "We need something for the other door."

"Use this." Michael pulled a towel off the rack.

Suki pushed it against the bottom of the door to the bedroom, plunging the small bathroom into darkness. "That's good." She got to her feet.

They stood in silence for a moment.

"Where's the dog?" Suki asked.

"I'm holding her in front of my chest," Angus said.

"I don't see anything. Can you turn her around?" Michael asked. A moment later he added, "Ow."

"What?" Suki said.

"Got a claw in the chin."

"You know," Suki said, "even if Lila was last night's ghost, someone could have given her a bath since then. I suppose we could ask."

Angus made a noise of disappointment. "Never mind. I was hoping for something conclusive. Oh, well. Someone get the door."

Michael fumbled with the knob, then opened the door a few inches until it stuck on the towel. He slid the towel aside with a foot and they went out.

Angus put Lila on the floor and straightened. "Bloody hell!"

"What?" Michael asked.

Angus strode over to the file cabinets. The second drawer was partially open, and he pulled it out the rest of the way. "Did anyone notice if this was open when we came in?"

"Sorry," Suki said. "I was watching you illuminate the dog."

"I know we locked the bedroom when we left this morning," Michael said, "but there might be another key somewhere. Did you lock the file cabinet last night before we went to sleep?"

"I honestly don't remember." Angus pawed through the files. "The private investigator files and the lawyer files are gone." He closed that drawer and opened another.

"The old investigator files or the new ones?" Michael asked.

Angus shoved the drawer shut. "Both. All. What was that investigator's name? Thompson? Patterson? Peterson?"

"I can't believe one of us didn't write it down," Michael said glumly. "I guess you figure something in a file is already written down."

"I'm pretty sure the name was Peterson," Angus said, "but I don't suppose he'll give us a copy of the records, even if we ask nicely."

Suki pointed upstairs. "What do you say we tell Charlotte and ask if we can search the place?"

Angus looked skeptical. "You think whoever took the files still has them in the house? They had the whole time we were gone to get rid of them."

"That's assuming the person broke into the room earlier," Suki said. "What if someone walked in while we were in the bathroom with the dog?"

Angus and Michael stared at her. Then they all made a concerted rush toward the door.

"Wait!" Michael said, as the three of them reached the foyer. "What exactly are we going to do?" He dropped his voice to a whisper. "Explain to Charlotte that we searched through her husband's files and found personal and embarrassing things about her?"

Angus chewed on the side of his thumb. "When you put it that way . . ."

"I suppose Charlotte might have taken them herself," Suki put in. "She seems like the kind of woman who would have a spare key to her husband's private room."

"But what if she doesn't?" Angus said. "What if she doesn't know they existed, and the person who took them was in cahoots with Thomas?"

"Thomas is dead, so cahoots are moot." Michael chuckled. "Is *cahoots* a Scottish word? It really sounds like it."

"Focus, Michael," Angus said.

"Right. It's not as though the files were harmful, since the investigator didn't find anything. In a perfect world, whoever took them is simply covering his or her tracks. Think of it this way—now Charlotte won't have to see stuff that would only hurt her feelings."

"I'd still like to know who it was," Angus muttered. "What do you say we search the downstairs, just to see?"

Michael shrugged and looked at Suki.

"Yeah, okay," Suki said. "While we're at it, keep an eye out for Lila. She must have run out of the room when you were looking through the files."

Suki had her head in one of the bottom kitchen cupboards when she heard Ellen's voice behind her.

"Can I help you find something?" Ellen asked.

Suki withdrew with a clatter of cookie sheets and stood. "Um, a waffle iron?"

"You want to make waffles?" Ellen held a pin cushion in one hand. It was in the shape of a Chihuahua's head.

Suki pointed to it. "I once dated a guy who did pet acupuncture. He said turtles were the worst."

Ellen looked at the pincushion for a moment, then back at Suki. "You want to make waffles?"

"Um, yeah," Suki continued. "I thought, since Charlotte was nice enough to put us up, we could make breakfast for everyone."

Ellen opened the cupboard beside the one Suki had been in and pointed. "There's the waffle iron." She smiled. "What a nice idea."

Suki squatted and eyed the machine's pitted chrome and

cloth-covered cord. "When was the last time you made waffles, 1949?" She pushed the machine to one side and looked behind it before standing and closing the cupboard door.

Ellen waved toward the stairs. "I've almost finished dressing Charlotte and Cheri for the Emma Crawford wake tonight, if you want to take pictures of them."

"I'll get my stuff and be right up."

In the parlor outside Thomas's room, Angus looked behind books while Michael got on his hands and knees and checked under the furniture.

Footsteps on the wood floor made them both turn.

Ivan sat down on an upholstered hassock, Lila at his feet. "If you are looking for dog, I have her." He eyed them curiously. "But surely you do not expect her to be behind books."

Michael sat back on his heels and brushed his hands on his pants. "We're, uh—"

"Looking for ghost spoor," Angus said, taking three books off the shelf and peering into the space behind.

Ivan crossed one leg over the other. "And why are ghosts poor?"

"Ghost *spoor*," Angus said, enunciating clearly. "Traces left by ghosts. It could be ectoplasm, unexplained piles of dust, even scraps of paper with cryptic writing. I found one of those once."

"Oh, please," Michael groaned. "What did this cryptic note say?"

Angus narrowed his eyes. "It said, 'Don't be a smart-ass.'"

Michael picked a pillow off the chaise and looked behind it. "Not so cryptic, then."

"We'd be happy to check your room for you, Ivan," Angus said. "I think Charlotte would want us to."

"Maybe later, when I can help," Ivan said. "And if we find something, we will give it to Lila to sniff. She can track it down, like a bloody hound."

"Bloodhound," Michael corrected.

Suki came in, carrying her tripod and camera. "Guys? Oh, hi, Ivan."

He grinned, crooked teeth on display. "Hallo, princess."

She turned to the others. "Ellen is putting the last touches on Charlotte's and Cheri's costumes for the Emma Crawford wake. I'm going to take some pictures. Do you want to ask them questions or anything?"

"I suppose we've looked in this room enough." Angus gave Suki a significant look. "We'll finish searching the rest of the house for *ghost spoor* later on."

"Ghost spoor . . . *riiight*," Suki said. "I wish you'd mentioned that to me earlier."

"Why?" Michael asked.

"Never mind, but you should know we're making waffles for everyone tomorrow morning."

They trooped upstairs, Ivan carrying Lila.

In Charlotte's bedroom, Suki set up her camera while Michael took out his recorder and muttered descriptive phrases into it.

Cheri stood in front of a mahogany-framed cheval mirror, wearing an old-fashioned white nightgown with a ribbon sash, puffed sleeves, and drawstrings at the wrists.

Noting her pale face and purple-shadowed eyes, Angus said, "If that's not makeup, you might want to see a doctor."

Cheri didn't smile, but went to the bed and sat on the edge of the mattress, her spine slumping. "It's makeup. I did it myself." She reached back and petted Chum, ensconced in the middle of the spread. He wagged his tail.

"Well, you make a lovely Emma, if a bit peaky." Angus took a notebook and pen out of his jacket pocket and turned to where Charlotte sat on a wooden chair, very upright. "And tell us who you are again."

"Cara Bell. Wife of the founder of Manitou Springs, Dr. William Bell." The dress she wore was of matte black silk. The high, close neck led into a ruffled yoke that decorated her bosom. Additional fabric draped her hips, making her waist look tiny.

Ellen stood at her shoulder, stitching the top of one of the close-fitting long sleeves.

"Is that dress an antique?" Michael asked.

"No." Charlotte put a hand flat against her stomach. "I'm wearing a corset, but unless I want my liver and kidneys to be even closer neighbors, I'd never get into an actual dress from that time. Those women were so small."

"This is a reproduction." Ellen took a pair of scissors off Charlotte's lap and snipped the needle free of the seam she'd been stitching. "Unfortunately, Charlotte snagged the sleeve on the hinge of her closet door this morning."

"Did you make the dress?" Angus asked Ellen.

She laughed. "No way. Dog costumes are child's play compared to this."

"I bought it from an online site," Charlotte explained. "It wasn't cheap, but I've wanted to play Cara Bell for years. I'm older than she was at the time of Emma Crawford's death, but I have a wig." She motioned to the bureau, where a Styrofoam head held a brown wig pulled into a bun. "What time is it?"

Angus looked at his watch. "Just after four."

Charlotte ran her hand over the mended sleeve. "Am I all set, Ellen? We should leave soon."

"Yep." Ellen went over to the bureau and stuck her needle in the top of the Chihuahua pincushion.

"I thought the first performance started at six," Michael said. "Should we go with you?"

"No," Charlotte said. "We're just taking care of last-minute preparations." She leaned forward very slightly, then stopped with a grunt. "Someone get me out of this chair."

Angus took her outstretched hands and carefully raised her to her feet. "Will you keep your costumes on?"

"No. We'll take everything off now and dress again right before the performance. This was just a trial run." Charlotte took a deep breath now that she was standing. "Whew. That's better. Ivan is going to help with the lighting, Ellen will check costumes, we need to make sure Cheri looks good in the coffin, and I want to go over my lines with some of the other historical figures."

Ellen gathered up her sewing things. "We haven't spent much time with the dogs today. Should I put Lila in her crate so she doesn't do anything bad while we're gone?"

"Would it help if I took her for a walk?" Suki asked.

Charlotte put a hand on her arm. "Oh, would you, dear?"

"Sure. As long as I can dress her up."

Charlotte laughed. "A woman after my own heart. Lila's clothes are in the bottom two drawers of this dresser, and her leash should be hanging on the coat tree by the front door."

"Is there any secret to dressing a dog?" Suki asked.

"Head first, but she won't give you any trouble. If you get back after we've left, you can just shut her in my room. She won't need to be crated after a walk."

In another twenty minutes, Suki was outside with Lila, and Charlotte and the Baskerville entourage were walking toward Miramont Castle, where Emma Crawford's wake was to be held. Cheri toted two garment bags, while Ellen and Ivan carried shopping bags.

Angus and Michael watched them through the window of the downstairs parlor.

"Time to do a more thorough search for those files," Angus said, letting the curtain fall. "You stay here and keep watch."

"Aren't you worried they'll realize the place has been searched?" Michael asked.

"Not really, but if anyone asks, you and I took a drive to Garden of the Gods right after they left."

"And if they come back for some reason and find us here?"

"The longer we talk about this, the less time I have to look around," Angus said.

"Fine." Michael moved one of the chairs so it faced out the window. "You know, if Ellen took those files, she'd put them in her workshop, and that's locked."

"I know." Angus sighed. "I don't really expect to find anything, but it's always worth trying."

Sixteen

Suki walked down Ruxton Avenue with Lila on her leash. She had dressed the dog in a pink silk skirt embroidered with black spirals, a black tutu, and a tiny vest in faux black leather.

Several people asked if they could pet Lila, and one small girl asked her mother for "a puppy like that," then burst into tears when one wasn't instantly produced.

"I'm sorry," the mother said, pulling the tot away. "She hasn't had her nap."

Suki watched them go, then looked at Lila, whom she had picked up when the child showed signs of being grabby. "It's hard being beautiful. Everyone wants a piece of you." She put Lila down and they continued up Ruxton.

As they came around a bend in the road, someone approached from the opposite direction, walking a white Chihuahua. As they neared each other, Suki saw it was Cheri's ex-boyfriend Jay, almost unrecognizable in jeans and a sweatshirt.

"Hi, Jay," she greeted him.

"Hi." He didn't smile. "Sorry, what's your name again?"

"Suki. Photographer for *Tripping* magazine. Is that your dog?"

"He belongs to my mom."

"What's his name?"

"Ludwig. He likes classical music."

Lila and the other dog sniffed each other eagerly, winding their leashes together.

Suki bent and untangled Lila, then scratched Ludwig's neck under his collar. "He feels a little damp. Did he jump in a creek?"

"No, Chihuahuas aren't that into water. I gave him a bath earlier." Jay stared across the street and sighed heavily.

"Are you going to the Emma Crawford wake?" Suki asked.

"Is Cheri going to be there?"

"She's playing Emma. The person who was supposed to do it got sick."

Jay's lips tightened. "I won't be there." He pulled Ludwig away from Lila and scooped up the dog. "I have to go now."

Suki watched as he strode back the way he'd come.

Angus decided to search Ivan's room first. The door was unlocked, and he slipped into the reek of stale cigarette smoke.

Ivan had his own closet and bathroom. Angus gave the bathroom a cursory look, noting that Ivan was a fan of Instinct body spray by Axe.

The closet held a modest selection of high-quality, rather slick clothes, with a few silk shirts still in their dry-cleaning bags. He pulled a cardboard box down from the upper shelf. It was full of unsorted papers, some of them with Cyrillic writing and red stamps. He looked through them briefly, but didn't see a file folder or anything that looked like the missing papers.

Another box held a few things that must have had sentimental value: paperback books, a lacquered box with a lock of hair and what looked like baby teeth, an etched glass in a tarnished silver holder, an enameled cross, and some photos.

Angus looked through the pictures. Two black-and-white prints with worn edges were probably ancestral wedding photos, the mustachioed men in suits with stiff-collared shirts, the women in white blouses tucked into slim, long skirts, their hair piled on top of their heads.

A stack of color Polaroids documented Ivan's time in the circus. Colorfully painted trucks sat on a snowy roadside, while bundled-up people sat by fires and steaming camp stoves. Three wolves slept in a straw-lined cage, the muzzle of one resting on another's back. A man knelt in the snow, holding a hoop overhead as a wolf leapt toward it. The camera had caught the wolf as it left the ground— haunches bunched with muscle, forepaws tucked, muzzle pointed like an arrow.

Angus squinted at the man, trying to see if it was Ivan, but a scarf and fur hat made identification impossible.

He gave up and looked at the last picture. A laughing woman in slacks and a puffy coat stood in front of a house, holding a tightly swaddled baby. The baby's eyes were mere slits in the chubby face, and the rosebud mouth looked faintly reproachful.

Angus studied the woman's high cheekbones and large, expressive eyes. Fair, wavy hair fell over her shoulders. "Quite a looker," he murmured, then put the photos back in the box and arranged things roughly as he'd found them. The only other thing on the shelf was a half-full carton of Chesterfield cigarettes.

He went over to the bureau. The surface was clear except for some copies of *Entertainment Weekly* and *Variety,* a hairbrush, and a small framed photo. He picked up the photo. He hadn't noticed it when they'd come in earlier to see the posters.

The picture showed a middle-aged couple with dark hair and Slavic faces, seated at a picnic table with a boy of about six. The lad's high cheekbones and smiling mouth reminded Angus of the woman in the photo from the box, but the boy's eyes were all Ivan—dark and intense, beneath straight black brows.

Angus opened one of the bureau's small top drawers. In addition to ties, it contained a tray with collar stays, cuff links, and rings, plus a small key. He picked up the key, but there was no imprint or other information that gave a clue to its use.

He slid open the next drawer and found a checkbook. "Ah, you beauty." Paging through the carbons, he noticed a torn edge at the top, where one of them had been ripped out. Checking the numbers, he saw that two more were gone.

Angus rifled through the rest of the drawers, but there were no other checkbooks. The rest of the contents revealed only that Ivan favored Kimono condoms and black boxer briefs. He felt the undersides of the bureau drawers and checked down the back. Nothing.

Turning, he noticed a trunk at the foot of the bed. "Aha." When the lid didn't budge, he got the small key from the bureau. It opened the lock easily.

The faint odor of mothballs wafted up as he raised the lid. A half-full bottle of vodka lay on top of some clothing. Angus set it on the floor, then pulled out a pair of black wool pants, an embroidered shirt, and some battered boots. Beneath those lay a folded quilt. He lifted one side and found two shallow boxes, one in black plastic, the other in gray.

He took the black box out and opened it. Inside, a foam tray held five black knives, each blade continuing up to form a metal handle with a small crossbar. Angus took one out and gingerly tested the tip. A drop of blood rose on his fingertip. He returned the knife to its place.

He opened the second box, expecting more knives, and froze with the lid open. The molded interior held a black handgun. It lay there, stark and threatening.

He closed the lid carefully, then got a pair of boxer briefs from Ivan's bureau and wiped the gun case clean of any fingerprints he might have left.

Beneath the other side of the quilt were a gun-cleaning kit, a box of ammunition, and a plastic tub of much-used theatrical makeup.

Angus put everything back and went to the bed to run his hand under the mattress, where he found a couple of fairly standard porn magazines. The bottom of the box spring yielded nothing.

He went down the stairs and into the downstairs parlor.

Michael turned from the window. "Did you find the files?"

"No, but I found Ivan's current checkbook, and a couple of the carbon copies are missing. Do you think Ivan was the one paying Thomas's bills?"

"It's suggestive." Michael thought for a moment. "Maybe Thomas promised to help Ivan with his TV show if he got hold of Charlotte's money."

"If that's the case, no wonder Ivan doesn't have the cash to get his teeth fixed," Angus said. "Thomas was bleeding him dry."

"Could that be a motive for murder?" Michael asked. "Ivan makes a ghost dog and uses it to lure Thomas into the street?"

Angus considered it. "Seems a bit extreme. Ivan could have just stopped paying."

"Maybe Thomas threatened to tell Charlotte about Ivan's involvement."

"Thomas would look bad as well," Angus said, "and remember, he'd just started to behave himself. But I do think Ivan is capable of violence. In addition to the checks in Ivan's room, I found a set of what I think are throwing knives, and also a gun."

"What kind of gun?" Michael asked.

"I don't know. A scary-looking pistol. Not being a gun person, I couldn't tell you more, except that it takes nine-millimeter bullets."

"How do you know that?"

"It said so on the box of ammunition."

"Did you find a permit?" Michael asked.

"No, but Ivan's filing system is a huge box of unsorted paper. I didn't take the time to go through all of it."

The front door opened, and they both jumped.

"Boy, that Garden of the Gods is spectacular," Michael said, a little loudly.

"It certainly is," Angus replied. "I particularly liked the rock shaped like a haggis."

Suki came into the room, Lila dancing at the end of her leash. "You went to Garden of the Gods without me?"

Angus slumped into a chair. "No. We thought you might be Charlotte or the others coming back for something, and I've been searching Ivan's room."

"Find anything good?" She bent and unclipped Lila's leash, then unfastened the Velcro at the bottom of Lila's vest.

"Knives, guns, photos, and a checkbook." Angus filled in the details of his findings.

When he had finished, Suki said, "Based on that photo, it looks like the story about Ivan's son is true." She put Lila's clothing in a tidy stack on a nearby table and sat down.

"Probably true," Michael said. "The woman with the baby could be Ivan's sister. Or maybe the kid *is* his son, but Ivan and the mom parted on perfectly cordial terms." He looked at their faces. "Hey, I take nothing on faith, okay?"

Suki patted Lila, who had jumped on her lap. "I have some news, too. Guess who we ran into on the street."

"Who?" Angus asked.

"Recent dumpee Jay, looking all depressed and walking his mom's pooch—a white Chihuahua."

"How do you know Jay was the dumpee?" Michael asked. "Maybe he broke up with Cheri."

"You're missing the point. Wouldn't a white Chihuahua make a great ghost dog?"

"It would at that," Angus mused.

Suki grinned. "*And,* Jay had recently given it a bath."

Michael's brow furrowed. "Cheri and Jay were each other's alibis on the night Thomas died. They could have been lying."

Angus frowned. "I hate to think of such a thing. Anyway, it sounded to me as though Charlotte would leave something to Cheri regardless of whether Thomas was still in the picture."

"Maybe they just hated him," Suki said.

Angus looked at his watch. "I was hoping to look at Ellen's and Cheri's rooms, but we need to get to the wake."

They headed upstairs to get their things.

In the parlor, Suki tried the connecting door that led to Charlotte's room. It was locked. "I hope the other door is open. I'm supposed to put Lila in there."

"I'll do it," Angus said, taking Lila from her. "Bring a camera to the wake, just in case. I don't imagine we'll be allowed to photograph the performance, but we might interview some of the audience afterward—see if we can get some good ghost stories."

"All right." Suki handed him Lila's clothing, which she had brought with her. "You might as well put these in there, too."

Angus went down the hall to Charlotte's room, the clothes in one hand and Lila under his arm. He opened the door and set her down. On the bed, Chum raised his head and gave a rusty yap.

"Just me," Angus said, putting Lila's clothes on the foot of the bed. He noticed a drop-front desk against one wall. "Pay no attention. Nothing to worry about." Both dogs' gaze followed him as he went over and carefully lowered the front of the desk. "Just harmless old Angus."

In the parlor, Michael checked his pocket for his notebook and recorder. "Did Angus go downstairs without us?" He went into the hallway, followed by Suki. "Angus? Where are you?"

Behind them, Angus appeared in the doorway of Charlotte's room. "Come here. I want to show you something."

"Lila didn't puke, did she?" Suki asked. "Because I swear she didn't get more than a lick of that dead squirrel."

"She's fine." Angus led them to the desk and pointed to a paper on it. "Look what I found."

"Oh, man. You searched *Charlotte's* room?" Michael asked. "Isn't there some sort of Old World code where you don't mess with your host's stuff?"

"I must have skipped school that day," Angus said. "Anyway, I only had a wee look around in case Charlotte had the lawyer and detective files herself. Then we could have saved ourselves worrying about them. Instead, I found her will." He held out a notarized piece of paper. "And if I could find it, anyone could."

Seventeen

"What's the will say?" Suki took it from him. "Whoa. Thirty thousand to Ellen, plus all rights to the Petey's Closet name and images. Ten thousand to Ivan, along with the dogs and money for their upkeep. The residual, including the house and all investments, to be split between Thomas and Cheri."

"Now that Thomas is dead, Cheri will get his share when Charlotte dies," Angus said. He took the paper from Suki, put it back in an envelope, and slipped it into one of the desk's cubbies. "Makes you think, doesn't it?" he said, as he closed the desk's front. "That much money could buy a lot of freedom for a young woman."

"Or dental work for Ivan," Suki agreed.

"Or advertising for Ellen's dog-clothing business," Michael added.

"C'mon, let's go." Angus led them outside, where he shut the door behind them. As they went down the hall, he paused and tried the door to Ellen's room. "Locked. Interesting."

"In all fairness," Michael said, "I'd lock my door if there were strangers staying in the house."

"I call that paranoia," Angus said, starting down the stairs.

"How can you call it paranoia when you just searched Charlotte's room?" Michael demanded.

"All right then, I call it inconvenient."

In the foyer, Michael took his leather jacket off the coat rack and zipped it over his sweater. "I'm starting to feel like we should tell Charlotte everything we know, even if we have to confess to rummaging through her house."

Angus blew out a breath. "Maybe so."

Suki settled a purple velvet tam on her head and picked up her camera bag. "Good thing we're making waffles tomorrow. Maybe that'll put her in a good mood."

Angus locked the front door behind them with Thomas's keys. Outside, dead leaves rattled across the sidewalk, driven by a chill wind. They crossed the street and walked the short distance to the Miramont Castle.

A woman stood at the door, wearing a wine-colored wool cape over her black Victorian dress. "Thank you for coming to pay your respects," she said solemnly. "Tickets?"

"Anne Marie said we could come in as long as we didn't eat dinner," Angus said. "We're with *Tripping* magazine, here to write up the wake for an article."

"She told me to keep an eye out for you." The woman leaned forward and lowered her voice. "You understand that there's nothing *funny* about this wake, don't you? I mean, we don't eat peyote or anything."

"I understand, ma'am. Our magazine title refers to travel, like *day tripping,* with perhaps a soupçon of the surreal."

"Oh, I see!" She opened the heavy front door for them. "Up the stairs, the room on your left."

They climbed the massive staircase, risers creaking under their feet. Candelabra bulbs flickered in the light fixtures, and the faint sound of a melancholy piano piece came from somewhere.

As they reached the large landing, the chatter of voices overlay the music. They turned left and saw a coffin on a metal stand with flowers around the base. Perhaps a dozen people milled around, wearing costumes.

A woman in a nun's habit saw them. "We're not ready!" she said, flapping her hands at them. "Go back!"

"It's all right," Charlotte said, coming forward. "They're with me."

"Oh." The nun subsided. "Sorry about that."

"Next time, smack 'em with your ruler," a man in a topcoat said, elbowing her in the ribs. She giggled.

Angus recognized the man as Shermont Lester, from the Chamber of Commerce. Angus lifted a hand in greeting and was rewarded with a stately nod.

Charlotte came over to them. "You'll want to go back down anyway. Diane, she plays Emma's mother, will be on the stairs in a minute, to give an introduction on what you're going to see."

"Where's a good place to stand for the show?" Michael asked.

Charlotte looked around. "It doesn't really matter. Maybe on that side."

"Then that's where we'll be," Angus said. "We'll go down now and wait with the punters. Break a leg!"

Charlotte smiled. "I haven't heard that in a while. Thank you."

The sound of voices became faint as they turned the corner onto the landing. At the bottom of the stairs, another woman in Victorian dress stood talking to three newly arrived guests.

As they descended, Michael spoke in an undertone. "It's so

weird that we're attending this made-up wake when Charlotte's husband died just yesterday."

"Presumably Emma Crawford was well liked, whereas Thomas was not," Angus murmured. "There's a lesson for all of us."

They waited downstairs as more and more people gathered around them. After fifteen minutes, Diane, the woman playing Emma Crawford's mother, took a head count and began her speech.

"Thank you for attending this wake for my beloved daughter. Tonight you will meet her fiancé, some of our friends, and other notable figures of our time. We ask that you remain quiet as we pay our last respects to Emma Crawford. Thank you. Now if you'll all follow me."

They trooped back upstairs, the floorboards' creaking drowned out beneath the clomp of shoes on wood.

Diane stood at the top, one arm extended in the direction they should go. "That way. You're welcome to file by the coffin as you go in. Then find a place to stand against one of the walls."

Angus and the others walked past the coffin. Cheri lay inside, hands crossed over her chest, looking young, virginal, and quite dead.

The parlor was large enough that everyone had a good view. The costumed men and women seemed unaware of their audience. Shermont Lester and Charlotte stood together, talking in low voices. Diane went to stand next to a young man with a sorrowful face—presumably Emma's beau. One woman sat in an upholstered chair and dabbed at her eyes with a lacy handkerchief.

When the audience had assembled, the young man stepped forward and introduced himself as William Hildebrand, a railway engineer and Emma's fiancé. "Emma was one of the sweetest women I've ever known. Always cheerful, always hopeful, and she knew that death is only a transition. A dozen of my friends and I are going to bury Emma in her chosen spot on Red Mountain, and I know she'll be watching." He choked up and went over to the coffin, where he retrieved a white rose from one of the vases around the bottom and laid it on Cheri's breast.

"Very affecting," Angus murmured.

One by one, the others came up, said something nice about Emma, then told their own stories. Charlotte, playing the wife of the founder of Manitou Springs, talked about the challenges of living in a fledgling town.

Local notables, such as Father Francolon, the first owner of Miramont Castle, were followed by more well-known figures— Wild Bill Hickock and deputy sheriff Wyatt Earp.

As the actor portraying the famous lawman began to talk, Suki leaned over to Angus and whispered, "I don't suppose Earp will reminisce about the time he spent pimping in Peoria."

"*No.* Really?" Angus whispered back.

She nodded. "Busted and fined twice. I wrote a paper on him in college."

Earp placed his rose in Emma's coffin before joining the ranks of the other costumed actors.

Finally the cast gathered in a line behind the coffin. "Again, thank you all for coming," Diane said.

The watchers, wondering if the show was over, began to shuffle and talk, but stopped as the lights dimmed and theatrical fog spilled across the floor.

Cheri sat up slowly in her coffin, scattering roses, her night-gown glowing white in what was probably the illumination from a black-light bulb. They heard the rustle of paper.

"I am Emma Crawford," Cheri intoned. "My spirit guide, Eddie

Five Eagles, told me to come to Manitou Springs. While it's true that I died before I could wed, I believe the healthy waters—"

"Healthful," Michael muttered.

"—extended my life and allowed me to know love, however briefly." Cheri looked down, then up again.

"She must have the script in her lap," Angus whispered. "I wondered how she'd learn her lines at the last minute."

"I ask you to remember that death is but a veil . . ." Cheri glanced down again. Her mouth, poised for the next word, opened wide. She began to scream, the sound thin and frantic as she gripped the sides of the coffin. "Get it off me! Get it off!" The black light showed the whites of her eyes around the irises.

Charlotte rushed to Cheri's side. "Get what off you?" She looked into the coffin and stepped back with a shriek.

A black-and-brown tarantula crawled into sight, long legs tapping on the white cotton of Cheri's gown as it slowly traversed her rib cage, toward her throat. She craned her head away, panting and wide-eyed.

"We need a glass, or a bowl!" Shermont said, looking around the room.

Angus started toward Cheri, but then he saw Charlotte. Her face had paled to the color of paper, and strangled noises came from her writhing mouth, as if she couldn't catch her breath. He caught her as she slumped.

The rest of the cast milled about uncertainly, shouting suggestions, while the audience gasped and babbled. A little girl hid her face against the legs of her mother, who patted her back and said, "They should really warn people before we buy tickets. This is too scary for Hannah."

Doors opened at the other end of the parlor, and light from the hall outside shone into the room. The fog swirled and thinned.

Ivan trotted into the room. "What is this noise?" He pushed several people aside and reached the coffin. Moving quickly and decisively, he snatched the spider off Cheri, threw it on the floor, and stomped it several times under his black boot.

"Ew!" several watchers exclaimed, as he lifted his foot. The woman playing Emma's mother gagged noisily.

Ellen came running in from the other room, followed closely by Bob Hume. "What happened?" She flicked on a light switch and glanced at the mess on the floor. "What *was* that?"

Angus lowered Charlotte to the floor as the last shreds of fog dissipated. She still breathed, but it sounded strained and difficult. "Someone call 911!"

Almost as one person, everyone in the audience took out their cell phones.

Shermont Lester pointed to a woman close to him. "May I use that to make the call? Everyone else, put your phones away and follow Diane to the buffet. Charlotte will be fine. I'm sure she's just fainted, but better safe than sorry."

As people began to file out, Ellen rushed over and knelt by Charlotte's side. "I should get the corset off her. She could barely breathe in it."

"Just like in *Pirates of the Caribbean*," Bob Hume said, looking worried. "The movie. Not the ride."

"Bob, you're in my light," Ellen said. "Why don't you go unplug the fog machine?"

"All right. I hope she's okay." He wandered off.

Ellen deftly unbuttoned the front of Charlotte's dress.

Cheri came over and stared down at her grandmother. "Did she have a heart attack?" Her voice was very small.

"I don't know." Ellen looked at Angus. "Hold her in a sitting position so I can pull the dress off her shoulders."

Angus put his hands under Charlotte's arms and pulled her limp torso upright.

Ellen tugged the dress down to Charlotte's waist, revealing a tightly laced corset. "Now lean her forward."

Charlotte's head lolled forward, her chin resting on her chest.

As Ellen loosened the corset's laces, Cheri stood and watched, her hands clasping and unclasping.

Ivan came over. "Cheri, you are all right?"

"Of course I'm all right," she snapped. "I just wanted the spider off me. You didn't have to kill it!"

Ivan threw his hands in the air. "What should I do? Pat it on the head and tell it to run along?" He made a noise of disgust and stuffed both hands in his pockets.

Ellen gave the corset laces a last tweak. "Okay, lay her on her back."

Angus did as she directed. Shermont Lester handed Ellen his frock coat and she covered Charlotte with it.

Charlotte's breathing seemed easier, and some of the color had come back into her cheeks.

Angus got to his feet and looked over to see Michael and Suki standing by the coffin. Michael made a small but urgent *come here* gesture.

Angus strolled to the wall that ran behind the coffin, passing unnoticed behind the backs of the other actors. Their attention was all for Charlotte, lying motionless on the floor.

"Take a look," Michael whispered, pointing to the interior of the coffin.

Angus looked inside. A full-length pillow, covered in white satin, cushioned the bottom of the mock coffin. Cheri had kicked it askew when she got out. Several small, muddy paw prints were visible on the white lining below.

Suki set her camera to video and hit RECORD as Angus carefully lifted the cushion.

"What are you doing?" Shermont Lester had turned and spotted them.

"Making sure there are no more surprises in here," Angus said, peering beneath the cushion before he pulled it all the way out. "But it turns out there's one surprise left."

The woman playing Marie Francolon shuddered. "Not more spiders, please."

"No, not that." Angus put the cushion on the floor.

The others came over, except for Ellen, who stayed by Charlotte.

Inside the coffin, the muddy paw prints trailed across the white satin, spelling out a single word: *Death.*

Suki switched to still photos and framed her shot. The resulting flash made everyone wince.

"Oh, my God," Cheri whimpered, putting both hands up to her mouth. "Which one of you did it?" She backed up against Ivan, then jerked away, stumbling over one of the vases and knocking it over. Water and white roses spilled across the floor.

Ivan grabbed Cheri's waist to steady her.

"Let go of me!" she shrieked.

"Calm down, Cheri," Shermont said.

"What if *he* put the spider in there?" Cheri demanded.

"What if *you* did?" Shermont shot back.

"I didn't!"

On the floor, Charlotte moaned. The group rushed to her side, except for Suki, who was focusing her camera on the spider's pulpy corpse.

Charlotte's eyes fluttered open.

"The paramedics are on their way," Ellen told her.

Charlotte nodded weakly. The brown wig looked oddly young above her face, which was haggard. She put a hand under the coat that covered her. "It felt as though something was crushing my chest. What time is it? I must be holding up the next performance."

Ellen shook her head in wry disbelief. "It's not important, Charlotte."

"Of course it is. The castle can't afford to refund those people's money. Will someone call Peggy and see if she can play my part? She did it last year."

Shermont Lester started toward the door. "If it'll make you feel better, I'll call her."

"Thank you," Charlotte whispered, closing her eyes.

"Maggie," Shermont called over his shoulder to another actress, "you tell the next group there's going to be a delay."

Maggie trotted after him, passing Bob as he returned to the room.

Cheri hugged herself and shivered. "What about my part? I'm not getting back in that coffin."

"No one's getting in that coffin until the police look at it," Angus said firmly. "This is vandalism, if nothing else."

"We can roll the coffin into the next room," one of the actors suggested. "Cheri, you can lie on a table."

"How will I hide my script when I'm lying there in plain sight?" Cheri protested.

"We'll stick it in a bunch of roses."

As the actors discussed the best way to salvage the show, Bob sat down on the floor. "I hope the police don't take too long. The buffet's going to get cold."

Eighteen

The paramedics came, followed closely by Officer Deloit and her partner, Officer Boyd.

While a second, modified performance of Emma Crawford's wake took place, the police took the nonperforming witnesses into the room with the coffin and questioned them.

Angus went first, then jerked his head at Michael, who volunteered to be next.

When Michael finished, he rejoined Angus. "What's up?"

"I want to go back to the Baskerville house while everyone else is here."

Michael looked over to where Suki was showing Officer Deloit the photographs she had taken. "What about Suki?"

"It can't wait. C'mon."

They strolled out of the room and found a stairway leading downstairs. As soon as they were out of the castle, Angus broke into a jog.

"What do you want to do at the house?" Michael asked, trotting beside him.

"I think Cheri is trying to claim her inheritance a bit early. I want to search her room."

"But Cheri was at most risk from the spider," Michael protested.

Angus made a rude noise. "A tarantula bite isn't any worse than a bee sting. Not only do they have weak venom, but they're not aggressive toward humans. No, I think it was there to frighten Charlotte."

"It did a good job," Michael said. "Where would you get a tarantula, at a pet store?"

"Yes, but they're also native to Colorado. You can find them crossing the road in late summer. I don't know if they're still about in October."

"Why do you know so much about tarantulas?" Michael asked.

"*Tripping* had a story on giant spiders of the Congo. I did some general research."

They reached the street, looked both ways, and jogged across.

"Cheri isn't the only one who benefits from Charlotte's will," Michael said. "Is she top of your list because her inheritance is biggest?"

"That, and she had the best chance of putting the spider in the coffin," Angus said. "She was also angry that Ivan killed it, and finally, she hangs out with that goth boy, Jay. He looks like someone who keeps spiders."

"I'm not sure he's strictly goth," Michael hazarded. "He looks more industrial to me."

"Do those people keep spiders?"

"Now that I think of it, industrial is an accepted goth subset. You see—"

"He's a young man with sideburns and a long black coat," Angus said loudly. "Don't you think he's the most likely to keep a tarantula?"

"I really can't commit to that sort of gross generalization."

They had reached the house. Angus took Thomas's keys from his pocket and unlocked the door. Once inside, he waved toward the downstairs parlor. "Keep an eye out through that window."

"Got it," Michael said.

Cheri's room was the last door on the right. Angus breathed a sigh of relief when the knob turned. Lock picking wasn't one of his skills.

He opened the door and recoiled slightly as fake strawberry scent hit him in the face like a damp, pink sponge.

Cheri's furnishings consisted of a four-poster bed with eggplant-colored hangings, a bright red recliner that faced a flat-panel TV mounted on the wall, and a walnut bureau that took up half of one wall, its top cluttered with makeup and jewelry. Two open doors on the side wall revealed a closet and a bathroom.

A few neoclassical prints hung on the walls, their subjects' flowing robes in imminent danger of revealing nipples and crotches. Magazines, cast-off clothes, and other detritus littered the floor.

Angus made his way over to the unmade bed, being careful not to step on anything.

Bending, he lifted the edge of the mattress and slid his hand almost to the back edge. Nothing. He looked under the pillow, just to make sure, then saw the edge of a laptop computer peeping out from beneath the sheet.

He lifted the lid and the machine hummed to life, but it was password-protected. Angus closed the lid with a slight feeling of relief. Unless Cheri had named a document something obvious, like "Care and feeding of spiders" or "How to kill Grandma," it would have taken too long to search through everything.

He made his way to the closet, where he switched on the interior light and shoved a laundry basket aside with his foot so he'd have a place to stand.

Cheri's clothes were packed on the rod so tightly, it was a miracle they hadn't turned to shale. Something pink caught Angus's eye, and he shoved at the clothes on either side until he could make it out—a quilted nylon jacket with a hood.

"That's something," he muttered. *Cheri might be the person who had gotten out of Bob Hume's truck and gone all the way around the block before coming home. Why would she do that?*

He shoved the jacket back and felt under sweaters and jeans piled haphazardly on the top shelf, then inside several pairs of boots on the floor, half expecting to feel a bottle. There was nothing but one knee-high nylon, wadded and dusty.

The bureau was next, and he went through all of the drawers, pushing aside thong underwear and shaking paperbacks of vampire erotica to make sure nothing hid between the pages.

He checked beneath the drawers, behind the bureau and prints, and under the chair and box springs. There was certainly no file folder, although he couldn't imagine how Cheri would fund Thomas's investigations.

Wondering if Cheri did drugs in addition to alcohol, he went inside the bathroom and checked the toilet tank, but found nothing. Cheri's signature scent was more concentrated in the small room. Pink bottles and tubes held strawberry-scented shampoo, body wash, lotion, and something called Pink Glimmer.

He left the bathroom and took a final look around to make sure things looked relatively the same as when he'd come in.

Angus shut the door behind him and went down the hall to Ellen's room. Its door was still locked. He continued downstairs to the parlor.

Michael turned from staring out the window. "Find any bags of spider chow?"

"No. I did find a pink coat with a hood."

"Then it was probably Cheri I saw from the Miramont Castle window."

"You'd have known for sure if you'd been close enough to smell her. Her room reeks of strawberry perfume." Angus held up his arm and sniffed it. "Might have to take a shower if I don't want to incriminate myself."

"Let me smell." Michael sniffed Angus's proffered hands and shook his head. "It's probably in your nose. What's next?"

"I don't know." Angus looked at the floor and rubbed his forehead. "Cheri, Ellen, and Ivan all have something to gain if Charlotte dies from a heart attack. They were all there today, so that's no help." He smiled faintly. "I wonder if Ivan's talents extend to teaching dogs to walk in the shape of letters."

"I'd use a fake paw from a stuffed animal or something."

Angus and Michael looked at each other.

"Like the stuffed Chihuahuas Bob Hume used to decorate his coffin for the race," Angus said.

"But Bob's not in Charlotte's will, and his buddy Thomas is dead. What could he hope to gain?"

Angus turned toward the door. "I don't know, but let's take a look at that coffin, shall we?"

Darkness had fallen. Next door, a television screen flickered through a downstairs window, but no lights showed in Bob's upstairs apartment.

Angus pushed open the gate and they walked quietly around to the back of the house. No coffin sat on the concrete patio.

"Maybe it's in the garage," Michael whispered. "Do you have a flashlight?"

"No." Angus walked to the side of the garage and tried the handle of the door there. "Locked." He walked along the wall to a window and peered inside. "I can't see a damn thing. Let's try the front."

They went back through the yard and out the gate. Michael bent and tried to lift the garage door. It moved a few inches and stopped. "Automatic door opener," he said, straightening. "I don't think we can get in."

Angus put his hands on his hips and thought for a moment. "It's time for the direct approach." He walked toward the front of the house.

Michael shoved the garage door to its original position, then trotted after Angus. "What are you going to do?"

"I have always depended on the kindness of strangers." Angus reached the front door and pushed the bell.

After a few moments, a tall man opened the front door. He was skinny except for a slight beer belly, and wore jeans and a grubby T-shirt. "Yeah?"

"I'm sorry to bother you," Angus said. "I was visiting Bob earlier today and I think I left my cell phone in the garage. Is there any way you could open it so I can check?"

"Hold on." Leaving the door open, the man disappeared into the house.

Angus and Michael stood on the front step, listening to the sound of the TV. Michael clasped his hands behind his back and rocked on his feet.

Angus chuckled quietly. "You know, I really should have turned my cell phone off before I started this lark. Hope it doesn't ring."

Michael waved his hand in a shushing gesture.

The man returned, holding a bunch of keys. "I don't use the garage, but I think this has a key to the side door." He pointed to a small, cluttered shelf, just inside the door. "Just leave 'em here when you're done. You don't need to knock."

"Thank you very much," Angus said, taking the keys.

"People are so trusting," Michael whispered, as they walked to the side of the garage.

"There's a lesson there." Angus tried a key without success.

"Not to trust people?" Michael said.

"Not to leave your keys lying about so your roommate can give them to strangers. Ah, here it is." Angus opened the door and slid his hand along the wall until he found a light switch. The over-head bulb revealed Bob's racing coffin, with a stuffed Chihuahua at each corner. "You check the two dogs in back, I'll check the front."

Angus went to the front of the coffin and grabbed the foreleg of a dog. Like every other part of the toy, the fur was crunchy with black paint. He bent the leg up to catch the light, then let it flick back into place. "That settles that."

Michael straightened. "They don't have paw pads."

Angus crossed his arms, patting one elbow thoughtfully. "I suppose we might as well look around while we're here. See if we can find anything suspicious." He pointed. "You take that half, I'll take the other."

Michael lifted the top of a standing toolbox. "I have to say, I'm starting to understand why people rave about Petey. I don't think even Lassie knew her letters."

"*Death*. Do you suppose that's a threat, or a reference to Thomas?" Angus asked.

Michael shrugged. "Could be it just sounded spooky and fit well in the available space. It's not easy to spell things using paw prints." He lifted a tarp. "Just out of curiosity, have you finally given up on the idea that we're dealing with a real ghost?"

"Of course not." Angus poked through a box of plumbing supplies. "It's just that ghosts aren't known for trying to kill people."

"Why not?" Michael asked. "If they can toss chairs around, why can't they pull the trigger of a gun? You know, I've noticed this double standard before. The public is fine with ghosts as long as they're moaning around in their jammies, but when a real crime happens, people stop looking for paranormal evidence and start looking for forensic evidence. If I were a ghost, I'd be pissed."

Angus pulled a stack of plywood away from the wall. "Interesting."

"Thank you."

"Not you. I stopped listening to you awhile back. Come look at what I found."

"What?" Michael came over to see.

Angus dragged out a box and flipped open the cut top. "Would you have taken Bob for a strawberry schnapps drinker?" He lifted one of the pink bottles inside. It was half empty.

Michael raised his eyebrows. "Not unless it's colored with açaí berries. He mentioned beer when he asked us to come over for chips and dip."

"Is this about the size of the box you saw him take out of his truck?"

"Pick it up," Michael suggested. "That'll help me judge."

Angus did, and stood for a moment holding it against his stomach.

Michael nodded. "I'd say it's a ringer. In fact, I think I even saw that red logo on the side."

Angus put the box down. "Combine that with the pink coat, and it looks like Bob is secretly buying liquor for Cheri. What a nice neighbor."

"Why would he do that?" Michael made a face. "Ew. You don't think they're having sex, do you?"

Angus raised his brows. "It's not as though he's covered with scales. And remember—she broke up with Jay. Charlotte described Jay as a decent kid. Presumably he wouldn't give Cheri liquor."

Michael raised a hand. "Hold on. Maybe it isn't booze or sex. Thomas is dead and Cheri is one step closer to being an heiress. What if Bob is counting on a different Baskerville to fund his business? He could be behind the Petey hoaxes."

Angus looked thoughtful. "Trading liquor for sex is one thing. Counting on an alcoholic girl to give you a packet of money after her grandparents die is another. I'm not sure even Bob is that much of a fool."

"Unless Cheri's in it with him."

"Maybe. Hold this plywood while I put the box back."

Michael held the plywood away from the wall. "It's difficult to think of Cheri and Bob as criminal masterminds. Maybe the booze has nothing to do with Cheri. Maybe Bob sits in his garage mixing up Tickle Me Elmos and getting hammered."

"*Tickle Me Elmo?* Is that a real drink?"

Michael nodded. "Strawberry schnapps, pineapple juice, and Everclear. I bartended briefly in college."

Angus shuddered. "Okay, you can lean the plywood back now.

The thing is, if the schnapps is Bob's, I wouldn't expect there to be a half-empty bottle out here. It'd be in his kitchen."

"I guess. Are you going to tell Charlotte that you think Bob is giving Cheri booze?" Michael asked.

"Not tonight, but assuming Charlotte recovers, yes." Angus swiped his hands together to get rid of dust. "Strawberry schnapps . . . That would explain Cheri's choice of strawberry perfume. Of course, nothing completely covers the smell of alcohol after it's gone through your system. It's the bits you don't metabolize that stink up the breath." He looked around. "I think I'm done. Did you find anything?"

"A bag of plaster," Michael said. "You could use that to make some sort of paw-print device, but from the looks of the spiderwebs, it hasn't been touched in years."

Angus nodded. "Let's go back to Miramont Castle and see what's going on."

They closed the garage door and went back to the house, where Angus placed the keys on the shelf. "Thank you!" he called out.

"Did ya find your phone?" came an answering shout.

"Yes! Thanks!"

They closed the door and walked past the Baskerville house.

As they crossed the street and neared Miramont Castle, Angus said, "Let's go around the back and see if someone could get inside without being noticed."

Miramont Castle was built into a slope. Stairs led up the left side, faintly illuminated by a streetlight on the road above.

"There's a terraced garden up here," Michael commented. "I remember that from the brochure."

Angus stumbled slightly on the edge of a concrete step. "Why do I never have a flashlight?"

They wound their way up the hill, following the path as it looped through planted beds, past bedraggled flowers that had gone to seed this late in the season.

When they were most of the way up, Angus stopped and pointed. "See that pipe coming out of the ground? That's a spigot. And what's that lying beneath it?"

"A bucket," Michael said, "and *mud*. Whoever made those muddy paw prints could have done it right here."

They went over to investigate. The spigot dripped slowly onto the churned ground beneath. The metal bucket sat upside down. Angus reached for it.

"Wait a minute!" Michael said. "Shouldn't we leave that for the police? We might have already messed up footprints or something."

"At the moment, we're standing on a gravel path."

Michael pointed. "Your toe is in the mud."

Angus lifted his foot carefully and took a step backward. "Fine, but what if the bucket is gone when the police come?"

"I'll keep watch." Michael looked around and pointed to a carefully manicured seating area. "On that bench over there."

Angus looked up the hill. "There's the back entrance to the castle. I'll go in and see what I can find out."

The back door led directly into Miramont Castle's gift shop. The woman seated behind the small counter looked up in surprise as Angus entered. "I didn't expect anyone to come in this way. Are you looking for the wake?"

"I've already been, thanks," Angus said. "I'm with *Tripping* magazine. We're doing a story on the wake, but right now, I'm interested in who could have brought a bloody great spider inside Miramont Castle."

"Wasn't that *awful*? Poor Charlotte." She shuddered. "As for who could have brought it, people have been coming and going all day, setting up for the wake and the dinner. It's one of the biggest events of the year."

Angus thought for a moment. "I don't suppose you've seen a boy called Jay hanging around. Dresses a bit goth."

"Barb Metcalf's son? I haven't."

"How long have you been at the castle today?"

"Oh, since about three. Mindy would have been here before that. I think she got in at ten."

"Thank you." Angus turned and took in the rest of the shop. The room was long, narrow, and lined with shelves containing everything from candy and toys to Victorian-style hats and cloisonné trinkets.

He went over to a rack of small stuffed animals and picked up a poodle, then a cat, and examined their feet. The toys didn't have pads, just fur. He put them back. "Is there anything in here that could be used to make paw prints on fabric?"

"We have some rubber stamps. One of the designs might be paw prints." She came out from behind the counter and led him through the main room and into a second section, filled mostly with books. A small Peg-Board hung on one wall, with rubber stamps hanging from metal rods. "Here we are."

"Wait . . ."

Before Angus could ask her not to handle it, she had taken one of the stamps from the rack and turned it over to show him the bottom. The raised rubber surface looked very similar to the prints in the coffin.

"I don't suppose it has any mud on it," Angus said, sighing.

"Mud? No," she said, running her finger over the rubber. She stopped and bit her lip. "Should I not have touched it?"

"Now that you have, does it feel damp, as though it's been washed?" Angus asked.

She pressed on the rubber again. "No. It's perfectly dry."

"Then I imagine it's all right. But you might want to keep an eye on the others and not let anyone handle them until the police get here. Do you know if the last performance is over?"

She looked at her watch. "It should be, even with the delay."

"And how can I get there from here?"

She pointed. "Go down that hallway, through the tearoom, and keep going. You'll run right into it."

When Angus reached the parlor, Officer Deloit was taking a statement from Ellen while Officer Boyd dusted the coffin for fingerprints.

Suki had apparently been co-opted as police photographer. She waved at Angus before focusing her camera on the coffin interior.

Shermont Lester, standing by the wall, looked even gloomier than his Victorian mourning garb could account for.

Angus walked over and joined him. "I don't suppose anyone has confessed yet?"

"No." Shermont pointed to the officer who was working on the coffin. "All that fingerprint dust is going to ruin the cloth, you know. The paw prints we could have sponged off, but now we'll have to reupholster the entire coffin, and for what? Everyone in the world touched that thing this evening. I think he just wants the practice."

"I can hear you, Sherm," Officer Boyd said.

"Good," Shermont shot back.

Officer Deloit finished talking with Ellen, and Angus went over to speak to her. She finished writing a note and looked at him expectantly.

"My writer, Michael, is sitting outside in the garden, guarding a tap, a bucket, and some mud."

Officer Deloit raised her head and spoke to the room at large. "Did anyone wash something off in the garden?"

Ivan raised his hand. "I washed spider off my boot."

"Did you use a bucket to do that?"

"I turned the bucket over and put my foot on it—the one without the shoe—so my sock would not get wet."

Officer Deloit looked down at her notebook and made a note. "I'll have my partner dust it anyway. He wants the practice."

Angus lowered his voice. "Have you searched people's belongings? I'm thinking the spider might have needed a special container—a box or jar with holes in it, for example."

"Good point. We'll look." She flipped to a new page of her notebook. "I might as well take your statement, since you're here."

Angus went over the evening's events, leaving out his searches at the Baskerville house and Bob's garage. He finished by asking, "How much longer before you can look at that bucket? It's just that my writer is out there guarding it."

"James!" she called. "You about finished in here? There's a bucket outside for you to work on."

He straightened. "Regular-size bucket?"

Officer Deloit looked at Angus, who nodded.

Officer Boyd smiled. "Excellent. I'll get the fume box."

"Fume box?" Angus asked.

"He puts the item in a box with some heated glue, and the glue shows up any prints."

"You're taking this seriously, aren't you?" Angus said.

She made a rueful face. "I have to tell you, if a robbery call came in, we'd be out of here. This doesn't even involve breaking and entering. Vandalism is the worst I can call it."

"Perhaps," Angus said, "but I think someone may be trying to scare Charlotte Baskerville to death by giving her a heart attack. She makes some pretty sizable bequests in her will."

Officer Deloit's eyes narrowed. "How do you know that?"

"She mentioned something about it. You might want to check pet stores and see if any of her employees recently bought a tarantula. Bob Hume spends a lot of time at that house, as well."

Officer Deloit tapped her pen against her thigh. "If I have time, I'll do that. I'll say one thing for this case—it's weird, and weird is always interesting."

Angus reached into his jacket pocket and pulled out a business card. "In that case, you might enjoy our magazine."

Nineteen

Angus and Michael waited around until Suki finished taking pictures. As the three of them walked down the front steps of Miramont Castle, Michael said, "Wouldn't it take a fair amount of time to spell out *Death* in paw prints? And the cushion would be out of the coffin the whole time. You'd think someone would have noticed."

"It wasn't done there," Suki said. "Turns out the paw prints were on a separate piece of cloth that was put into the bottom. It would have taken less than a minute to tuck it inside."

"I still think Cheri must be involved in tonight's business," Angus said. "Wouldn't she have noticed a spider when she got in the coffin? Or have crushed it?"

Suki shook her head. "There was a bunch of swagged material lining the sides. They found a slit where someone could have put the spider. Apparently they're attracted to warmth, so it was only a matter of time before it climbed out and snuggled up to Cheri. Or maybe it was just exploring. Poor thing."

They crossed the street, carefully looking both ways first. "Hold on a mo," Angus said, when they reached the other side. "Let's talk out here a bit before going in. That piece of fabric—"

"I've been wondering about that," Michael said. "Ellen has all that cloth lying around, and she has the most compelling reason to be angry at Charlotte."

"Yeah," Suki said. "But anyone could have gone into Colorado Springs and bought fabric, or even ordered it online. I wonder if the police are going to try to track it down."

"I don't think so," Angus said. "Officer Deloit told me they're treating it strictly as vandalism right now. It's not exactly high on their list." He looked at the Baskerville house, lit from top to bottom. "Shall we go in?"

Ivan came out as they stepped onto the front porch, a pack of cigarettes in his hand.

"Any word on Charlotte?" Angus asked.

"No." He shook a cigarette out of the pack and put it in his mouth, where it bobbed as he talked. "But I know these old women. They live forever."

"Let's hope so. About that spider . . . ," Angus said.

Ivan rolled his eyes as he applied flame to his cigarette. "Not you, too. Cheri was angry because she *loves all creatures*." He invested the words with a wealth of sarcasm.

"Actually, I was going to say you were very brave," Angus went on.

Ivan exhaled smoke and grinned on one side of his mouth. "Exactly! When something is dangerous and in the way, it needs to be eliminated, yes?"

"Sometimes, yes." Angus pointed at the door. "Is everyone else inside?"

Ivan waved a negligent hand. "Go in. They are all there." He reached out and caught Angus's shoulder, his gaze suddenly intense. "Later tonight, I will have surprise. It will be good for your magazine."

Angus glanced at the others. "Um, we'll look forward to it, won't we?"

They nodded.

Once inside and with the door closed, Michael shook himself slightly. "That guy gives me the creeps."

"Oh, I don't know," Suki said. "That much confidence is kind of sexy."

"Oh, please," Michael said. "He's a total cliché. Dramatic Russian Guy, twelve ninety-nine plus shipping."

Angus, Suki, and Michael were in the upstairs parlor discussing photos for the article when they heard the heavy front door close, followed by the sounds of Ellen's and Charlotte's voices downstairs.

Angus checked his watch as he got to his feet. It was a little after 11 P.M. "They didn't keep her overnight. That's a good sign."

The three of them went into the hallway, where they met Ivan coming out of his room.

Charlotte reached the top of the stairs. Instead of the Victorian gown she had been wearing when the paramedics took her away, she wore knit slacks and a matching tunic in turquoise. Several hospital bracelets wrapped her wrist.

Beside her, Ellen carried their purses and a garment bag.

Lines of weariness drew Charlotte's mouth down, but she smiled when she saw them waiting for her. "A welcoming committee. That's nice."

"You are well?" Ivan asked.

"A touch of angina, that's all. Just a few more pills to remember."

"So it wasn't a heart attack?" Suki asked.

"Thankfully, no."

"But it does mean she needs to take better care of herself," Ellen said. "More exercise, and less saturated fats."

Charlotte shook her head slightly. "That's the least of my worries." Her voice broke as she said, "If only the doctors could find out who would do something like that."

Ivan stepped forward and took both of Charlotte's hands in his. Gazing into her eyes, he said, "We will find out who tortures you, and stop it. I will do séance, now, tonight. We will ask Petey."

"Cool!" Suki said.

Ellen put a hand on Charlotte's shoulder, as if to pull her away from Ivan. "Don't be ridiculous. It's late, and Charlotte needs to sleep."

Charlotte looked into Ivan's dark eyes for a few more moments. Then she said, "Let's do it. I'm too worried to sleep anyway."

"I will prepare." Ivan released her hands and rolled his shoulders.

"Take your time. I need to eat something." Charlotte went down the hall and knocked on Cheri's door. She waited a moment, head bent, before turning to go downstairs.

Ellen followed her, speaking urgently. "Charlotte, I really think that paying attention to this will make it go on that much longer."

Charlotte shook her head impatiently as she started down the stairs.

"Ivan," Angus said, as the Russian started toward his room. "Would you like us to film the séance and put it on our Web site? It would be good exposure for you—as well as practice for television."

Ivan pursed his lips as he thought. "I will get ready and let you know."

"What does it take to get ready?" Michael asked. "Making sure you have a tippy table and some clear fishing line?"

Ivan gave him a cold look. "It requires meditation. I will commune with wolf spirits." He went into his room and closed the door.

"He's good," Angus said admiringly.

Suki turned toward the stairs. "The kitchen is pretty much the only place to have it. I'm going to scope out places I can put a tripod."

They followed her downstairs and found Charlotte seated at the kitchen table while Ellen made her a peanut butter and jelly sandwich.

Ellen gave them an unfriendly look as she put the plate and a glass of milk in front of Charlotte. "I have to wonder if having magazine people in the house is the best idea. It's as if whoever is behind this is showing off for them."

Charlotte picked up the sandwich. "I saw Petey before they got here."

"But things have gotten steadily worse." Ellen fumbled the lid of the jelly jar as she tried to put it on. It fell to the floor with a small metallic clatter, and she made a frustrated noise.

Angus picked up the lid and put it in her outstretched palm. "We don't want Charlotte to get hurt any more than you do."

"Really? I'd think it would be good for business. Now that I think of it, maybe you people are behind the whole thing." She gave the lid an angry twist and put the jar in the fridge.

"Ellen," Charlotte chided, but Ellen left the kitchen without acknowledging her.

Angus turned to Charlotte. "If you think it would help, we'd be happy to go back to the motel."

Charlotte shook her head as she swallowed a bite of sandwich.

"I feel safer with you here." She plucked a napkin from the jaws of a ceramic Chihuahua and dabbed at her mouth.

Angus pulled out the chair next to her and sat. "We weren't much help this afternoon."

Charlotte shuddered and took a gulp of milk. "I *hate* spiders. My brothers locked me in the basement once. I walked through a web in the dark and a big spider got on my face. Now it's an actual phobia."

"Who knows that?" Angus asked.

"I'm not sure. Thomas did, of course, and I told Ellen when she wanted to use fabric printed with spiders for a dog costume. I don't talk about it, because people don't understand real phobias. They think it's all right to tease you."

"Charlotte," Angus said gently, "given how few people know about your fear, do you think it might be someone close to you who is behind all this?"

"I don't know." Charlotte pinched the bridge of her nose, then let go and took a deep breath. "Anyway, it may have had nothing to do with my phobia. I'm sure there's no shortage of people who are afraid of tarantulas. Poor Cheri certainly was. Which reminds me, have you seen her since you got back from the castle?"

"No," Angus said. "Have you tried calling her?"

Charlotte nodded. "It went straight to voice mail. I'd call Jay, but she made it clear that they weren't even speaking. Surely the police aren't still talking to her."

"She left before I did," Suki said.

"I'll tell you what," Angus said, resting a hand on Charlotte's shoulder. "We'll take a quick walk down to the Happy Mountaineer and see if she's there."

"Would you? She and Jay went there all the time."

"We'll be back soon. Don't let Ivan start without us." Angus left the kitchen, followed by Michael and Suki.

"Hold on," Michael said. "I want to get some fresh batteries for my recorder." He started up the stairs, two at a time.

"And I think I left my coat up there," Angus said. "We'll be right back, Suki."

Upstairs, Michael unplugged his battery charger from the wall. "I don't know why we're bothering with the Happy Mountaineer. Cheri's probably over at Bob's, getting hammered on strawberry schnapps."

"I was just being diplomatic," Angus said, taking his coat off the back of a chair. "We'll check Bob's first."

Downstairs, they found Suki peeking through a gap in the curtain that covered the window of the front door.

"I heard a car pull up," she said. "Take a look outside."

Angus pulled the eyelet curtain to one side. Michael leaned in so he could see.

Jay's Explorer sat at the curb in front of the house. As they watched, the headlights shut off, but no one got out.

"I can't tell if there are two people in there or one," Michael muttered. "Maybe he's stalking her."

Ivan's voice, behind them, made them all jump. "What is outside?"

"Jay's car," Angus said. "We're wondering if Cheri is in it."

"Let us find out." Ivan opened the front door.

The others followed him onto the porch. As they did, the front passenger door opened.

Cheri slid down from the seat, dressed in jeans and a jacket and holding a plastic bag. "Just shut up. I'm not doing it, and that's final. See ya." She slammed the car door and started down the sidewalk, but halted when she saw the group on the porch.

On the other side of the car, the driver's door opened and closed. Jay stalked around the car. "Cheri, don't be stupid."

"Shhhhh!" she hissed at him, as Ivan strode down the sidewalk. To Ivan she said, "Grandma left me a message that she was home. Is she okay?"

Ivan crossed his arms. "Charlotte is as well as she can be when her family is not here to help her."

Cheri put a hand on one hip. "Speaking of family, I don't see where you get off scolding me, Ivan. You're an employee."

"Sometimes that is better than family." Ivan drew himself up. "We are having séance tonight. I will contact Petey to ask who is responsible for the evil influence on this house. Charlotte would like you to be there."

Jay put his hands in the pockets of his coat. "Can I come?"

"You're not invited," Cheri said, turning to glare at him.

Ivan studied Jay for a moment. "Yes, he is."

The sound of footsteps pattering down the sidewalk made them all turn.

Bob Hume slowed to a walk when he saw everyone's attention on him. "I was just out for a walk. What's going on?"

"Nothing." Ivan started toward the house.

Cheri's mouth turned up in an evil smile. "We're having a séance, Bob. Do you want to come?"

Ivan stopped, his back hunched.

"A séance? Wait . . ." Bob's forehead wrinkled. "Charlotte didn't die, did she?"

"No, she's fine," Cheri said. "Are you in?"

Bob bounced on the balls of his feet. "When is it?"

"Tonight. Come on." Cheri linked her arm with Bob's and walked with him toward the house.

Jay followed hard on their heels.

Angus looked at Suki and Michael. "This should be interesting."

Twenty

As Suki had predicted, Ivan decided that the large kitchen table was the most logical place to hold the séance.

Michael squeezed a folding chair into the last remaining space. "It's going to be a tight fit."

"The vibrations will travel better." Ivan, already dressed in black, hadn't changed clothes. He had taken off his boots, saying that they interfered with spiritual impulses. Now he padded around the kitchen in his socks, looking short.

He straightened the last chair and nodded to Suki, who stood by the door to the hall. "You can bring them in now."

Suki had changed and now wore a red velvet housecoat over her long black skirt and ruffled white blouse.

Michael trotted after her, leaning in and whispering as they went through the hall. "Did Ivan say you could take video?"

"No, but he's okay with a still photo."

"Huh. As far as I can tell, he hasn't set up any props or tricks.

He took his shoes off, so maybe he's going to pop his toes to make noise, but other than that, I've been in there the whole time."

"Except for now," Suki pointed out, as they reached the door to the parlor.

"*Shit.*" Michael darted back toward the kitchen.

Suki opened the door to the parlor.

Inside, Charlotte sat in her usual velvet chair, Ellen beside her. Bob sat next to Angus on the chaise, extolling the virtues of the açaí berry.

Cheri and Jay stood at windows set in different walls, looking outside. They glanced at each other, then looked quickly away.

"If you'll all follow me." Suki led the way through the hall and into the kitchen.

Ivan sat facing them as they filed in, his hands spread flat on the table. "Thank you for coming. Please quiet your thoughts as you sit."

Suki ushered them to their places. "Charlotte, you're here on Ivan's right, I'll be on his left."

"I want to sit beside Ivan," Michael said.

Ivan ignored him. "Angus, you sit beside Charlotte. Then Cheri, *then* Michael, Bob, Ellen, and Jay."

Cheri scooted her chair up to the table. "I read about this. You sit boy-girl because of the energy or something." She looked around. "Except, don't we have one extra guy?"

"Trust me, it will not matter," Ivan said, sneering at Bob. "And it is good that our number can be divided by three."

Nine people made for a tight fit around the table. Suki was the last to take her place. Before she did, she put a camera on the kitchen counter and checked the viewfinder. Then she pushed a button and took her seat. "The timer's on. Everyone hold hands and look mystical."

As the red light blinked, they groped quickly for each other's hands. Ivan closed his eyes and tilted his head back.

The flash went off, and Suki got up and checked her camera. "Thanks, Ivan."

"You are welcome," he said. "Switch off the light, please. It will be easier to see any spirits in the dark."

"And harder to see how you make them appear," Michael muttered.

"What was that, dear?" Charlotte asked.

"Nothing. Just repeating my spiritual mantra." Michael held Bob's hand loosely in his right hand. On his left, Cheri changed the position of her fingers yet again.

Despite Michael's complaint, it wasn't truly dark in the room. Light from a streetlight filtered in from the window behind Ivan, leaving his face completely in shadow but casting a dim light on most of the others.

Ivan waited until everyone's fidgeting calmed before intoning, "We invite the spirit of Charlotte's beloved Petey to enter our circle. All dogs are spiritual children of Anubis, god of the underworld. Anubis, please guide Petey's spirit to us, so he can fight the shadow that torments his mistress."

Angus looked at Suki across the table. *Good stuff,* he mouthed at her.

She lifted her brows and nodded.

For a while, nothing happened. Cheri fidgeted some more. Bob cleared his throat. Ellen shifted in her chair, kicked something, and muttered, "Sorry."

Ivan began to rock back and forth. "I feel something," he gasped, his accent becoming thicker. He panted, swaying faster and faster. Then he stopped.

The sudden silence was broken by the sound of a dog's faint howl, ending in a yodel. It seemed to come from Ivan's general direction, but his shadowed face betrayed no movement.

Seated next to Ivan, Charlotte gasped. "He's here! I felt him nose my ankle!"

"Petey," Ivan said, his voice calm, "Charlotte needs your help. Will you help her?"

Two enthusiastic yips, sounding faint and distant.

"Should I say something?" Charlotte whispered.

"Ask for the winning lotto number," Michael suggested.

"Hush," Angus said. "You might ask who was behind that spider trick."

"Right," Charlotte said. "Petey, who put the spider in the coffin with Cheri?"

Out of the dark came a series of whimpers and barks, now louder, now fading away, but all sounding somehow worried.

Ivan began to sway again. "He says . . . He says there is someone nearby who means you harm."

In the dim light, faces turned and looked at each other, then looked away.

"How nearby?" Charlotte whispered.

"Close. Too close." Ivan's head lolled back and forth, his chin almost on his chest. "But do not lose hope. There is a man, from the east. He will . . . protect you. Keep you safe."

"Why can't he just say who it is?" Jay asked, from the other end of the table.

A doggy whine came in answer.

"Petey is afraid," Ivan said.

"Of what?" Michael asked. "It's not like he can get any deader."

"He is afraid of what might happen to Charlotte."

"What might happen if he tells who it is?" Charlotte asked.

A series of high excited barks, still faint, was the answer.

The refrigerator clicked on.

Ivan's silhouetted head tilted to one side. "What? I can't hear you." He turned this way and that, as if searching. "The refrigerator—the electric field is interrupting my contact."

Jay scooted his chair back slightly. "I could pull it out from the wall and unplug it, but we'd have to turn on the light."

"Petey?" Ivan groaned. "Where are you, Petey?"

"Turn the thermostat down and it should click off," Angus whispered. "Cheri, you're closest."

Cheri's chair was jammed between Michael and Angus. She scooted out enough to get her legs over the side of her seat and stand. "Where's the thermostat?" she asked, opening the fridge door. Cold white light illuminated the room.

"There should be a dial at the top," Angus said. "Turn it away from the snowflake."

Cheri reached up and twisted. The hum stopped. She shut the door. "Now I can't see to get in my chair."

"I'll push it out for you," Michael said. The chair's legs squeaked across the wooden floor.

"Thanks." Cheri said. "Hey, what'd you put in my seat?"

"I didn't put anything there," Michael said. "Hold on." He leaned back in his chair and managed to open the fridge door with his fingertips.

The resulting light showed Cheri holding up a ratty stuffed toy.

"Wormy!" Charlotte said. "That was Petey's favorite toy, but he lost it." She turned to Michael. "Shut off that light!"

Michael closed the fridge door, plunging the room into darkness.

Silence. Finally Ivan grunted. A high, wailing howl sounded faintly.

"Petey?" Charlotte asked.

"It is a message for Cheri," Ivan said, his voice slow and tired-sounding. "He says he forgives you."

"What does Petey have to forgive me for?" Cheri demanded. "I never did anything to that dog."

"Not Petey," Ivan slurred. "Someone else. He is passing on the message. Also, you must give up your bad habits. Only then will you be able to forgive yourself."

"I have no idea what he's talking about," Cheri said, her voice high and tight.

"Cheri," Jay said.

"Shut up!" In the dark, they heard her sniffle.

Ivan moaned. "Petey grows tired. Does anyone else have any questions?"

"I have a question," Angus said. "Something has gone missing from Thomas's room. Who has it?"

After a pause, they heard one quiet bark.

"He says it is not your concern. Anyone else?"

"Yeah, me," Suki said. "Was I a Mongol princess in another life?"

"Oh, for—," Michael began.

"What?" Suki demanded. "That's the sort of thing you're supposed to ask."

Ivan swayed toward Suki. "He says you were the bravest and most fierce of Mongol princesses."

"I didn't hear any barking," Michael said.

"He is fading." Ivan let out a deep sigh. "He is gone. I will turn on lights." He pushed back his chair and got up while the others broke into a babble of conversation.

The overhead light came on. Ivan stood next to his chair and rolled his shoulders. "It has been a long time. I forgot how tired it makes me."

"You did a wonderful job." Charlotte applauded, followed by the others.

Michael brought his hands together twice and let them fall. "We didn't learn much, though."

"It was enough to know Petey still exists, on some level," Charlotte said. "Also, that I can rely on help from a man from the east." She smiled up at Ivan.

"I grew up in Nebraska," Bob offered. "That's east of here."

"I think Ivan probably comes from the farthest east," Charlotte said.

Ivan put a hand on her shoulder. "I will always work to keep you safe, Charlotte, but you know that already."

Cheri threw the dog toy in the center of the table. "I'm going to bed." She glared at Michael with pink-rimmed eyes. "Move!"

Michael maneuvered his chair out of the way.

Cheri got up and walked stiffly from the kitchen.

"Poor Cheri," Charlotte sighed. She picked up the dog toy and held it tenderly. "Maybe what Petey said will help. What do you think, Ivan?"

"Why ask him?" Ellen demanded. "Is he an expert on troubled youth now, in addition to dogs?"

Charlotte looked taken aback. "Okay, then what do you think, Ellen?"

"It doesn't matter what I think." Ellen shoved back her chair. "It's late, and I have to get up early tomorrow." She left the kitchen.

Bob straightened Ellen's chair so he could get up. "I should go, too. The race is tomorrow, and I still have a lot of work to get ready.

Thank you, Ivan and Charlotte. That was fascinating." He headed toward the front door.

Jay stood. "Thanks for the invitation, Ivan."

Ivan nodded. "It is no problem."

"Take care, Jay." Charlotte gave him a sympathetic smile. "I hope we'll still see you."

He turned away, his neck bent. "Yeah, maybe."

Ivan leaned down to Charlotte. "I will make sure all the doors and downstairs windows are locked," he said quietly.

Charlotte turned her face up to his. "I can't thank you enough, Ivan."

He nodded solemnly and followed Jay toward the front door.

Charlotte put her hand to her chest and blew out a breath. "What an amazing man. I couldn't believe when I felt that touch on my ankle. It was *exactly* the way Petey used to nose me when he wanted to be picked up. And then to have Wormy appear out of nowhere!"

"Very impressive," Angus agreed. "I had Michael record the sound, so we can include a transcript of the most exciting parts."

"We should also put the dog sounds online," Michael added. "People love that kind of cr . . . um, stuff."

Charlotte clasped her hands. "You'll stay tonight, won't you? Tomorrow is the big race."

Angus nodded. "We can stay for that, but then we'll have to be going. I can't thank you enough for your hospitality."

She shook her head. "I should be thanking you. It's been a little frightening at times, but I have the feeling that things are going to settle down now."

"Why?" Michael asked.

She smiled. "Because Petey would have told me if I should be worried. Anyway, I'll see you all in the morning."

"That reminds me," Suki said. "What do you like on your waffles?"

Angus and his crew decided to shop for waffle supplies that night, so they could discuss the séance away from the house.

Charlotte gave them directions to a twenty-four-hour grocery store, about ten minutes away.

Once they were on the road, Michael blew out his breath in an irritated huff. "I guess there's nothing like a completely bogus display of otherworldly tripe to lay all your fears to rest. A little ventriloquism and Petey says whatever Ivan wants."

"You don't believe I was a Mongol princess?" Suki asked.

"Or that the ghost of Petey touched Charlotte Baskerville on the ankle and put his missing toy on Cheri's chair?" Angus asked.

"Please," Michael scoffed from the backseat. "Why do you think Ivan took his shoes off? I'm sure he got rid of at least one sock, too, so his clammy toe could pass as Petey's nose and also so he could toss that dog toy into Cheri's chair."

"How could he know Cheri would be the one to turn the refrigerator thermostat?" Angus asked. "For that matter, how could he count on the refrigerator starting up?"

"He didn't have to know any of that. He just had to be prepared to take advantage of a distraction, like a phone call, or the wind. And he would have had something to say for whoever got up from their chair. If no one got up, he could have left the toy at Charlotte's foot and poked her ankle like Petey."

"And the fact that it was Petey's *favorite* toy?" Angus asked.

Michael made a derisive noise. "Every toy is a dog's favorite at some point. That particular one might not even have belonged to Petey. Ivan could have bought a new one and roughed it up when he got the idea for the séance."

Angus stared out the car window. "It would be a lot of trouble to go through, but on the other hand, Ivan certainly made an impression on Charlotte tonight. I wouldn't be surprised if she changes her mind and helps his TV career."

"Ellen and Cheri definitely seem to think there was a shift in power," Suki said. "Did you notice how pissed they both were? And what did Ivan mean by that business of forgiving Cheri?"

"That was just a safe, vague thing to say," Michael said. "Everyone has something that needs forgiving."

"Especially alcoholics," Angus said.

"And who was forgiving her?" Suki went on. "He left that up in the air."

Michael thought for a moment. "The most *logical* assumption, and I use that word reluctantly, is that if it isn't Petey, it's someone else who's dead. Thomas, for example."

Angus nodded. "Maybe Ivan thinks Cheri was behind the ghost dog that Thomas followed into the street."

"Or maybe Cheri brought the spider to the wake, and he's talking about that," Suki said.

Angus sighed heavily. "It's horrible to think that a young woman would want to scare her own grandmother to death."

When they reached the store, the parking lot was almost empty.

"I assume there's some kind of mix for waffles," Angus said, as the store's sliding doors whooshed open and they walked into the glare of fluorescent lights.

"We used Bisquick when I was a kid." Michael flagged down a passing employee. "Excuse me, where's the baking aisle?"

The man pointed. "Four aisles that way."

"I'm kind of glad I volunteered us to make waffles," Suki said, as she and Angus followed Michael. "Charlotte's pretty cool. Of course, there's always the possibility that she's the one behind all this."

Michael turned and looked over his shoulder. "How do you figure that?"

"She could have done it for the publicity."

Michael snorted. "She should have researched the magazine a little more, then."

Angus frowned. "Mark my word, the local papers will get wind of our article, or it could get picked up on the wire—from there she could wind up on a talk show."

"Or maybe it's not for publicity," Suki said. "Maybe she's crazy and wants the attention."

"Or maybe it was all a clever way to get rid of Thomas," Michael said.

Angus turned down the aisle marked BAKING. "I don't see how Charlotte could have worked that hoax on her own."

"You have to think outside the box," Michael said. "We don't absolutely know that Charlotte and the people in the car didn't know each other. Or maybe Thomas didn't actually slip in the road. He could have been shot by Ivan, who was hiding in a tree, in cahoots with Charlotte."

"And a car just happened to run Thomas down moments after he was shot?" Angus asked.

Michael shrugged. "It's not as though cars never come down that road. Ivan could have been up in his tree, giving the ghost dog instructions to run around the yard until the right moment."

"Assuming such a ludicrous thing happened," Angus said, "and the coroner didn't notice a bullet hole in Thomas, why would the pranks continue? Why put a spider in the coffin?"

"How about this," Suki chimed in. "Charlotte gets rid of Thomas, then decides to scare her slacker granddaughter away so she can live in peace with her Russian lover."

"Does that mean Ellen is the next to go?" Angus asked.

"Nah," Suki said. "Someone has to answer the door and bring the drinks."

Angus pointed to a shelf. "Waffle mixes."

"I hope there's one without trans fats," Michael said, picking up a box and checking the ingredients. "This one looks okay." He pointed farther down the shelf. "And a bottle of maple syrup. Charlotte might not have any." He chose a bottle and started walking.

"The exit is this way, Michael," Suki said.

"But whipped cream and frozen strawberries are this way," Michael said.

"Oh, for crying out loud," Angus said. "You'll be wanting chocolate sprinkles next."

Michael turned uncertainly. "Those would be back in Baking."

Angus gave Michael a little push. "No sprinkles for you. Get your berries and cream and let's go."

"*No sprinkles for you* would make an excellent T-shirt slogan," Suki said.

Twenty-one

The next morning, Ellen came down in her robe at seven thirty and found the staff of *Tripping* making waffles. Pouring a mug of coffee, she said, "I thought you people would have left by now."

"We still have the coffin race to cover," Angus said.

"Hmph." She went back upstairs.

Ivan came down a little later, looking dressy in charcoal slacks and a silky shirt the color of blood.

"Going to the casino today?" Angus asked, as he gathered silverware from a drawer.

"No. Today is coffin race." Ivan pulled out a chair and slouched elegantly, legs straight out and crossed at the ankles. "People will make videos, and you never know who will see it or if I will be interviewed." He pointed at Angus. "You will send me copy of your magazine article."

"I'll be glad to." Angus took a stack of plates from the cupboard and began to set the table. "Your séance was very impressive last night."

"Ivan has many talents."

"What do you think the spirits meant about Cheri being for-given?"

Ivan shrugged. "It could be many things. She has been worse recently, getting angry and not doing chores. If Ivan had his way, Cheri would straighten up and fly right on." He made a scooting gesture with his hand.

At the sound of the front door opening, Ivan sat up straight.

Angus looked down the hall and saw Charlotte with Lila on a leash and Chum in a shallow purse. Both of them wore little coats. "I hope you're hungry," he called to her.

She gave him a little wave. "I saved myself. All I've had is cof-fee."

Ivan got up and went to join Charlotte.

Angus watched as he murmured something to her, put a hand on her arm, then picked up Chum in his carrier and headed up-stairs.

Michael put the butter and syrup on the table and followed Angus's gaze with his own. "Looks like he's got her on the hook and is reeling her in," he muttered.

"It does," Angus said. "I have to wonder, was he behind the ghost from the beginning?"

"Make her afraid and then save the day?" Michael said. "Possibly."

Charlotte came to join them, Lila trotting beside her. "This looks very nice. Thank you."

"It's the least we can do for all your hospitality." Angus pulled out a chair for her. "How are you feeling this morning?"

"Wonderful. Luckily, angina doesn't have much in the way of lingering symptoms." Charlotte sat and patted her lap for Lila, who jumped up immediately. "I can't tell you how relieved I feel this morning. It's as if there was a thunderstorm looming, and that séance cleared the air."

Ellen clattered down the stairs and came into the kitchen, dressed this time.

"Good morning, Ellen," Charlotte said cheerfully.

Ellen stared at her for a moment. "I'd like to set up a time for you and me to meet with my lawyer."

Charlotte's face fell, but irritation quickly replaced the hurt. "I'm sure we can resolve this without resorting to lawyers."

"I don't think we can." Ellen clasped and unclasped her hands, but her mouth was firm and set. Then she saw Ivan returning and sneered. "Come to protect your investment?"

Ivan went to Charlotte and put a hand on her shoulder. "Charlotte is my friend, and our employer. You and I owe what we have to her."

"Charlotte owes a lot of what she has to my designs!" Ellen said.

Lila raised her head and gave a peremptory bark.

"Ellen," Charlotte began.

Ivan took a few steps toward Ellen. "Perhaps you should go cool yourself."

"You . . ." Ellen took a deep breath through her nose. "I have things to do anyway." She walked to the front of the house and left, slamming the door behind her.

Charlotte put her elbows on the table and rested her head on her fingertips. From outside came the sound of a car starting. She looked up and gave Angus a sheepish smile. "There's nothing like airing your dirty laundry. At least you're not filming a documentary on me."

Suki came to the table with a waffle stuck on a fork. "Hey, that's why we had you sign a video-release form."

Angus cleared his throat.

"Just kidding," Suki said, putting the waffle on Charlotte's plate.

Ivan sat next to Charlotte and put a hand on her back, rubbing it in soothing circles. "If Ellen leaves, there are other businesses you could try."

Charlotte reached for the syrup, shrugging Ivan's hand off in the process. "If things don't work out with Ellen, I'll find someone else, or go back to designing the clothes myself."

The back door opened and Cheri walked in. Her hair was flattened on one side of her head, and dark circles of smeared eye makeup ringed her eyes, which were mere slits. She closed the door slowly behind her.

Charlotte frowned. "Are those the same clothes you wore yesterday? Where did you sleep last night?"

Cheri edged along the opposite side of the table from Charlotte, not looking at her. "Can we talk about this later?"

"How about some breakfast?" Suki plucked a waffle off the iron and held it in front of her.

Cheri averted her face. "No. God, no."

"Suit yourself." Suki put the waffle on Ivan's plate.

Ivan reached for the butter. "At the restaurants, they serve these with whippy cream. Is there any of that?"

Michael handed him a can of whipped cream. "Sorry. I was busy thawing the strawberries." He opened the microwave and took out a bowl, which he put on the table.

As Cheri left the kitchen, she said, "That's right. We all have to make Ivan happy now."

"Cheri!" Charlotte said.

Suki pointed a fork at Cheri's departing back. "No sprinkles for you!"

Charlotte got up, her face grim. "Excuse me, please." She trotted after Cheri.

Ivan watched her go. Then he stuck his fork in her untouched waffle and moved it to his plate.

Angus wiped his mouth on a napkin. "That was delicious. Thank you, Suki and Michael."

Suki sat at the table finishing a waffle, while Michael loaded the dishwasher. Ivan had finished his breakfast and gone upstairs.

Charlotte had returned after fifteen minutes, during which they could hear her and Cheri shouting at each other. Now she wiped her mouth on her napkin and glanced at her watch. "Thank you for a wonderful breakfast. I'm helping with check-in at the race, so I should leave soon."

Angus pushed his chair back. "We'd better get moving. I didn't realize everything started so early."

Charlotte waved a hand. "You have plenty of time. The parade doesn't start until twelve fifteen, and the race is after that."

"Ah." Angus subsided. "Charlotte, I hate to add to your burdens, but there are a few things we should probably tell you."

Charlotte tucked her paper napkin under the side of her plate. "Such as?"

Michael came over, wiping his hands on a dish towel. "While we were staying in Thomas's room—"

Angus interrupted. "We were looking for the instructions to the clock radio, and happened across a file of Thomas's."

Charlotte frowned. "You *happened* across it? What kind of file?"

Angus made a regretful face. "A file that showed your husband hired a detective to prove you were cheating on him or that you were crazy, presumably so he could take the business away from you or get a big settlement in a divorce. He was also working with a lawyer."

Charlotte's mouth dropped open slightly, but she recovered quickly. "Where is this file?"

Angus's regretful expression deepened. "The thing is, someone took it."

"When did this happen?"

Suki swallowed a bite of waffle. "Probably while we were holding the dog up to the light."

"Why would you . . . what?" Charlotte sputtered.

Angus gave Suki a quelling look. "Animal fluorescence is a key part of many paranormal investigations. Regardless, someone came into Thomas's room and took the file. The cabinet wasn't locked to begin with, you see."

Charlotte studied their faces, her expression grim. "Any idea who took it?"

Angus looked at the others. "No. But I'd be careful about trusting anyone in your household too much."

Charlotte slumped in her chair. "Wonderful."

"There's more," Angus said apologetically, "although it probably won't come as a surprise. Cheri's appearance this morning did suggest that she was a bit—"

"Hungover?" Charlotte finished. "I'd like to know how she got hold of alcohol. I'd hate to think Jay would get Cheri drunk in order to get her back."

"I don't think she spent the night with Jay." Angus cleared his throat. "I'm hesitant to say this, because it's very circumstantial."

Charlotte's eyes narrowed. "Do it anyway."

Angus looked at Michael. "Tell her what you saw."

Michael pulled out a chair and sat. "I was at Miramont Castle when I looked out the window and saw Bob Hume and a woman in a pink hooded jacket get out of his car. Bob unloaded a box. The woman walked all the way around the block before entering your house, as if she didn't want to be seen coming from Bob's."

"Cheri has a pink coat with a hood," Angus said.

Charlotte frowned. "Not to be blunt, but did they kiss or something? I mean, it is odd, but—"

"Later, we were in Bob's garage looking for Angus's cell phone," Michael went on. "We came across a box of strawberry schnapps. I'm pretty sure I recognized it as the box Bob took out of his trunk."

Charlotte stared at the table. "That must be why Cheri wears that terrible perfume all the time." She sighed. "Bob Hume, huh? And to think, I even wondered if Ivan was giving her liquor in his room."

"I'm not saying Ivan is lily-white," Angus said, "but I don't think his sense of self-preservation would let him liquor up his employer's granddaughter."

"When you put it that way, it does seem unlikely." Charlotte shook her head sadly. "I'm not sure what to do, but at least I have the information. Thank you for telling me." She looked at her watch and stood. "I'd better get going."

After she left, Angus blew out a breath. "That could have gone much worse."

"I notice you didn't tell her about the missing copies in Ivan's checkbook," Michael said.

"True." Angus squinted and scratched his chin. "It was difficult enough to tell her we'd *stumbled* across that file. I'm not sure how we'd explain searching everyone's rooms. Anyway, after Ivan's triumphant performance last night, he can probably get more out of Charlotte alive than dead."

"Unless she changes her will to favor him instead of Cheri," Michael said.

Suki shook her head. "Charlotte's no pushover. Did you see her ease out from under Ivan's hand when he hinted about changing businesses?"

Angus sighed. "We've told her what we can and searched everywhere we can search. I think we've done all we can do."

The front door opened and Charlotte walked determinedly back. "It occurs to me that you haven't had much access to the workshop in your paranormal investigation." She handed Angus a key. "Here. Knock yourself out."

Angus looked at the others as Charlotte marched away. "Or maybe we *can* do more."

The stone workshop looked like someone had already searched it. File drawers stood open, and stacks of binders littered the tables.

Michael lifted the edge of an empty binder and let it fall. "Presumably Ellen made this mess, but why?"

Angus squatted next to a file cabinet and looked at a stack of folders on the floor next to it. " 'Design notes, 2007,' " he read. He flipped open the manila cover. "Some of the phrases are highlighted. 'You asked for three new skirt designs. Here's my take on a sport jacket.' If I had to guess, I'd say Ellen is putting together proof that she's responsible for all of Charlotte's designs."

"I smell a lawsuit," Michael said.

"Hey, guys?" Suki said.

They turned to see her in front of the wall rack that held bolts of fabric.

She grabbed the edge of one and waggled it, making the cloth ripple. "White satin."

They hurried over.

Michael pointed to the cut edge of the cloth. "Dirt. Right there. Could be the edge of a muddy paw print."

Suki shook her head. "Ellen wouldn't work with the whole bolt of cloth. She'd cut off what she needed. Anyway, if you look closer, you can see it's not mud, just general grubbiness."

Angus bent and examined the fabric's edge. "It looks like a smudge from the edge of a shoe."

"Man's or woman's?" Michael asked.

Angus gave him a look. "I'm not bloody Sherlock Holmes, Michael." He let go of the fabric. "I can't see Ellen routinely treading on the goods."

"You can't tell anything from a dirt mark," Suki said. "Someone could have stepped on the edge at the store, and Ellen hasn't used it yet."

"So it's no help," Michael said.

Angus shrugged. "It tells us that Ellen has access to white satin."

"Along with Charlotte," Suki pointed out.

Michael gave a short laugh. "You really want Charlotte to be behind this, don't you?"

She shrugged one shoulder. "It'd be more interesting."

Angus put his hands on his hips and surveyed the workshop. "Let's see what else we can find."

While Angus looked through the files for Thomas's reports, Michael felt under tables and looked behind the whiteboards that hung on the walls. Suki busied herself with the sewing things.

"Hey, guys," she said, after a few minutes.

"Again? You found the last clue!" Michael tugged at the yardstick he was using to poke behind a cupboard, but it was stuck. He left it there and joined Suki and Angus at the end of one of the big tables, where Suki had been searching through the drawers of a plastic organizer.

"Take a look at this." Suki poked at a plastic-wrapped lump that lay on the table. It looked like clay but had a silver color.

"What is it?" Angus asked.

"It's a modeling compound. Ellen used it to make what I think are zipper pulls." She stirred her finger through a drawer of handmade charms. "Little bones, little dog dishes . . ." She picked out a charm that dangled from a key chain. "And little paw prints."

Angus took it from her. "This is far smaller than the paw prints on the coffin lining."

"But it shows Ellen could have made them," Michael said. "She probably forgot these were here." His hand hovered next to Angus's, fingers reaching toward the charm. "Can I see?"

"In a minute." Angus tapped the charm on the table, then prodded the wrapped lump of raw material, leaving a dent in the surface. "How do you get this stuff to harden?"

"You bake it," Suki said.

"Would she have risked doing that at Charlotte's house?" Angus gave the charm to Michael's twitching fingers. "Oh, for crying out loud, here."

Michael tapped the charm. "She could have baked it at a friend's."

Angus tilted his head skeptically. "She'd have to really trust that person."

The door to the workshop opened, and Ellen entered, carrying a covered file box. "What are you doing here?"

"Who is it?" a voice asked from behind her. Barb Metcalf, Jay's mother, edged into the doorway so she could see. "Oh, the magazine people!" She saw Ellen's expression and wiped the eager smile off her face.

"How did you get in?" Ellen demanded.

Angus reached in his pocket and held up the key to the workshop. "Charlotte gave us this so we could do some paranormal investigating."

"And what are your EMF detectors and thermometers telling you?" Ellen looked around, her expression sardonic. "Oh, wait, you don't have any."

"We're not dependent on gadgetry," Angus said. "Suki here is a bit of a medium."

"Actually," Suki said, "I've never been above a size six."

"Rim shot." Michael held out his fist and Suki bumped it with hers.

"I've never seen a medium work," Barb said. "Can we watch?"

Ellen set her box on the worktable. "They're not contacting the spirits, Barb. They're snooping for Charlotte." She glared at Angus. "You can tell her from me that I have a perfect right to make copies of *my work*."

Angus held up a calming hand. "I assure you, we're simply doing research for our article. But since you brought it up, I think you have a case against Charlotte."

Some of the anger left Ellen's face. "You do?"

"It won't be cheap. These lawsuits often depend on who outlasts the other, but a jury could very well decide that Charlotte isn't giving you proper remuneration, given the role you've had in Petey's Closet."

Ellen spread her arms. "*Thank* you."

Barb put another box on the table. "Especially since Charlotte made her sign a noncompete agreement. That's just not fair."

"They don't need to know the details," Ellen snapped, then turned back to Angus. "You still haven't explained how going through my drawers helps you find ghosts."

"Psychometry," Angus said. "Suki can detect psychic vibrations from objects. Go ahead, Suki."

Suki put a hand to her forehead and sighed. "You know, I've been working all morning and I'm beat. Let Michael do it. He's just as good." She patted Michael's shoulder as he stared at her. "Go on, sport."

"This is so exciting!" Barb said.

Ellen pursed her lips. "Doesn't he need to hold something?"

Michael held out his fist. "I'm already holding something." He shut his eyes and waved his closed hand in front of his face. "I sense a lot of rage. Rage and resentment. But there's more. The color white, and a word, a word that begins with *D* . . ."

"Dog!" Barb squeaked. "It's Petey's ghost!"

Ellen grabbed Michael's hand. "What have you got there?" She opened his fingers and picked up the paw-print charm. "Anyone could look at this and get *dog*." She tossed it on the table. "C'mon, Barb. I think we can get the last of these files in one load."

The *Tripping* crew watched as the two women swapped files between the cabinets and the boxes.

Ellen opened the door for Barb and then picked up her box. "Make sure to lock up when you leave." She hooked the door with her foot and slammed it shut.

"Not very mousy anymore, is she?" Michael said.

"That's the thing about doormats," Angus reflected. "Once they get ruffled, you can suffer a nasty fall."

· · ·

Angus, Suki, and Michael searched the rest of the workshop but were unable to find anything else of interest. Angus locked the door and they crossed the yard to the house.

"Are we going to leave right after the race?" Michael asked.

"Since I can't come up with any more excuses for staying, yes." Angus opened the back door and led the way through the kitchen. "We have more than enough for an article."

"Especially since we can't prove it isn't a ghost," Suki said.

"As far as *Tripping* is concerned, it *is* a ghost."

As they reached the foyer, Barb Metcalf came down the stairs, carrying yet another cardboard box. She gave them a smile before going out the open front door. A minivan stood in front of the house.

"They're not taking things from Charlotte's room, are they?" whispered Michael.

Angus held a finger to his lips and looked upstairs.

Charlotte's voice floated down to them. "Ellen, honey, there's no need for this."

A pause, but Ellen's voice was too quiet to hear.

Charlotte went on. "It'd be silly to let something like this get in the way of our friendship, not to mention what we've built together."

Angus went up the stairs quietly, the others following.

Charlotte stood in the doorway of Ellen's bedroom. "Honey, we've had disagreements in the past and always worked them out."

"Because I always gave in," Ellen said from inside her room. "If we're going to work together, things will have to change. I mean it, Charlotte." She came out, a load of clothes slung over one arm, a desk lamp held in her other hand. "You'll be hearing from my lawyer."

She passed Angus and the others without a word.

Charlotte looked distraught, but she pushed her hair back and straightened her spine when she saw the *Tripping* crew. "I only came back for a moment, to change clothes. It got warm outside." She went down the hall to her room and closed the door behind her.

Angus and the others went into the adjoining parlor. "I suppose we may as well pack anything we don't need to cover the race this afternoon."

Suki opened a bag and began to load it with cables. "At some point, I'll need to check that I didn't leave anything in Charlotte's room when I slept there."

Michael picked up a pen and looked around. "Some of my stuff is downstairs in Thomas's bedroom."

"I left some things, too," Angus said. "We might as well get them now."

They went down the hall, slowing to look into Ellen's room. The doors to her empty wardrobe stood open and the top of the desk was clean. Folded bedding lay stacked on the bare mattress.

"She's really moving out," Michael said.

When they reached the foyer, Angus went to the front door and pulled the curtain aside. The minivan pulled away from the curb, Barb at the wheel, Ellen beside her. "There she goes."

Michael sniggered. "It's just like when Tom Ford left Gucci, only with Chihuahuas."

It took only minutes for Angus and Michael to pack. Angus was deciding whether there was enough toothpaste left in his tube to justify taking it when he and Michael heard the front door open.

Michael went quietly out of the room, then came back and whispered, "It's Ivan."

Footsteps sounded up the stairs, accompanied by whistling.

Angus and Michael went to the foyer in unspoken agreement and stopped at the foot of the stairs to listen.

Ivan's footsteps paused as he reached the upstairs, then continued briefly. "Hallo, princess," he said.

"Hey, Ivan," Suki said.

"Ellen has left?"

"Yep."

"And you also are leaving today?"

"Sometime after the coffin race."

"Will you give Ivan your phone number, for when I need photos?"

"Sure." A pause. "Here's my card."

"Excellent. Someday I will be famous, and then I will take you on date you will never forget."

"I'll look forward to it."

Ivan's footsteps continued to the end of the hall, and they heard him knock. "Charlotte?" he called.

Upstairs, a door opened, then closed.

When they didn't hear anything more, Angus gestured at Michael to follow him, and they ran lightly up the stairs. They found Suki in the parlor that adjoined Charlotte's room, ear pressed to the wall.

Angus shut the door to the hall and joined her, jockeying with Michael for position.

"—worry," Ivan said, on the other side of the wall. "You will make other business. Television business. Everything you need is right here."

"Ivan, I spent ten years building Petey's Closet. I'm not going to give it up because of a temporary difficulty."

"It will take time to find other designer. Take that same time and spend it on Ivan. I have five brilliant ideas for television show. First idea. Americans love baby animals, but they also love to be afraid."

"I don't want to hear . . ." Charlotte hesitated. "Scary baby animals? No, forget it, because I am not in the entertainment business."

"But you should be!"

"Ivan, we are not having this discussion. I have to get back to the race now. Do me a favor and take Lila for her walk."

Lila gave a short bark.

Charlotte's door opened, and they heard the tap of her heels as she left her room and went downstairs.

"She is ungrateful, Lila," Ivan said heavily. "But she will learn."

In the hall outside, they heard the click of Lila's claws as she passed the parlor door and followed Ivan downstairs.

Twenty-two

The *Tripping* crew arrived an hour early for the Emma Crawford Coffin Race. They staked out their place by setting up Suki's video camera on its tripod.

Sun beat down on the milling crowd of locals and tourists, many of them dressed as if for Halloween. A woman in a tattered wedding dress hurried by, her skirt hiked up. Sweat streaked her white makeup. Stilt walkers stalked the street, costumed as surreal birds and giant eyes.

Over the noise of the crowd, a loudspeaker amplified the voices of the two official announcers, who chatted about the race's history and its sponsors.

Angus snagged Shermont Lester as he walked by, carrying a case of bottled water. "Is this a good place for our camera?"

"Sure is."

"And can you give us a brief idea of what happens?"

Shermont set the box down by his feet. "The parade starts with the procession of hearses." He waved at a contestant. "Cathy, did you get a new helmet? Looks good!" He went on. "After the hearses, the contestants come by, following the Chamber of Commerce pace coffin."

Michael, holding up his recorder to catch Shermont's remarks, chortled. "Isn't the proper pace for a coffin *dead still*?"

Shermont rolled his eyes. "I've never heard that before. Anyway, the pace coffin doesn't actually participate in the race, since they do that in heats. But it adds a touch of ceremony and shows people where to line up in the parade."

"Is there a favorite to win?" Suki asked.

"Usually, but the team is out of town. I'm betting on the Dirty Grannies this year. They have some really strong pushers." Shermont noticed a race official waving at him. "Gotta go. The parade's about to start."

The announcer's voice boomed over the crowd. "And here comes the Hearse of Fire!"

Huge bat wings extended from the roof of the hearse in the lead. A man dressed in black leather and dark glasses stood on its roof, behind something that looked like a mounted machine gun. His head was shaved except for a red and black bihawk about eight inches high. As they watched, a gout of flame roared from the gun.

"Dude," Suki said. "That is *awesome*."

Other hearses followed. One dark, metallic blue beauty paused, revved its engine, then peeled rubber. "Nothing but pure power," the announcer crooned.

"I guess if you have a hearse, you wait all year for an event like this to show it off," Michael mused, as a hearse with accompanying Ghostbusters went by, the costumed team strutting to the movie's theme song. "What complicated impulse makes someone take up hearse rallies as a hobby?"

"It probably starts when someone offers you a really good deal on a hearse," Angus said.

The pace coffin came next, occupied by someone in a tiger costume. The tiger waved at the crowd.

The announcers ratcheted up their enthusiasm a notch. "And here come this year's contestants!"

The assembled teams included Elvis impersonators in canonical white jumpsuits, people dressed as garden gnomes, and faux Rastafarians. Most of the coffins rested directly above an axle with wheels of eight inches or less. A welded frame rose from the sides of the coffin, apparently for the pushers to hold.

"Hey, there's Bob Hume," Suki said, pointing. "I guess he managed to round up a team."

Bob's coffin still had black Chihuahuas at each of the four corners, but now they wore tiny top hats. Black tulle draped the sides, gathered into swags with rhinestone collars. Unlike the majority of coffins, his race vehicle sat at the top of its metal frame, with handles just below the bottom of the coffin.

Two of his three pushers looked like they might be high school football players. The third, a bearded man in his forties, wore a knee brace. All of them, including Bob, sported headbands with dog ears on them.

The team's Emma, seated inside the coffin, looked to be in her mid-forties and had a smoker's leathery skin and whippy build. Her costume consisted of jeans and a white T-shirt with the slogan *I'm Dead* painted on it. She flipped lank brown hair over her shoulder and lit a cigarette.

Bob caught sight of them and waved at the video camera. "Hello, *Tripping* fans! Try Petey's Pride dog food, with cancer-preventing açaí berries, available soon at a store near you!"

Keeping his lips still, Angus said, "We'll put music over that part of the video."

Michael nodded. "I have to admit, the black Chihuahuas go great with the story, even if they are tasteless as hell."

"Speaking of the story, we should try to find Charlotte and interview her about the parade." Angus stood on tiptoes and looked over the crowd. "The judge's box is over there. Michael, you come with me. Suki, stay here, unless you see something better to film. Actually, just do whatever you think is best."

Suki's gaze remained fixed on the camera's screen. "I usually do."

Angus and Michael wormed their way through the crowd until they reached the reviewing stand. Speakers mounted on the corners blasted the voices of the announcers, who riffed on the dangers of driving dead drunk.

"I don't see Charlotte in there," Michael shouted.

"There should be stairs around back," Angus shouted back. "We'll go ask if anyone knows where she is."

They squeezed between the side of the stand and a cluster of trash and recycling bins. Angus stopped as they rounded the back corner.

Behind the stand, Charlotte Baskerville held on to her granddaughter's arm with both hands.

Cheri was dressed in the white Emma gown she had worn at the wake. Her face and hair were both painted white, and purple makeup ringed her eyes. She pulled against her grandmother's hold and stumbled.

Charlotte tried to pull her upright. "I warned you from the beginning, you can't live with me if you're drinking!"

"I'm not drunk!" Cheri wailed, slurring the words. She changed direction and fell against her grandmother, knocking Charlotte against the back of the stand. Cheri dissolved into giggles and slid to the ground, her gown riding up to her thighs.

Charlotte pushed herself off the wall and caught sight of Angus and Michael. She shook her head in a helpless gesture.

"Can we do anything to help?" Angus asked.

Charlotte bent and pulled Cheri's dress down. "I'm going to call Jay and see if he'll take Cheri home and stay with her." She straightened. "Can you make her stay until he gets here?"

Cheri kicked out and caught Angus a glancing blow on his shin. "Noooo!" she howled. "I wanna see the race!"

Angus took a step back and rubbed his leg. "I'm fully prepared to sit on your head, lass."

Charlotte pointed at the reviewing stand. "My phone's up here. You shouldn't have to wait too long. Jay's probably somewhere around here." She went up the stairs and disappeared inside the box.

Michael took up a position on the other side of Cheri. "Hey, Cheri, I've got a joke for you. What's brown and sticky?"

Cheri gave up trying to stand and squinted up at him. "What?"

"A stick."

After a moment, she began to laugh. "A stick!"

Angus smirked at Michael. "You should rent yourself out for kids' birthday parties."

"Don't knock it," Michael said. "I tended bar in college, and there's nothing like a stupid joke to calm an angry drunk." He looked down at Cheri, who was trying to stand again. "Hey, Cheri, what kind of mistakes do ghosts make?"

She frowned and looked away. "I don't like this one."

He nudged her hip with his shoe. "They make boo-boos."

She laughed, slumping against his leg.

. . .

Jay joined them about ten minutes later, wearing his long black coat and with his face painted like a skull. He squatted and hauled Cheri to her feet. "C'mon. Let's go."

Michael blew out a breath. "Finally. I was about to start on the knock-knock jokes."

Angus watched Jay get a firm grip on the limp girl. "Charlotte wants you to take her home and stay with her."

"Yeah, she said."

Cheri pouted and tried to pull out of Jay's hold. "I don't wanna go with you."

"Well, you don't have much choice," he said. "That's what you get for being stupid."

"Bob!" she called. "Where's Bobby? He's fun!"

Jay got Cheri's arm around his shoulder. "You don't need any more fun."

"I don't envy you trying to get her through that crowd," Michael said.

Jay pulled Cheri upright as she lurched to one side. "Don't worry. I can handle her."

"You've been gone awhile," Suki said, when Angus and Michael rejoined her. "Did you get a good interview?"

Angus shook his head. "No interview. Things got a bit complex."

"Cheri," Michael said, and mimed drinking.

"Bummer." Suki turned back to the racecourse. "It's good you made it back. Bob is racing in this heat, and he's up against the Dirty Grannies."

They looked down the hill, to the start of the race. The Dirty

Grannies had curly white hair and wore housedresses, but looked improbably burly. At the starter's flag, the two teams charged up Manitou Avenue, legs pumping.

"Man, those Grannies are fast," Angus said.

As the teams came closer, the Dirty Grannies were revealed to be a group of tough-looking men in their thirties, wearing wigs.

About halfway up the course, one of Bob's pushers let go of the coffin and stumbled to a halt.

"It's the guy with the knee brace," Suki said, as someone from the crowd helped him off the street.

The announcer chimed in. "Oh, that's a shame. Petey's Pride won't be disqualified, but the team's time will definitely suffer from having only three pushers."

As the Dirty Grannies pounded across the finish line and whooped as loud as their heaving sides would allow, Bob and his remaining two pushers labored the rest of the way up the street.

With the two athletes at the back and only Bob in front, the coffin veered sideways as they made their final approach.

"He's going to push it into the crowd if he's not careful," Angus muttered, as people on either side of the track yelled warnings.

Bob, apparently trying to correct course, hauled sideways on his side of the coffin. The rear pivoted, the wheels juddering along the asphalt, and then the whole thing slowly tipped over as the pushers grabbed at the sides, trying to keep it upright.

Their helmeted Emma spilled onto the street in a flurry of arms and legs, then bounced to her feet and did a rubber-legged dance as the audience hooted in appreciation.

Bob's two remaining pushers sat on the ground and panted, while Bob ran around the coffin, checking for damage.

Suki shook her head in admiration. "Now that's entertainment. Shall we go interview the Grannies?"

Michael raised his brows. "Just for winning their heat?"

"Odds are, they're going to win the whole thing, and we'll have trouble getting near them if they do," Suki said, pushing her tripod legs closed. "Just don't ask questions about this heat and no one will know we didn't interview them after the race."

"And if they don't win?" Michael asked.

"Then we'll interview the winner."

"I bow to Suki's experience," Angus said. "Let's go."

Suki led, the tripod giving her an official air, not to mention making people duck aside to avoid the panning handle.

The Dirty Grannies were holding court at the race-end staging area. Suki pushed her way to the front of their fans and set up her tripod with a few deft movements.

The Grannies had pronounced five o'clock shadows, hairy bare legs, and were sweating profusely. Two of the coffin pushers wore high-top athletic shoes, one wore work boots, and the fourth had on enormous bedroom slippers.

Inside their race coffin was a slight but hirsute man dressed as a baby, with a girlish blonde wig. He got out and tugged on the rear of his onesie, then noticed Suki and her camera. Jerking his head by way of greeting, he said, "Yo, sexy mama. How 'bout a diaper change?"

Michael held his recorder in front of the largest Granny. "Hi, I'm from *Tripping* magazine. Is there a secret to your impressive speed?"

"*All My Children* is on in half an hour. I don't want to miss anything." He took a chewed cigar from the pocket of his housedress and stuck it between his teeth.

Angus addressed the Granny in boots. "I love your hair. Where do you get it done?"

The man dragged the curly blonde wig off his head and used it to wipe sweat from his neck. "At my neighbor's. She breeds poodles." He held up the bedraggled wig and wiggled it. "Arf, arf."

"What makes a Granny dirty, exactly?" Michael asked.

The one in the slippers answered. "Gardening. But really, it's a state of mind."

Suki picked up the camera, and they moved back toward the middle of the racecourse.

"Oh, jeez," Michael said, "here comes Bob."

Bob Hume waved as he made his way through the crowd toward them. "Can you help me push my coffin back home? I can't find my team, and one of the wheels isn't working very well."

"We're covering the race for our magazine, Bob," Angus said, his voice chilly. "We can't leave."

"Where's your truck?" Michael asked. "Didn't you bring the coffin in that?"

"Parking is so hard, and it was just a couple of blocks." Bob looked around distractedly. "Maybe Jay or Ivan could help. Have you seen either of them around?"

"I haven't seen Ivan." Angus folded his arms. "As for Jay, Charlotte asked him to take Cheri home after she turned up completely drunk."

Bob's attention snapped back to Angus. "Cheri was drunk?"

Angus scowled at him. "The poor girl will have to find other living arrangements now."

"Oh, yeah, I guess they had an agreement." Bob glanced past

Angus. "Oh, there's James. Excuse me." He struck out through the crowd, waving and yelling. "Hey, James!"

Angus shook his head. "Not a bit of remorse for what he's done. What a complete bastard."

Michael looked thoughtful. "Is it possible he doesn't know about the liquor?"

Angus raised his brows. "It's in his garage. How could he not know?"

"I saw him take a box out of his truck, and it looked like the schnapps box, but what if it wasn't? Cheri could have hid the liquor in Bob's garage without him knowing. It's all circumstantial."

"How would she get into Bob's garage?" Angus asked.

"The same way we did, or maybe the roommate is responsible."

"I still think it's Bob." Angus shook his head sadly. "Cheri's problem is not our business, but it makes me sad to see someone so young bugger up her life."

"You'd rather she was older," Michael said, "with more family to be affected and a real job to lose?"

Angus rolled his eyes. "Come on, master debater. Let's get back to the racecourse."

They pushed their way through the crowd, the announcers' voices booming above them. Suddenly Angus stopped.

Michael walked into his back. "What? If it's a Porta-John, I need one, too."

"Look over there." Angus pointed surreptitiously toward the sidewalk, a little ahead.

Michael and Suki craned their necks to see over the crowd.

Ivan and Ellen stood beneath the awning of a store, their heads close together.

"They look surprisingly cozy," Michael said.

They watched as Ivan spoke rapidly, punctuating his speech with urgent hand gestures. Ellen nodded, looking intent. Then she said something and touched his arm, smiling.

"Proposal," Suki said quietly. "I saw him say the word *proposal* right before she nodded."

"Business proposal?" Angus wondered.

"I doubt it's a marriage proposal." Michael turned toward the racecourse. "Did you hear the announcer? The two Elvis teams are going to race each other next. Let's get going!"

"All right, keep your shirt on." Angus moved through the crowd again. "It's not as though Elvis was ever a sprinter."

They made it to the course's side in time for Suki to catch the tail end of the heat on video, as eight Elvii thundered across the finish, white capes flapping behind them.

The crowd went wild when the Dirty Grannies pounded across the finish line to win the Emma Crawford Coffin Race.

"They didn't look that much faster than the other teams," Michael said. "I mean, they don't look like they're marathon runners or anything."

Angus scanned the crowd for the thinnest spot. "Perhaps they just wanted it more."

"I'm betting it's weight." Suki collapsed the tripod's legs. "Baby Emma can't weigh more than a hundred and twenty pounds, and the coffin could be fiberglass. Most of the others look like they're made of half-inch plywood, and that stuff's heavy."

"Bob's was certainly plywood," Michael agreed, as they waited for a mother with a stroller to cross in front of them. "And it was almost full size, whereas the Grannies' was at the minimum. He had his legs tucked into that thing like it was an Indy race car."

"Maybe one of their team is an engineer," Suki said. "My money's on the one in boots."

They moved slowly down the street, surrounded by people. Suki had switched to still photographs and took pictures as she went.

Angus looked around admiringly. "Wonderful town, Manitou Springs. Has a real sense of community."

Michael gave him a look. "The kind of community that lures old men into traffic and puts tarantulas in coffins with young women?"

Suki snapped a photo. "Oh, that's just the Baskervilles and their crappy luck."

Angus looked thoughtful. "We should write a mini article on families who have had bad luck, like the Kennedys."

"And a sidebar on ghost dogs through the ages," Michael said, as they turned left onto Ruxton Avenue. The crowd had thinned, and now only twenty people or so walked on either side of the street.

Angus's phone rang. "It's Pendergast," he said, flipping it over and pushing a button. "What's up? You're on speaker."

"Are you done with that dog thing yet?"

"We just finished the coffin race. I wish we could stay longer. I'm worried about your cousin's safety."

"Yeah? Don't tell me the ghost dog has rabies."

Angus filled him in, finishing with, "I should have called earlier, but it's been a little fraught."

"Angus, I've missed the way you talk. Too bad about the old man dying, but does this story get better and better or what? Listen, don't worry about Charlotte. I'll tell my wife she needs to go to Manitou for a week and kick some ass."

"Tell your wife to be careful."

"Don't worry about her. She once got mad and broke a mechanical bull. Hey, get this—I've already got a lead on a new story."

"What is it?"

"Twin sisters and a creepy painting. I gotta go. Some kid's got my assistant's finger between his teeth. Ciao."

Angus closed the phone.

"He sure doesn't sound like someone named Pendergast," Michael said.

"He's one of the Trenton Pendergasts," Angus said absently. "I wish we could stay longer and keep an eye on Charlotte, but I have to be at work on Monday."

"Me, too," Michael said. "I'm doing the graphics for a tech manual. High-tech compost bin. Where do you work?"

"At the moment, file clerk in a law office," Angus said.

He and Michael looked at Suki.

"Trust fund." She shrugged. "Sorry, kids."

As they reached the Baskerville house, the rest of the pedestrian traffic continued up the hill, to less historic homes. They went up the walk and into the house.

Suki pointed to a stack of boxes just inside the door, filled with sewing supplies. "Looks like Ellen's getting the last of her things."

"It's awfully quiet," Angus said. "I wonder where Cheri and Jay are."

"Cheri's probably passed out in her room," Michael said.

They went upstairs. Ellen's door stood open, but she wasn't inside.

"Must be in the workshop," Michael said. "Do you think Charlotte knows about all this coming and going? If there's going to be a lawsuit, she might want to change the locks."

The tinny sound of a television came from behind Ivan's closed door. Farther down the hall, Charlotte's and Cheri's doors were also shut.

They went to the parlor that adjoined Charlotte's room, where Suki's equipment bags lay, mostly packed.

"Make sure to check the outlets for chargers." Michael pulled one free and handed it to her.

Suki opened one of the other bags and stuck it inside, then unclipped her camera from the tripod.

From downstairs came the sound of someone knocking on the front door. Suki looked up. "Should we get that?"

"Let Ivan answer it," Michael said.

The knock came again. Angus looked into the hallway, but Ivan's door remained closed. "He probably can't hear it. I'll go."

Downstairs, Angus opened the front door to find Bob Hume holding Lila's leash, the little dog jumping and yapping at the end of it.

"Is Charlotte home?" Bob asked. "I found Lila running around loose on the street. She could have gotten hit by a car."

Angus took the leash from him. "That's strange. Thank you for bringing her back."

"No problem. Tell Charlotte she needs to be more careful. I have to get back."

"Thanks again." Angus shut the door and bent to stroke Lila's head. She dodged and barked sharply into his face.

Angus winced at the noise. "Hush." He took her upstairs, where he knocked on Charlotte's door. "Charlotte?" When no one answered, he pushed it open.

Chum turned cloudy eyes toward Angus from his place in the center of Charlotte's bed.

Angus let go of Lila's leash. She ran up the little bedside stairs, barked at Chum, then jumped down and ran out of the room.

"Lila!" Angus went into the hall and saw her go down the stairs, the leash slithering behind.

Ivan looked out of his room. "What is happening?"

"Bob found Lila wandering in the street with her leash on, and I can't find Charlotte. She's not in her room."

Michael came out of the parlor, followed by Suki. "That's not good," Michael said.

"Charlotte!" Ivan called. "Where are you?" He took a few steps down the hall and opened Cheri's door. "No one here."

"That's weird," Michael said. "Jay was supposed to have brought Cheri home from the coffin race. She was drunk."

Ivan took a cell phone out of his pocket, dialed, and listened for a few moments. "Charlotte's phone went to voice mail." Punching a number, he said, "I will call Ellen. Go look in the workshop."

Angus and the others went quickly downstairs, where Lila pawed at the front door, panting and wide-eyed.

"Should we take her with us?" Michael asked.

Angus picked up the end of the leash. "I think so."

They went down the hall and through the kitchen, to the back door. As soon as they opened it, Lila lunged this way and that, barking.

"I'd let her go, but I don't want her to run into the road," Angus said, as they walked through the backyard. He opened the workshop door.

Ellen stood inside with her cell phone to her ear, looking

concerned. She held up a finger as they came in, and spoke into the phone. "I haven't seen Charlotte or Cheri since I got back."

Lila strained toward Ellen and gave a bark.

"Hush." Angus picked up the trembling dog.

Ellen cupped a hand over her non-phone ear. "They just walked in, Ivan. I'll call Cheri and meet you at the front of the house." She pressed a few buttons and waited. "Cheri, we're looking for Charlotte. It's urgent. Call me." She snapped the phone closed. "Cheri's phone went straight to voice mail. Jay could have taken her to his mom's house, but where on earth could Charlotte be?" She headed toward the door.

They followed her to the front of the house, where Ivan stood on the sidewalk, peering down both sides of the street. As they approached, he put his cupped hands to his mouth and shouted, "Charlotte!"

"Did you check Thomas's room?" Ellen asked him. "You don't suppose Charlotte forgot to take her new medicine and is lying unconscious somewhere?"

"I looked in Thomas's room." Ivan's mouth turned down, deepening the furrows on either side. "She is not anywhere."

"Charlotte!" Ellen yelled.

Bob came out of his garage, maneuvering past his truck, which was backed up to the entrance with the tailgate down. "Did you find her?"

"No!" Ellen chewed her lip. To Angus she said, "Should we call the police?"

"I think so. They could at least keep an eye out."

Bob walked over and joined them. "Do you want me to help look? I'm about to take this coffin back to the guy I borrowed it from. Let me load it up and I'll drive around Manitou first. Maybe I'll see Charlotte."

"Thanks, Bob," Ellen said. "Keep your eyes open for Cheri, too."

"You want help with the coffin?" Michael asked Bob.

"That's okay. I already unfastened it from the frame. It slides right off and into the truck." He scratched his head. "I'm wondering if Lila pulled loose from Charlotte at the race, and Charlotte is looking for her there. You might want to try that." He walked back to his garage.

Ellen shook her head. "Charlotte wouldn't take Lila to the race. There's too much danger of her getting stepped on."

"I will look anyway," Ivan said, already turning toward the street.

"Wait a minute." Ellen grabbed his arm. "We need to be organized about this." She yelled over to Bob, who had pulled the coffin frame up to the back of his truck. "Bob, will you look on Ruxton Avenue when you go? Drive up the hill."

He raised a hand. "Got it!"

Ellen turned back to the rest of them. "Ivan, you go back to the race and ask the officials if they've seen Charlotte."

Michael took out his phone. "We should all exchange numbers."

Suddenly, a faint wail floated through the air. Lila stiffened in Angus's arms, then pointed her nose at the sky and howled.

Next door, Bob stopped pushing, the coffin halfway in the truck. "Petey's ghost!"

"It must mean Charlotte is dead," Ivan said grimly.

"Oh, God." Ellen put a hand to her mouth.

The faint, wailing howl came again. Lila barked and struggled in Angus's hold.

"Ow!" he said, as her hind claws raked his arms. He put her down, where she strained toward the house next door. "Let's see where she goes." He walked, letting the frantic dog lead.

The others followed, crossing the strip of lawn between the Baskerville house and Bob's driveway.

"Sounds like it might have come from around back," Bob said, still struggling under the back end of the coffin. He shoved it another foot into the truck bed, but the iron frame rolled out from under the tail end. He staggered under the coffin's weight as it threatened to slide onto the ground.

Michael darted forward and helped push it the rest of the way into the truck. "Good thing you had the lid strapped on."

"Yeah. Thanks," Bob said. He pointed toward the rear of the Baskerville house. "I'm pretty sure the howl came from the workshop."

Angus stared at Lila, who stood on her hind legs and lunged toward the truck. "I don't think it did. In fact, I don't think it was Petey at all." He handed Lila's leash to Ellen and shoved Bob out of the way. "We need to get that coffin open. *Now.*"

Ivan put a hand on the side of the truck bed and vaulted into the back.

"Hey!" Bob said. "I just got it in there!" He grabbed at Michael's ankle as Michael clambered over the open tailgate.

Angus grabbed Bob's arm and pulled him back.

Ivan pried at the clip on one of the straps. "How does it open?"

Suki climbed into the truck bed. "Let me." She got her fingertips under the buckle and loosened it as Michael pulled his strap free. "Got it."

They lifted the lid and shoved it to one side, Ivan scrambling to get out of the way.

"Oh, Jesus," Michael said.

Charlotte Baskerville lay motionless inside the coffin, her hands, like frozen claws, clutching a folded blanket that lay half over her face. Her eyes were closed, and pink suffused her skin.

Michael pulled the blanket off and threw it aside. A muscle twitched slightly in Charlotte's cheek.

"She's alive!" Ivan said.

"Is it Charlotte? I had no idea she was in there, I swear!" Bob said.

Suki grabbed one of Charlotte's arms. "Let's get her out of there. She needs air."

As Suki, Michael, and Ivan lifted Charlotte from the coffin, Jay's Ford Explorer pulled up.

Jay got out of the car and ran over as they carried Charlotte to the lawn. "Oh, my God, what happened to her?"

The Explorer's passenger door opened. Cheri slid bonelessly out, but managed to stay upright by falling against the car. "Jay!" she squalled. Her face and hair were clean, but she still wore the white Emma gown.

Jay ran back to her as the others laid Charlotte on the grass and knelt beside her.

Michael tilted Charlotte's head back and started artificial respiration.

"Why is she pink?" Ivan asked.

"Carbon dioxide poisoning," Suki said. "She must have run out of air."

"I've called an ambulance," Ellen said. She looked at Bob, still in Angus's grip. "And the police."

"I didn't do anything!" Bob said. "She must have gotten in there herself, or someone put her there!"

"Grandma?" Cheri pulled away from Jay and stumbled to her grandmother, landing on her knees by Charlotte's side.

Charlotte's rib cage lifted, and they heard a slight breath pass through her slack mouth.

"Good!" Suki said. "You can stop, Michael." She raised and lowered Charlotte's arms a few times, until her breathing deepened and became more regular. The pink color faded from her skin.

Cheri took her grandmother's hand. Ellen came over, still holding Lila's leash. The little dog licked Charlotte's face.

Charlotte's eyelids fluttered, then opened.

Ellen picked Lila up. "Good girl," she whispered. To Charlotte she said, "The ambulance is on its way."

Charlotte nodded very slightly before she looked away from Ellen and found Cheri. She frowned slightly before her gaze passed to Ivan, then Jay, and finally to Bob Hume.

"You," she said, her voice thready. "You tried to kill me."

Cheri squinted up at Bob. "You tried to kill my grandma?"

"I didn't! She's out of her mind!" Bob struggled with Angus briefly, but Ivan got up and grabbed his other arm.

Charlotte glared at Bob. "I came back from the race and took Lila out to pee, then decided to go over to Bob's and read him the riot act for giving liquor to Cheri." She looked around at the others. "When I turned to leave, he held something over my face until I blacked out." She shuddered. "I woke up in the dark and screamed, but I couldn't get enough air to make it very loud."

"We heard you and thought it was Petey's ghost," Angus said.

Charlotte nodded. "I could feel the air running out, and then I passed out again. I thought that was it for me."

Cheri let go of Charlotte's hand and struggled upright, where she glared at Bob. "You tried to kill my grandma! Why would you do that?"

Bob's wild-eyed expression became pleading. "Because she's not your grandma."

Cheri shook her head in confusion. "What are you talking about?"

"Cheri, I had an affair with your mother before you were born." He straightened. "Randolph Baskerville wasn't your father. I am."

"No, you're not." Angus and Ivan said it together.

Angus looked at Ivan, who looked away.

"What do you mean, I'm not Cheri's father?" Bob asked.

"Thomas suspected his daughter-in-law was having an affair," Angus said. "So he got Randolph to have a paternity test done. The results showed that Randolph was definitely Cheri's father."

"That can't be right." Bob twisted his neck to look at Cheri. "Betsy told me she hadn't had sex with her husband for months!"

"But she didn't leave him," Suki said. "Instead, she called it quits with you."

"Well, yes," Bob admitted. "We'd been seeing each other for a few weeks when she said she wanted to make things work with Randolph." He swallowed. "Something about family and responsibility."

Suki smiled grimly. "She lied to you about not having sex with her husband. She must have found out she was pregnant, and further along than a few weeks."

Bob sagged against the arms that held him. "Oh, shit."

Cheri shook her head. "I still don't understand. Even if you thought I was your daughter, why did you want to kill Grandma?"

Bob looked at the ground. "You were always talking about how you'd get your life on track if you could just get away from your family. I thought if Charlotte died and left you her money, you'd be free. Then I'd tell you I was your dad, and we could make Petey's Pride dog food a family business."

Charlotte bent her legs to one side and propped herself up with one arm. "Did you put the spider in the coffin, Bob?"

He nodded slowly. "Cheri told me you were deathly afraid of them. We used to talk for hours."

"Because you gave me schnapps!" Cheri said.

He lifted one shoulder. "I didn't think it would hurt in the long run. Neither Betsy's family nor mine has a history of alcoholism."

Charlotte rolled her eyes. "Hoo, boy."

"So you killed Thomas, too?" Ellen asked.

"Oh, no, you can't blame everything on me." Bob straightened a little. "I had nothing to do with anything before the spider."

The sound of sirens had been growing more audible in the distance. Now an ambulance rounded the corner of Manitou Avenue and screamed down Ruxton, followed closely by a police car. Lila barked frantically, and Bob began to struggle again.

Ivan grabbed Bob's face, a snarling growl rising in his throat.

Bob whimpered as Ivan's thumb dug into the side of his jaw.

"I always knew you were a *pig*," Ivan said. "Be glad you are going to jail. You will be safer there." He released Bob with a contemptuous jerk of his hand.

The ambulance and squad car pulled up to the curb, sirens cutting off with a final *whoop*. Paramedics ran across Charlotte's lawn toward them, Officer Deloit and her partner following close behind.

Charlotte pointed to Bob. "This man tried to suffocate me. He almost succeeded."

"Oxygen," one of the paramedics said to the other, and they trotted back to the ambulance.

Charlotte turned her attention to the police. "Also, he confessed, and everyone here heard it."

Officer Deloit unclipped her handcuffs from her belt. "Gotta love that."

Twenty-three

Hours later, when Charlotte had been declared recovered, the police had taken statements, and Bob Hume, weeping, had been taken off to jail, the *Tripping* crew gathered in the kitchen of the Baskerville house with Charlotte, Ellen, Ivan, Cheri, and Jay.

The sun had dropped below the edge of the canyon. Ellen switched on the overhead lamp. Warm light displaced the cool autumn atmosphere, casting everything outside the windows into darkness.

Charlotte went to the counter for coffee. Lila ran over to where her mistress stood and put her forepaws against Charlotte's leg as she filled a mug.

Charlotte looked down at the little dog. "I think you deserve a treat." She got a bone-shaped dog cookie from a jar shaped like a Chihuahua.

Lila took the cookie and crept under the table to crunch it.

Charlotte sat down between Cheri and Jay and took a sip of coffee, then looked at the mug she held in both hands. It had a photo of a white Chihuahua on it. "I guess Petey really did come back."

Jay took a deep breath. "Cheri and I rigged the ghost."

"Jay!" Cheri shoved his shoulder.

"I can't keep it a secret anymore, Cheri. It's killing me." He looked down the table at Charlotte. "We didn't mean for Thomas to get hit. That was an accident, I swear."

"Why on earth would you do such a thing?" Charlotte asked Cheri.

"It was just for fun." Tears welled in Cheri's eyes. "I used some glow paint of my own to paint a Chihuahua shape on a balloon. Jay hid in the neighbor's yard and held on to the end of the balloon's thread."

Suki shook her head. "So low-tech."

Jay continued the story. "When Thomas was so horrible to you afterward, saying you were crazy and all, Cheri decided to make Petey tell you to leave him. She got me to help make the dog voice."

"*Divorce Thomas,*" Charlotte said.

"But you took him back," Cheri said glumly.

Michael looked at Jay and Cheri. "How did you make Petey talk?"

Jay answered. "There was a recording of Petey on the Web site. Cheri did the talking part. I modified her voice and tacked it on to the end of Petey's howl. We put about twenty minutes of silence in front, so Cheri could hide the player and some mini speakers in the dog tunnel out back and have time to get away."

Cheri nodded. "And after everyone went to bed, I snuck out and brought the equipment inside."

Jay looked at Charlotte. "When you gave Thomas another chance, Cheri decided Petey's ghost should come back and let you know you were doing the wrong thing. She'd found a glow costume by then, and we put it on Ludwig, my mom's dog."

Cheri wiped at the tears running down her face. "I put Ludwig in our front yard and told him to stay. Then I ran across the street to hide."

"I was in the backyard, behind the workshop," Jay said. "We had our cell phones, and Cheri was going to tell me when to whistle, so Ludwig would run around the back of the house. Then I'd grab him and go through the gate into the neighbor's yard."

"But the costume made Ludwig all nervous," Cheri continued. "When Thomas started chasing him, he totally freaked out and ran into the street." She began to sob. "Grandpa was awful, but I didn't mean to kill him, I swear."

Charlotte leaned over and put her arm around her granddaughter. "I believe you, honey. What did you do with the glow costume?"

"I put it back in Ellen's room, where I found it."

Charlotte slowly turned her head to look at Ellen, seated across the table.

Ellen stared at the ceiling for a moment, exhaling slowly. "I love you, Charlotte, I do, but you can be so controlling."

"Someone has to be the boss, you know."

"You're more like a parent, talking about how we're in this together, *you and me, kid,* and then handing over my allowance like I'm a child who does chores instead of the designer for this company." Ellen shook her head in frustration. "I guess we should talk about that part in private."

"I think so, yes," Charlotte said. "Just tell me about this costume."

Ellen smiled wryly. "Well, as my lawyer will point out, it was for my own personal use, and designed for a cat, not a dog."

Charlotte gave a sharp laugh. "I think I would have noticed if you owned a cat."

"I have friends who own cats," Ellen said.

Cheri rolled her eyes. "It fit Ludwig perfectly."

Ellen nodded. "Chihuahuas are very similar to cats in shape. My lawyer would also point out that I could press charges against you, Cheri, for coming into my room and stealing my property."

Cheri slumped in her chair and stared at her mug of hot chocolate.

Suki looked at Ellen. "Was the costume in the shoe box you took to your car?"

"Were you spying on me?" Ellen demanded.

Suki raised her brows. "I happened to be sitting in the parlor, looking out at the moon."

"Wait a minute." Charlotte raised both hands. "Ellen, you must have realized the costume was involved in Thomas's death. Why didn't you tell me or the police about it?"

"Are you kidding? When that costume showed up in my room that night, wet and muddy, I figured whoever put it back had killed Thomas and was trying to frame me." She gestured to Angus. "It didn't help that these jokers told the cops there was glow-in-the-dark paint in my bathroom. It seemed safest to get rid of the costume, so I took it out of the house and burned the damn thing."

"You *burned* it?" Charlotte looked disgruntled. "Did you at least keep a pattern? Was it any good?"

Ellen leaned forward. "It was outstanding. That is, as cat costumes go." She smiled and took a sip of her coffee.

Cheri bit her lip and looked at Charlotte with pleading eyes. "Do we have to tell the police about this? No matter what happens, I promise to stop drinking."

Charlotte gazed at her sadly. "I don't think we'll bring the police into this, but you do know you're going to rehab, right?"

"Yeah," Cheri sighed.

Ivan crossed his arms. "She has been in rehab twice, yes? I don't think it is working."

Jay turned to Cheri. "He's right. I think you're mostly bored. Why don't you find something you want to do and start taking classes?"

Cheri huffed sarcastically. "This from a guy who lives with his mom."

Jay pointed at her. "Hey, I'm looking at sound-design schools in Europe."

"You're leaving the country?" Cheri pouted.

Charlotte sighed. "It's hard for me to believe all this was going on, right under my nose." She glanced at Angus. "You must think I'm very foolish."

"No, just wrapped up in your business," Angus said. "Bringing things out into the open should help clear the air." He gave Ivan a significant look. "Confession is good for the soul."

Ivan returned his gaze blandly.

Charlotte pushed back her chair. "Angus, I'd like to talk with you in the upstairs parlor, if that's all right."

"Certainly." Angus rose and glanced at Ivan again.

Ivan stared implacably back, his throat vibrating in a barely audible growl.

Suki got up from the table as well. "Hey, Ivan. Want to go for a walk?"

His head swiveled toward her and the growl vanished. "Okay, Princess."

Upstairs, Charlotte ushered Angus into the parlor that adjoined her room and closed the hall door behind them. Then she sat on the settee and patted the spot next to her. "Let's talk business—specifically, the magazine business. You and your staff have been very helpful throughout this ordeal."

Angus leaned against the upholstered seat back and crossed his legs. "I saved your life."

"Yes, you did. And in return, I think you should be able to publish the story of Petey's ghost. Minus the spider, of course."

"As I see it, the main question is whether you can keep your people quiet."

Charlotte nodded. "I have to make Ellen partner, that's clear. She'll see the wisdom of not dirtying the family's image." Charlotte drummed her fingers on one knee. "Perhaps Cheri would enjoy going to a school in Europe. I always said that Jay was a smart boy."

"And then there's Ivan." Angus opened his mouth to say more, but remembered the growl and kept silent. Yes, Ivan had known about the paternity test, but that didn't absolutely mean that Ivan had paid Thomas's lawyer and detective bills. And it wasn't as if those activities had put Charlotte in real danger.

Charlotte looked thoughtful. "Ivan would sell the whole story without a second thought. It might be time to throw him a bone. Maybe Petey's Closet is ready for some television ads, or Ivan could appear on a few talk shows, to promote the company."

"He'll need to have his teeth fixed," Angus said.

Charlotte slapped her thigh. "Teeth fixed, and out of the will."

"Good idea. I'm sure he'll do Petey's Closet proud," Angus said.

Charlotte nodded. "Then that's settled. Write all you want about a ghost, but if you mention my family's part in it, I'll sue you from here to hell and back."

Angus grinned. "It's a deal."

"And I'll need your subscription list, so I can mail a Petey's Closet catalog to all of *Tripping*'s readers."

Angus's grin didn't falter. "Possibly. Of course, you'd miss newsstand readers that way. I recommend a year's worth of advertising, just to be sure. *Tripping* has some very attractive rates."

Ivan and Suki walked uphill along Ruxton Avenue. A cold breeze blew, and black tree branches waved in front of lighted windows. A few TV screens glowed and flickered inside the houses they passed.

Suki linked her arm through Ivan's. "Did you take the file with the detective reports?"

He stared ahead, stone-faced. "Ivan would not take anything that wasn't already his."

"So you gave Thomas money to hire them, and he promised to help you once he got control of Charlotte's money."

Ivan frowned. "I admit nothing. But business is like war. Sometimes you make alliances with people you do not like."

"And now Thomas is gone, Bob is gone, and Cheri is going into rehab. You have Charlotte almost to yourself, but she's no pushover, Ivan."

"A dog-training show would make Petey's Closet famous!" Ivan's dark brows pulled together, and his chin jutted slightly. "Ellen will help convince Charlotte to make the show, and I will convince Charlotte to make Ellen partner."

"That must be what you two were talking about at the coffin race," Suki said, almost to herself. "I saw you say the word *proposal*."

"You have been watching Ivan," he said complacently. "That is good."

Suki rolled her eyes. "It seems to me that a dog-training show isn't an ideal vehicle for advertising Petey's Closet, unless you're going to train dogs while they're wearing costumes."

"Ivan has four other brilliant ideas for TV shows," he said, putting his arm around Suki's waist.

"Let's hear these brilliant ideas. My father works in L.A. He might be able to make some calls."

Twenty-four

Two Months Later

Suki and Angus sat at a table in a pizza place on Boulder's Pearl Street Mall. The steamy windows looked out on scurrying holiday shoppers, loaded with bags and hunched against a light but wet snow.

Michael pushed open the door and walked back to join them. He slapped a damp copy of *Tripping* on the table, sending stray specks of Parmesan flying from the table's surface. "I can't believe you did this! Half my article gone, and no mention that the ghost turned out to be a hoax."

"Keep your voice down," Angus said, wiping grease off his chin.

Michael grabbed an empty chair from a neighboring table and sat. "I didn't even know the issue was out until I saw a copy on the newsstand."

"I got mine in the mail weeks ago." Suki wrapped scarlet lips around her drink's straw.

Michael shook his head, his expression bitter. "I should be calling TV reporters right now, to tell them the truth."

"You can't," Angus said hurriedly. "It's against your contract, not to mention that I promised Charlotte Baskerville to keep Cheri's part out of it." He took a spare plate, loaded it with two pizza slices, and slid it in front of Michael. "Eat something."

Michael crossed his arms. "I'm too angry to be hungry."

Angus picked up the copy of *Tripping* and gently brushed it off. "It's not as though the article is an out-and-out lie. If you'll notice, I edited it to use the words *image* and *apparition* a lot. We saw those things, even if they didn't turn out to be a ghost."

"The title was 'Ghostly Dog Walks'!" Michael grabbed a napkin and shook it out angrily. "Talk about poor word choice. It sounds like a dog owner's tour of graveyards."

"Yeah, I got that from it, too," Suki said.

Angus lifted one shoulder. "Perhaps I meant it to be ambiguous."

"Did you?" Michael bit out.

"No." Angus looked askance and mumbled, "Should have read it out loud, I suppose." Straightening, he said, "We couldn't have printed the article any other way, or Charlotte would have sued us. Instead, she bought a lot of ad space. She's also sponsoring Manitou Springs' new pet parade, and the Chamber of Commerce is going to advertise it in *Tripping*'s Halloween issue next year."

Michael swallowed a bite of pizza and spoke with somewhat less rage. "You think there'll be a next year for *Tripping*?"

"I do. Pendergast is talking about getting us an office."

"Dibs on a window," Suki said.

"You can't—" Michael broke off with a sigh. "You'd get one anyway, dibs or no dibs."

She smiled at him. "You can visit."

"The reason I called you both here is that I have some outstanding news." Angus wiped his hands on a napkin before reaching into the inner pocket of his coat, which hung on the back of his chair. Taking out a folded page of magazine, he said, "Charlotte Baskerville sent me this. It's from *Entertainment Weekly*." He unfolded the page and read. " 'Next fall will see the debut of a new sitcom that makes extensive use of dogs. The brainchild of animal trainer Ivan Blotski, the show is set in the cutthroat world of New York fashion, but with a twist. Missy Bijon is a designer of canine fashions who actually *is* a canine.' "

"So Ivan is getting his TV show," Michael said.

Angus went on. " 'Eighty percent of the performers will be dogs, who rely on humans for such lowly jobs as hailing taxis and fetching liver Frappuccinos with grated Milk-Bone on top. Costumes will be provided by Petey's Closet, a real-life canine clothier owned by Charlotte Baskerville, with designs by Ellen Froehlich. In addition to making sure the doggy models can navigate a catwalk without barking, Ivan Blotski plays the part of Gregor Poochi, Missy's rival designer.' "

"I wonder if they'll make him gay," Michael mused.

Suki chuckled. "Does the article mention us?"

Angus pointed to the page as he continued. " 'Petey's Closet recently made a splash in the press when it was revealed that the ghost of the company's namesake, a Chihuahua named Petey, appeared several times to Charlotte Baskerville. The story appears in this month's issue of *Tripping*, a magazine that covers vacation destinations with paranormal aspects.' "

Michael stood and punched his fist in the air. *"Yes!"*

Angus smiled and folded the article again. "I told you this story could lead to great things. *Tripping* is on its way."

Michael was dancing around the restaurant, still punching the air and whispering, "Yes! Yes!"

"Sit down, Michael," Angus said. "You're disturbing the other diners."

Michael plopped down in his chair. "I'm putting a link to my Web page on the magazine's site, tonight."

"That's fine, as long as your page doesn't reflect badly on *Tripping* in any way," Angus said.

"Might have to make the blog private," Michael muttered.

Suki used her straw to poke at the ice in her cup. "What's the name of Ivan's TV show? You didn't say."

Angus tucked the article back in his pocket. "Given that it stars doggy fashion divas, I think they came up with the only name possible. They're calling it *Bitches*."

Ghostly Dog Walks!

Charlotte Baskerville's dog refuses to lie down, even though he's dead.

Shortly before All Hallows' Eve in the mountain town of Manitou Springs, Colorado, the spectral form of Charlotte's dead Chihuahua appeared to his beloved mistress.

"I was lying in bed when I heard Petey's unmistakable howl," Charlotte Baskerville (69) remembers. "I rushed to the window and looked out into the backyard. In the cold and dark, I saw the glowing form of a Chihuahua, floating across the lawn. I thought I must be dreaming."

But it was no dream. Before Charlotte's astonished gaze, the ghostly apparition floated onto the roof of an old stone hut, remnant of the town's historic past. She ran outside, but Petey had disappeared into thin air. For the moment, only one thing remained—a set of glowing paw prints in the damp earth.

(cont. on page 13)